THE MINNESOTA KINGSTONS | BOOK FOUR

AUSTEN

THE MINNESOTA KINGSTONS | BOOK FOUR

AUSTEN

SUSAN MAY WARREN

Austen
The Minnesota Kingstons, Book 4

Copyright © 2025 by Susan May Warren
Published by SDG Publishing
Print ISBN: 978-1-962036-56-6
Ebook ISBN: 978-1-962036-57-3

This book is a work of fiction. Names, characters, places, and incidents are either products of the author's imagination or used fictitiously. Any similarity to actual people, organizations, and/or events is purely coincidental.

Scripture quotations are from The ESV® Bible (The Holy Bible, English Standard Version®), © 2001 by Crossway, a publishing ministry of Good News Publishers. Used by permission. All rights reserved.

Scripture quotations are also taken from the Holy Bible, New International Version®, NIV®. Copyright© 1973, 1978, 1984, 2011 by Biblica, Inc®. Used by permission of Zondervan. All rights reserved worldwide.

Scripture quotations are also taken from the (NASB®) New American Standard Bible®, Copyright © 1960, 1971, 1977, 1995, 2020 by The Lockman Foundation. Used by permission. All rights reserved. lockman.org

For more information about Susan May Warren, please access the author's website at the following address: www.susanmaywarren.com.

Published in the United States of America.

Cover design by Emilie Haney, eahcreative.com

For Your glory, Lord

ONE

RULE NUMBER ONE: DON'T RUN AWAY FROM *the shark.*

Of course, when Austen said exactly that to her two dive clients, they stared at her as if she'd told them to stand in front of a moving freight train.

"Listen. You panic, you start splashing and swimming away— you become prey." She'd been checking their tank connections and opening the air valves as she said it.

Elise Jameson sat on the seat of the dive boat, holding on as the private charter banged through the waves. Spray coated the deck, but it landed warm, refreshing, the sun high as it baked the cloudless day.

It would be a perfect day to dive the *USNS Vandenberg*, seven miles off the coast of Key West. The waters glistened a deep blue, and the sun's rays just might reach all the way to the massive sunken ship, some ten stories tall, over five hundred feet long, and settled into the sandy bottom at one hundred forty-five feet.

The artificial coral-reef habitat of moray eels, green turtles, stingrays, barracuda, and, of course . . . sharks.

Mostly nurse sharks and nonaggressive reef sharks, but okay, occasionally Austen had seen a tiger shark snoozing in the shadows of the upper decks.

Hence the warning.

"I heard you should just hit them on the nose." This from Hunter Jameson, Elise's husband and a seasoned diver, so yeah, Austen might have guessed he'd heard that.

She pulled on her BCD and tank, strapping them on and reaching for her mask. "If they get that close, it might be too late."

The boat slowed, and she reached out to steady herself, glancing back at Hawkeye, who stood at the center console, under the bimini, his hat on backward, wearing aviator sunglasses, sporting a tan against his white Ocean Adventure Divers swim shirt.

He pointed, and she followed his gaze to the dive buoy, an orange floating ball onto which Hawk would moor his forty-foot dive skiff. The divers would follow the line down, sink into the quiet, and . . .

And she'd be flying. It happened every time she dove. As she descended, the ocean turned into the sky, and even as she swam through schools of fish, somehow the world dropped away into peace, only her heartbeat and her rhythmic, slow breathing tethering her to reality.

For those brief moments, she was free.

She turned to Hunter. "Just follow me, and should we startle anything down there, remember these rules: Don't panic, maintain eye contact, and back away slowly. Feel free to shout through your regulator, to blow out bubbles, but don't thrash. Even better—tuck your hands under your armpits. Your gloves can reflect light and look like fish, so—"

She stopped talking at Elise's wide-eyed look. She held up her hands. "Listen. This is a great dive. The ship is covered in barnacles and green and yellow algae, with coral already growing in areas. It'll be inhabited by all sorts of fish. We might even see a goliath grouper, and definitely parrotfish and angelfish, lionfish, maybe silvery tarpons, and hopefully, Millie, our resident loggerhead." She pulled on her mask. "Just stay with me. I promise—I'll keep you safe."

Then she sat on the edge of the boat and backrolled into the water.

Promises, promises.

She'd seen Hunter and Elise dive before—they knew how to handle themselves in the water. And Hunter had been in the military, so he didn't seem like a guy prone to panic.

They descended the line, no problem, and Austen had called it—the light pierced the depths even this far, although she needed her dive light to illuminate the inner passageways of the ship.

The first time Austen had dived the former transport ship, the length had shaken her. The second-largest intentionally sunk dive ship in the world, it stood ten stories tall, with nooks and crannies and stairwells and compartments. But she'd dived the wreck for the better part of the last four years, so she easily guided them along the upper deck, then down a stairwell to the mess hall, where a bright green eel emerged from the empty burners of the large rusty stove.

They watched a parrotfish scrape algae from a bloom on a railing, the crunch echoing in the depths. And Millie rose from one of her favorite spots under an anchor winch on the bow, paddled into the current with her flat oar arms.

Hey, Flash, Austen wanted to say as Millie struck out for the great beyond. *Wait for me.*

Austen checked her time—thirteen minutes down. Four more minutes and they'd head up. Time enough for a quick trip to the satellite dishes.

Rule number two: Keep your eyes on the shark.

It might have helped if she'd seen it lurking, but she'd already swum through the spokes of the satellite array.

Not until she turned did Austen see Elise at the bottom, her tank hooked on the array.

In all her attempts to break free, she'd kicked up dust and splashes and ... yep, awakened a tiger shark sleeping in one of the superstructure sublevels.

It edged out, curious.

Hunter swam down to help his wife, and the two got jammed up in one of the spokes. Worse, Elise's mask had dislodged, and she struggled to clear it.

So she was clearly not watching the predator as he circled.

When the shark darted in and veered off, Austen knew she had to engage. She swam down, outside the satellite, reaching back for her tank tapper, the metal ball strapped on a band that encircled her tank. The tapping might scare him away.

Nope. He circled just below them, then darted in again.

Elise had broken free, her mask on but still half filled with water, in full-out panic as she swatted and kicked away.

No—stop!

The tiger shark jerked away, but Elise's movement only fueled his curiosity.

Austen grabbed Elise's hands. Shook her head. Glanced at Hunter.

He got it, nodding, and took Elise's hands. She struggled, but Hunter gripped her BCD, stilling her.

Of all the places to have a panic attack, a hundred feet down on the ocean floor might be the worst.

Stay calm. Austen tried to communicate with her eyes while also looking for the tiger.

Go down. She pointed to the upper deck of the structure, flattened her hand, and indicated that they should sink down to the platform.

Sharks typically attacked from behind or below—

Hunter pointed behind her, his eyes wide.

Austen turned, and *yep,* he'd come in for another look-see.

A shout filled her regulator. The sound echoed in her head, but it might startle the shark. Then she blew out hard—bubbles rising around her.

The shark jerked away some six feet from her.

Glancing down, she spotted Hunter and Elise on the platform, also blowing bubbles. Hunter had put himself in front of Elise—*sweet*—and pulled out his dive knife.

Okay, everybody calm down.

Austen sank down to them, held up her hand, shook her head. Indicated that Hunter should put the knife away. But he shook his head and she turned. *Oh no.* The tiger wanted a taste.

Most likely it was just very, very curious about these erratic seals. But she faced him, stayed vertical, and despite the thundering of her heart, she kept her eyes on the animal and Didn't. Move.

At the very least, the tiger wanted a bump, but she put her arm out, kept her elbow stiff, and caught it on the snout.

It had opened its mouth, but she deflected it even as it started to roll.

She pushed with her other hand, moving herself away from the shark.

It darted away, probably a little stunned. Hunter was right about the snout being sensitive, but she hadn't hurt it.

The shark swam around the end of the superstructure as if retreating. Her watch beeped, a tiny shrill in the depths. Austen gestured toward the line leading to the surface, and Hunter grabbed his wife's hand.

Turning her back to them, Austen searched for the shark as she grabbed the thick rope with her glove. Then she let out the air in her BCD and started to ascend. Twenty feet from the ship, a dark shadow still circled the superstructure. She didn't take her gaze from the shark as they rose to their deep deco stop at fifty feet. Her dive watch settled into a three-minute countdown and she searched the water.

So much for flying. She hung here like bait, waiting, the outline of the ship below.

A shadow in her peripheral vision caught her eye and she glanced over. Stilled.

A barracuda. Long and silvery, but not a threat as long as No. One. Panicked.

Her timer beeped, and they ascended up the line to their fifteen-foot safety stop. From here, the white hull of the boat dipped in the water, and Hawkeye had already put down the ladder.

Elise seemed to have calmed, but Austen's gaze swept the depths, her breaths hard. A glance at her O2 levels said her tank had emptied faster than usual. *Well, no duh.*

The alarm dinged and Elise shot to the surface, Hunter behind her. Austen hung on the line, floating up slowly, watching.

Elise pulled off her fins, unsnapped her BCD, and let her tank float in the water. From above, Hawkeye fished it out of the drink.

Hunter did the same, disappearing next, and Austen was just reaching for the ladder when she spotted him.

Tiger, back, and maybe angry.

He darted from the depths, hot for the surface, probably attracted by the splashing. She kept her eyes on him, her hand on the ladder, her heartbeat in her throat.

Stay calm.

She put him at a good eight feet, so not the monster great whites she'd seen in Hawaii, but big enough to inflict damage.

She preferred to keep all her appendages.

There was shouting above her, but she sank in the water and put the ladder between her and the tiger.

Then she hung below it, waiting.

He came at her faster than mere curiosity would explain, but not in full attack, so maybe intending to bump her again. She hung on to the ladder with one hand and set her other cupped hand on his snout. He reared up, and she rode with him, her elbow stiff.

Her hand dislodged. But she flipped above him, moving over him, and pushed him away. He shook his tail fin and darted away.

She chucked off her fins and dove for the ladder. Scrambled up, still wearing her vest.

Hands grabbed her and hauled her onto the boat, dumping her into the bottom.

A splash and a scream, and she guessed the tiger shark had found a fin still floating in the water. She unsnapped her BCD, then rolled out of it and lay, breathing hard, the sun hot on her dive skin.

"You okay?" Hawkeye stood over her, then picked up her vest and set it in the rack at the back of the boat.

"That just might have been the bravest thing I've ever seen," Hunter said.

She pressed her hands over her face. Closed her eyes.

There was a vast difference between bravery and desperation.

She finally scrubbed away the shaking and sat up against the side of the boat. "Anybody see my fins?"

"Sorry, Austen. I think they're at the bottom." Hawkeye had started the boat, probably not wanting to stick around.

She scooted up to the bench, the adrenaline still ripping through her.

"Wow. That was . . ." Elise wiped her hands across her face, clearing more tears than saltwater. "Thank you."

Austen held up her hand, nodded. "It's my job."

Hunter shook his head. "Declan said that you were some sort of shark expert, but I didn't . . . I guess I thought it was a euphemism."

Declan. The urge to ask about the philanthropist rose inside her. He'd hired her to lead a dive expedition for his big charity event earlier this summer on the island of Mariposa, and she'd thought . . .

Well, she'd been a little stupid, really. The man had the body of

Henry Cavill, including the jawline, and his dark-gray eyes could turn the ground under a woman to sand. Clearly, all the sunshine and seafood—not to mention how he'd handled unexpected trauma—had gone straight to her sun-bleached head. Plus, the man helped fund an orphanage while managing to run a large tech firm. According to her sister, Boo, he was worth billions.

So there was that too.

She hadn't heard a word from him since she'd returned to Key West. Probably because she'd just been the hired help. *Hello.*

Still, if she'd known how uber-wealthy he was, she might have given him the same stiff-arm she'd given the tiger shark.

Austen picked up a towel and started to dry her hair. "I studied shark behavior for two years in Hawaii. I was on a shark preservation and tagging team." Hawkeye had picked up speed, and she turned her back to the setting sun. Her stomach growled.

"Dinner is on us," Hunter said. "We have reservations at Latitudes. I'm sure they'll let us add another person."

She held up her hand. "No, I'm good. I'm heading out for a week of vacation tomorrow, and I need an early night." In the distance, the city of Key West edged the horizon, the ocean a vivid aquamarine.

"Oh, Declan will be sad to miss you."

Declan?

"He's picking us up on his yacht in a couple days."

The bait just hung there, and she couldn't resist. "Really? Why aren't you flying in? My brother Doyle is on his way back to the orphanage on a seaplane."

"The airfield is still torn up on the island, and Declan's chopper is being used to shuttle supplies back and forth from St. Kitts. And"—Hunter glanced at his wife—"one of us isn't a fan of small planes."

"I've tried the patch. I just can't make it work," Elise said. "We had an ugly incident over Denali once." She made a face. "Thankfully, Dec offered to pick us up."

Huh. Austen shouldn't immediately assume it was because they were massive donors. Declan wasn't like that.

But who was she kidding? He was probably just like every other billionaire. Still, she drew up a knee, wrapped her arms around it. "How is he?"

Elise had grabbed a towel, worked it through her dark hair, turning it curly. Petite and sweet, she and Hunter had been among Declan's guests during the charity-event-turned-earthquake trauma. "Good. He set up the court date for us to adopt Jamal and Kemar from the island, which, after the landslide, was no small feat. I think he wants to get them out of there and into their new lives as soon as possible. We already had our home study done, so . . ." She reached for Hunter's hand. "We're very excited to bring the boys home."

Austen had met the two boys during her stay. Jamal and his older brother, Kemar. "They're very blessed."

"Oh no. We're the ones who are blessed." Hunter wrapped his arm around Elise. "We've been waiting so long for a family . . . It hardly feels real."

Elise nodded, tucked her hand into his.

"It's like being set free from a long prison sentence," Hunter said. "I'd sort of given up."

"Not me," Elise said. "I knew God had a family for us. We just needed to wait for it." She turned to Austen. "You know the saying—'A longing fulfilled is a tree of life.'"

Huh. Austen nodded as the boat hit a wave, thanks to a catamaran flying past them, and water sprayed them.

Elise laughed.

So apparently they were over their scare from the depths of the sea.

"Where are you going on your vacation?" Hunter asked as they slowed, moving toward the green buoys.

"Oh. Um . . . I'll be doing some diving off Sosúa, in the Dominican Republic."

"Dominican Republic?" Hunter said. "We dove the *Zingara* wreck there a few years ago."

"That's not the wreck she's diving," said Hawkeye as he cut the motor. They were puttering into the Key West Bight harbor. "She's looking for the *San Miguel*, a Spanish ship that went down in 1551."

She made a face. "No, I'm not looking for the ship."

"Okay, Spanish gold, then." Hawkeye's mouth tightened around the edges.

"What's that face for?"

"It's the middle of pirate country," Hawkeye said as they turned into their canal. "Right off Haiti."

"Calm down," Austen said. "My boat is hardly a yacht worth attacking. And I'm not looking for Aztec gold." She stood up. "I'm looking for the statue of Santa María de la Paz." She picked up the rope, ready to catch the dock. "It's a sixteenth-century statue of the Black Madonna, about three feet tall, inlaid with pearls and rubies, sent by the King of Spain to a monastery on the island of Hispaniola—a.k.a., DR. It was sculpted by Diego de la Piedra, one of the king's private artists. He died shortly after he sent the statue to Hispaniola, so it's a one of a kind. The *San Miguel* went down on the Silver Bank after breaking up on coral in a storm. A few relics from the wreck have been recovered, but not the statue." She jumped onto the dock and wrapped the mooring rope around a dock post.

"And you hope to be the one to find this statue?" Hunter got up.

Hope might be a strong word.

"It's just a vacation." She jumped back into the boat and headed to the back to unrig the gear.

"Sounds like a job for Ethan Pine." Hunter gathered up their gear. Elise had already climbed out of the boat.

"The treasure hunter? No. I'm not looking to get rich."

She just wanted . . . *Aw, shoot.*

She stood, her gaze landing on a man standing at the end of the pier, long blond hair held back in a bun, wearing shorts and a tank. *Mo.*

And with him . . . *Oh boy.* Built like the ex-SEAL he was, dark-blond hair, sunglasses, and not appearing at all like he'd taken a bullet to his chest a couple months ago.

"Is that your brother with Mo Winters?" Hawkeye had hoisted the BCDs onto the dock.

She sighed. "Yes. Yes, it is."

So much for escaping town.

"Right. I forgot what the date was," Hawkeye said quietly as he unhooked another BCD from its tank.

Yep.

Mo and Stein headed her direction.

Hunter had gotten out. "Thanks again, Austen. Have fun on your trip. Should I say hi to Declan for you?"

While she debated her answer, her twin brother walked up, took off his sunglasses, held out his hand to Hunter, and said, "No. You most certainly shouldn't."

Then, even as he shook Hunter's hand, he glanced at Austen, his mouth grim, a definite we've-got-trouble expression on his face.

And she had the strangest urge to turn around and run.

———•———

Please let this plan work.

Declan stood in his office, leaning on his black marble desk, arms akimbo, listening to Zeus, his head of security, outline the operation. Operation Shell Game.

Whatever. The former SBS operative could call their bait-and-switch plan anything he wanted. As long as it worked.

He cast a glance out the window. His property sat atop a bluff overlooking the small seaside town of Esperanza, and now his gaze searched the harbor. He spotted his yacht, the *Invictus*, anchored to shore.

Crew loaded it up with food supplies, gas, and water. He checked his watch.

They should be landing soon.

Zeus was still talking. "The cargo ship will dock on the far shore, but only after it clears customs in the Mariposa harbor." Zeus wore a black T-shirt that seemed too small for his body, a pair of jeans, and a cap over his dark curly hair, his Bermudian English accent heavy. "We'll replace the crew with our own, then head over to the dock on the north side of the island." He brought up a picture of the mining company.

The mining company owned by the Russian mob.

Declan's mouth pinched. He shouldn't have let it get this far.

Beyond his property and up the hill rose Cumbre de Luz, the now-dormant volcano that had created the tiny island of Mariposa. A terrible scar of rock and debris cut down the face of the mountainside, the once-lush tropical forest at its base ripped up, shredded, and deposited into the small unsuspecting town along the harbor, taking out homes and destroying businesses.

Even now, some two months later, the locals struggled to rebuild their lives.

When he'd leased rights to the Russians, he'd known they weren't mining for sulfite inside the volcano like they claimed, but rather for obsidite. A rare mineral found only on Mariposa, a superconductor of electricity, and the hottest commodity in the terrorist market.

To get to the obsidite, the Russians decided to destroy the tunnels that ran through Cumbre de Luz like Swiss cheese. Which, as it turned out, caused the entire mountain to tremble, break free . . .

And slide down into the village.

The mining, the landslide—it was all his fault. And he had to do something about it. Especially now that they'd mined enough to create their first shipment off the island.

Declan blew out a breath, hung a hand on the back of his neck. "You sure they won't know we switched the boat crews?"

Zeus set down the remote control. "I hired our crew. One of the captains is Russian—he can do the talking. He can be trusted."

"And then?"

He turned. "Then we play a little game. We send out two more ships, one equipped with the AIS they expect—"

"Which will be the route they expect?"

"Cuba."

Of course, Cuba. The closest communist country and still in cahoots, apparently.

"Right. And our ship?"

"Two of them, using the same AIS—"

"They'll have different positions and speeds and courses but will offer the same basic signature."

"Yes," Zeus said. "They'll go two different directions, so even if the Russians do manage to find out the AIS, they won't know which one it is. I named them the *Niña*, the *Pinta*, and the *Santa Maria*."

"And the mining company?"

"Rigged, sir. Most of the workers will be leaving the island for R&R. Just a few security, but we'll escort them away before the mine is destroyed."

"Very good." Declan glanced again out the window, at the nearby orphanage, also positioned above the village. The slide had, providentially, narrowly missed taking out the centuries-old former monastery. A few of the kids played outside in the soccer field. Probably Rosa was making some of her delicious jerk chicken.

Maybe he'd have enough time to head over there after he picked up Doyle and Tia ...

He stood up. "I'm leaving this with you, Zeus." He held out his hand.

"Very good, sir. I'll be in touch." Zeus shook his hand, then headed for the door.

Declan locked his office, then headed to his bedroom.

The thick stone walls of his home collected the cool breezes off the ocean, the doors to his expansive terrace open to the lush tropical smells and salty breeze.

Shanice had just finished changing his sheets, and now she gestured to his packed suitcase. "According to your list, sir."

"I appreciate that. You can tell Javier that he can take it to the yacht when he's ready. I'll take the Alfa and leave it at the dock garage."

She left him and he stepped out onto the balcony jutting out over the pool deck, white travertine tile bright against the sunlight. Sometimes the view still stopped him—the expansive blue water of the Caribbean, the endless unfettered sky.

"You'd like this, Mom," he said, leaning on the glass railing, and he couldn't deny the smallest thickening of his throat. This place was so very different from the tiny bungalow in New Hope, Minnesota, where he'd grown up.

A buzz in the air turned him toward the harbor, and he spotted the small seaplane descending, its red-and-white body an albatross gliding to a landing.

He headed downstairs, then outside to the steps, and finally out to his four-stall garage. Keying in the code, he entered, grabbed his keys, and slid into his restored 1969 Alfa Romeo Spider, a tiny Italian car that barely fit his body. But he liked it.

Had restored it himself, back when he'd had time for things like that.

He should restore something else, probably. Air out his head from the tangle of intrigue woven by his we're-the-good-guys contact—a guy who went by the code name Texas. Texas had been the one to first suggest he sell to the Russians. *Keep your enemies close.*

Yeah, too close. Now Declan had to fix the mess.

The air cut through his hair, his linen shirt, the shocks terrible as he drove down the rutted dirt road into town. In the two months since the devastating landslide, they'd bulldozed the rubble, reconstructed a road through town, and now as he entered the outskirts, new construction evidenced the rebirth and resilience of the town.

And soon there would be a new trauma center, thanks to Tia Pepper and Doyle Kingston, his new secret weapons. Last he'd seen them, a month ago when he'd returned to Minnesota, they were finally dating too.

About time.

He'd tried to track down Steinbeck, his former bodyguard, who'd left him for the States after being shot a couple months ago. But he hadn't yet been able to connect with him. Which felt weird.

He had a plan to fix that too.

He slowed as he motored through town, past the new bank and the street vendors, hardy folks who still sold doubles—delicious flatbread filled with chickpeas—patties, and of course, conch fritters.

His stomach growled. But he'd have a decent dinner on the yacht, and Camille would murder him if he filled up.

That's what he got for hiring a French chef. But he wanted this voyage . . . Well, he wanted *so much* out of this voyage. Nothing could go wrong.

He pulled up to his private dock, waved at the camera, and the gate opened. Driving in, he parked at the small dock house and dropped the keys into the hands of Diego, his chauffeur. "Park her in the garage. They'll take the Jeep to the orphanage."

Diego nodded. *Good kid.* He was one of the oldest orphans rescued out of the terrible aftermath of the hurricane five years ago. Now he had a wife, a kid on the way, a home, and a job. Declan patted him on the shoulder, then headed out to the dock.

The seaplane sat secured, the pilot gassing up, the passengers already out, helping unload their gear.

"Doyle!"

The dark-haired man, dressed in a T-shirt and cargo shorts, loafers, turned and raised a hand. Doyle sported a hint of a beard too.

The woman with him, Tia, also turned. Dark hair pulled back into a messy bun, hazel-green eyes, and a tan, the woman smiled, waved. "Declan!" She picked up a satchel, put it on her shoulder, and reached for a rolling bag, but Doyle grabbed it from her.

Huh. So maybe she wasn't the boss of him anymore.

Declan came up to her, gave her a kiss on one cheek, then the other. "You look fantastic."

"All that time on Conrad's sailboat." She glanced at Doyle. "And Doyle just had to volunteer as a soccer coach for the last month, so I sat in the sun a lot."

"Oh no, that's on her. She's the one who hooked me up with EmPowerPlay, her family's charity. I had no choice." He glanced at Tia, grinning.

Oh yes, definitely together.

"Glad to have you both back." He reached for one of the rolling bags.

"Just in time for Jamal and Kemar to have their court hearing?" Doyle asked as he followed.

"In a couple weeks. I'm heading up to the Keys to pick up the Jamesons. Hunter and Elise are excited. And by the way, I heard from the Scotts. They finished their home study, so I think we'll be scheduling Lucia's court date soon too." He glanced back at Doyle. "Three down, forty to go."

"And I've landed a couple scholarships for Gabriella and others who might want to go on to college," Tia said, looking back at them. "But the biggest project is the trauma center. We got Compassion Corp to put up the initial payment—enough to get the plans drawn up and break ground."

"I knew hiring you two was a brilliant move." He reached the end of the dock, where Diego waited.

"Ranger is on his way, sir," Diego said.

"Ranger is still here?" Doyle said, carrying his suitcase to the Jeep, now pulled up in the gravel drive.

"He goes back and forth, but yes, he's been instrumental in helping organize all the cleanup." Declan spotted the man now, headed toward the truck. Tall, with dark-brown hair, he dressed in a T-shirt with *Jones, Inc.* written across the chest, a pair of light-weight pants, boots, and he still bore the swagger and build of the SEAL he'd once been. Declan had gotten to know him and his story over a few dinners and late-night street grub.

"Hey, cuz," Doyle said and greeted Ranger with a shake-slash-man-hug. "How's the baby?"

"Good. Although not a baby anymore. Walking. Terrorizing his mother. The other day he found a jar of peanut butter, took the top off, and managed to lather his hair with it."

"Nice," Doyle said. "So, trouble, just like his old man."

"Oh no, I wasn't trouble. That was my brother, Colt." He winked, then pointed to the plane. "That for me?"

"Yep. Thanks again, Ranger." Declan held out his hand. "Safe travels."

Ranger clamped him on the back and threw his duffel bag over his shoulder and headed out to the plane.

"You're not going with him?" This from Tia as Diego put her bag in the back of the Jeep.

"No, the Jamesons aren't big fans of flying, so I'm taking the *Invictus* to pick them up in Key West." He pointed to the yacht. A hundred twenty feet, all white, three decks, five staterooms, and a crew of seven.

"Oh, my dad would be jealous," Tia said, turning toward it, lowering her sunglasses. "He has a sailboat, but he's definitely thought of adding a yacht to his fleet."

"That's a beautiful yacht, Dec," Doyle said.

"Thanks." And he suddenly felt like a sixth grader showing off his new bike to his friends, hoping that . . .

Well, hoping he might impress the girl, Austen Kingston, once he found her.

Wow. He was *that* guy. The nerd who wanted the prettiest girl he'd ever seen to notice him.

Please let him not be reading the sparks between them wrong. He'd made his big mistake last time by hiring her. He could hardly have asked her out while she worked for him without it getting weird.

Although, showing up in Key West in his hundred-and-twenty-foot yacht, asking if she'd like to have dinner with him might be equally weird.

Hopefully, impressively weird.

Oh brother.

"Key West, huh?" Doyle grinned.

"C'mon, Doyle," Tia said, taking his hand, smiling. "Give the man some breathing room. He's just a guy, standing on a yacht, asking a girl to like him."

Declan's mouth opened.

"Good luck, boss," Tia said and pulled a smirking Doyle away.

They got in the Jeep, and Diego pulled out.

Declan turned, his hands in his pockets. Watched Ranger climb aboard. Then the pilot waved, and a few moments later, the plane pulled away from the dock, motored out into the harbor, then kicked up water and took to the air.

Right. Well then, everything seemed buttoned up.

This could work. It could really work.

He took a breath and headed toward the yacht.

Here went nothing.

TWO

TWO GLORIOUS DAYS ON THE OCEAN, THE sun spilling across the waves, turning the depths transparent and crystalline, the sun hot on her skin, miles away from her argument with Stein just two days ago, yet...

His words still sat inside Austen like a hot burr as she stood at the helm of her trawler-slash-floating-home, cutting through the waves to her dive location.

"Do not trust Declan. Don't even talk to him again. He's a criminal, Austen."

What-ever.

She sat on the captain's seat in the flybridge of the restored trawler, forty-three feet of head-to-toe gleaming teak (new fiberglass in places), with a freshly painted white hull, a blue racing stripe along the sides, and a Yanmar motor that hummed like a sleeping lion. The deep-blue canvas canopy flapped as the wind skimmed over the ocean. The air hinted at rain, and in the distance, a gathering of dark clouds edged the horizon.

But for now, blue skies, and according to her map, she'd nearly reached the shoal where she would anchor the *Fancy Free* for her dive. Yesterday's location had netted her a massive male lobster—in DR waters, legal to catch even this late in the year.

But no Virgin Mary statue, and yes, she could admit that her hunt might be just an excuse.

It got her out of yet another yearly reminder of Margo's death, so maybe not an excuse. A necessity.

"I've never heard of anything so crazy!"

Her words from the fight with Stein replayed as she slowed the boat over the shoal, some nine miles out from shore, searching for the right sandy bottom to anchor. Of course, he'd brought her to Sloppy Joe's for their epic showdown. None of the regulars there would care if she threw down with her twin brother—and a local reggae band drowned out the argument.

Still, her "Why would you say that?" could probably have been heard across the island.

Maybe she should have held back just a little—seeing Stein on the mend didn't mean he'd completely found his footing after yet another on-the-job injury. He still boasted his deep tan, however, and moved like a guy who'd taken his rehab seriously. He'd even helped carry her dive gear to her boat in permanent harbor in Key West Bight. She'd sprayed off her gear, then set it in the aft head to dry and locked the bridge, all while he updated her on the family news—Jack and Harper, still working on Jack's new bus, not engaged yet, but Stein thought it might be soon. And Conrad, heading back soon to Blue Ox hockey camp, spending the summer coaching in specialty camps, still dating Penny Pepper, who had started in on another podcast about a serial killer in Alaska.

And Doyle and Tia, of course, the surprising power couple, raising funds for a new trauma center in Mariposa.

"I guess we're the holdouts," she'd said to Stein as they'd headed to Sloppy's.

And that's when Stein had launched into his comments about

Declan being some sort of international handwriting mastermind, working with some evil Russian outfit trying to take over the world.

"You make him sound like *Pinky and the Brain.*"

Stein hadn't laughed. Just sat there, his mouth a grim slash, his blue eyes on hers. *Weird*—they might share the same birthday, but Stein seemed worlds different from her. He actually went looking for trouble. Thrived on it, maybe.

She preferred the wide-open spaces, the peace, of the sea.

Here. Where the sandy bottom seemed close enough to touch, despite being twenty feet down. She pointed the boat into the wind, then let out the bow anchor. It touched the seabed. Not much chop on the water, and she'd only be down for an hour, so she let out the rope to a three-to-one length, then reversed the engine and set the anchor. Turned off the boat.

But just to make sure, she headed out to the bow, along the narrow deck, and checked. Sand still clouded the water where she'd landed the anchor, but it seemed the boat was set. If she decided to stay all night, she'd set a stern anchor, but this would work for now.

Heading back to the stern, she pulled her gear out of the aft dive box and fixed her BCD onto one of her four tanks. She had topped them off with her personal O2 compressor.

"It's not a joke, Austen. I've been looking into him. Declan lied to me about selling his AI program to the DOD. And there are other things too—like his meeting with foreign agents in Barcelona when we were there. And maybe even a connection to the Russian mob—"

Their hot wings had arrived then, the reggae band stirring up the night's festivities. How often did she get a visit from her favorite brother, and he had to tell her she was an idiot?

Okay, maybe not an idiot. Stein didn't know how far Declan had gotten into her heart. Still . . .

She had sort of lost her appetite. "How do you know all this? You worked for the guy. I remember you liking him. You usually have great instincts, Steinbeck. What made you turn on him?"

At her words, Stein had pushed away the wings. Silence from him as he'd listened to the music, the wind stirring the palm trees, too much in his blue eyes for her to read. He'd shaken his head then and turned back to her. "Just . . . trust me."

She'd been the one to look away then. He'd put his hand on hers, squeezed. "I'm just trying to watch your back. Keep you from getting hurt."

She'd wanted to yank her hand away, round on him with *That's not your job!* But she got it—they'd always had a bond, and maybe if she'd let him protect her more, she wouldn't prefer the high seas and wide skies to . . . well, whatever the rest of her siblings had with their recent relationships.

So, even if she couldn't quite get her brain around Stein's words, she knew he was right.

Declan was trouble.

Now she changed into her dive shirt and shorts, grabbed her fins and mask, affixed the control box of her Garrett Sea Hunter metal detector onto her weight belt, grabbed the headphones, picked up the wand, which she'd use to probe the sand, then lowered her inflated BCD and tank into the sea.

Then she jumped into the water.

Five minutes later, she'd followed the anchor line to the bottom. According to a recent posting in one of her online dive communities, someone had picked up a piece of majolica pottery in this area, crusted over with sea barnacles and algae, but after cleanup, the shiny white tin glaze had revealed a coat of arms from the house of Philip II of Spain.

So, early fifteen hundreds. Maybe the *San Miguel* had broken up on the coral reef that edged the sandy shoal, scattering her debris along the reef.

And of course, as she swam toward the deeper water where the waves could have buried the heavier cargo, her old partner Margo's words hung in her brain: *"Today's the day, Tennie!"*

Not her original words—Margo had adopted the relentless optimism of Mel Fisher, but said it with her signature smile, her eyes shining as she jumped into the blue . . .

"Yes, today's the day, Marg."

Austen wove through a garden of coral life teeming with angel and clown fish, the coral itself a landscape of color and shape. She flicked on her dive light and glided around golden elkhorn spires, over green brain coral, around pink boulder coral, scattering clown fish embedded in the carpet of a magnificent red bubble-tip anemone.

A stingray lifted from the rippled layers of the sandy bottom, and her light landed on a lurking grouper. She checked her dive watch, then her O2. She had a good forty minutes of bottom time left. She pulled out a search-grid map on her diver's slate and marked it.

Settling just above the bottom, she pulled on her earphone and turned on the metal detector, keeping it parallel to the bottom. She'd work the grid in lanes, and should it ping on anything, she'd disturb the sand, raking up years of sediment.

The pulse whined over an area littered with shells and rock. She stirred up the sand, let it settle, and the whine sounded over a small barnacle-crusted object. Digging in, she found a ring. Probably a diver's lost wedding band. She pocketed it, then kept searching. Found a ring of keys, a watch, and even a couple coins.

From 1963.

A check of her O2 suggested she should turn home, but not before she searched another sandy pocket rimmed by boulder coral. She spotted a giant scallop, its mouth moving to collect plankton and algae, and imagined the pearls she might find inside. But she didn't have a permit.

Besides, she didn't need treasure. Just . . .

Closure. A promise kept.

The Sea Hunter pinged around the base of some elkhorn coral, and she stirred up the ground. Waved the metal detector over the sand, and the whine settled. She grabbed her Quest XPointer and searched.

There. Something metallic in the gleam of her dive light. She pulled a trowel from her belt and dug it up.

Oh, she wished she could turn to Margo and shout, or at least give a fist pump. A layer of verdigris turned it almost black, but it was clearly a mug, complete with a handle.

Like the kind a Spanish galleon might have for its crew.

Or a modern-day ship might offer to a sailor enjoying a sunset mule. But . . . *maybe.*

She pulled out a mesh bag and added the mug to it, then glanced at her O2. It had sunk toward the red. Turning around, she glanced at her compass and headed back to her down line, listening now to Stein's words as he'd dropped her off at her boat.

"You're diving by yourself?" He'd stood there, arms akimbo, his expression judgy.

"I'm not reckless, Stein. You know that. Besides, if anything happens, I always dive with a PLB."

"A Personal Locator Beacon isn't going to save you if you get tangled in netting or run into a gear issue." His phone had beeped then, and he'd pulled it out, frowned. Put it back. "I have something I need to do tomorrow, but wait for me—I'll go with you."

Yeah, maybe that would have been a good idea. But the trip took two days in good weather, and she'd wanted at least two decent days of diving.

So, "Not this time, bro." She'd hugged him, and he'd growled.

Now, as she searched for the down line, his growl thundered through her.

She checked her compass again, aware of the beeping from her watch. *Low air. Yeah, yeah,* she knew.

Except, where was the line? Around her, the ocean seemed

darker. She hadn't noticed the change, thanks to the depth and her dive light.

She let out her BCD air and ascended to her safety stop. She must have mistaken her GPS point.

Three minutes later, she reached the surface and inflated her BCD to float.

Rain pinged down on her, and the ocean had turned wild, the waves cluttered, disorganized, pitching her.

The squall had rolled in quicker than she'd thought it could.

But where was her boat?

She searched the water, the sun darkened despite the daytime hour, and a realization climbed into her gut and squeezed.

Somehow, her anchor had broken free.

The *Fancy Free* was adrift in the Caribbean.

And so was she.

———————— • ————————

Finally, a blue-skied day, and Declan stood on deck, searching the Key West Bight harbor as the *Invictus* pulled into dock. Two days of dodging intermittent squalls on his voyage north from Mariposa cut precious time from his trip.

Aw, who was he kidding? He should have gotten on that plane with Ranger for a hop to the Keys. It would have at least cut down the two days of trial-and-error conversation replaying in Declan's head.

"Hey, Austen. Thought I'd stop in and see if you want to have dinner."

Weird.

"Hey, Austen, how are you? Haven't heard—"

No. That was on him.

"Austen, what a surprise!"

Okay, so lying wouldn't be a great way to ignite their relationship.

Relationship? He had clearly flung his hopes far and long, but a guy who didn't have a vision couldn't create a strategy, right?

So, he would settle for, "Hey, Austen. I thought maybe we could start over. I'd really love to take you to dinner."

And if she wondered why he'd traveled fifteen hundred miles for a date, maybe that would work in his favor. Show her that, yeah, she meant something to him.

"Declan, you are a surprising man." Her words, spoken while he'd danced with her two months ago under a moonlit night at his charity event. She'd smiled up at him, her green eyes almost magnetic, and right then, the sense of her had crashed into him.

This woman.

Like a brilliant star, she'd lit up the darkness inside, and it had been all he could do not to dance her into the shadows, ask her if he could kiss her.

But . . . he was her *employer.* At least for that weekend, so . . .

Not today. Today he was just a guy—how had Tia put it? Asking a girl on a date?

For starters.

Standing in shorts and flip-flops, the sun baking through his linen shirt, Declan held on to the bow railing, searching the Key West Bight harbor for the *Fancy Free.* From the pictures Austen had shown him, it was an old fishing trawler with a blue canopy, maybe forty some feet long, and spiffed up as a liveaboard.

He spotted a few sailboats, their masts piercing the blue sky, a couple yachts, and a few dive boats, but no trawlers matching the description.

Maybe she'd put out for a day of diving.

He'd dock at his private slip, find hers, and wait her out. *Not creepy at all.*

"Sir, we're about to dock. Would you like a car to meet you?"

Jermaine Rhodes, his ship's steward, had come out of the salon, sliding the door behind to keep the air-conditioning trapped.

Declan turned, his hands in his pockets. "No, thank you. I'll wander around. Maybe grab a bite to eat at the Half Shell. I love Camille's coq au vin, but I need something from the sea today."

"Shall I ask her to pick up some fresh lobster from the market?"

Did Austen like lobster? *Maybe.* "And some shrimp and mahi-mahi, just in case."

"In case?" Jermaine raised an eyebrow.

Declan shrugged. "In case . . . I'm really hungry."

Jermaine offered a slight nod, then headed back inside, down to the kitchen.

Declan glanced up at the bridge, where his captain, Teresa, a petite, no-nonsense Portuguese woman in her mid-thirties, helmed his ship. Her first mate, a Swede named Ivek who dwarfed her and had a quiet solidness about him, stood on deck, radio in his grip, directing the deckhands—two men and a woman—as they maneuvered the ship into one of the larger slips. The woman had also helped in the kitchen and worked as a cabin steward. She was new to the boat, but Declan left the staff hires to Ivek.

In his pocket, Declan's phone buzzed. He pulled it out and then cupped his hand over the screen to read it. Couldn't quite make it out, so he headed inside to the salon.

The cool air prickled his skin, the boat motor quietly humming through him as he left the chaos outside. He sank onto one of his white sofas.

An update from Zeus.

Zeus
Cargo acquired. Ships deployed.
The game is on.

Declan shook his head, smiling as he sent a thumbs-up emoji. Okay, yes, it did feel like a clandestine operation.

A grand heist. Necessary, really, to keep the peace.

He pocketed his phone and headed back outside. They'd pulled alongside the outer docks jutting into deeper water, the deckhands busy securing the ropes to the dock cleats.

Ivek came over to him. "We'll have the gangway out in a moment, sir. We'll be ready to leave in about four hours."

"Thanks. I'm not sure how long I'm staying. Can you ask Jermaine to contact the Jamesons and send a car? Ask them to meet me at the Half Shell."

"Yes, sir," Ivek said and moved away with his radio.

The voice of Declan's former bodyguard raked through his head. *I think someone is after you, sir.* Words spoken in Barcelona after he'd been sideswiped by a scooter. Stein had suggested it wasn't an accident but a woman after the contents of his cybersafe in the country of Montelena, a woman who needed his blood to create a bio key.

Crazy, but the theory contained enough what-if plausibility that Declan had moved the AI program to his own vault in Mariposa. And of course, the vault had been destroyed during the earthquake, so two months ago, he'd finally moved the hard-drive backup copy to his safe at his estate in Minnesota.

But that's when Stein had gone missing and shown up shot, which had Declan a little unnerved as well. He'd airlifted his bodyguard to St. Kitts and then flown him home to Minnesota.

Maybe he should have replaced him, because Declan felt a little naked as he ventured down the gangway. On the island, and even in Minnesota, his security blanketed him from the sense of being watched, stalked. *Whatever.* Frankly, he'd thought Stein would return after he'd healed. But repeated texts and a couple phone calls had netted Declan zippo. As if he'd been ghosted.

Which felt even more weird because he'd sort of thought they were friends. He missed Stein's good-natured ribbing, his quiet confidence, his stalwart presence.

Declan simply didn't let people that close, really, so . . .

Aw, he hadn't had any trouble in two months, so maybe he'd imagined whatever danger had stalked him, his brain igniting paranoia after his cell phone was stolen at the Kingston family wedding. *Lost—not stolen. See? Paranoid.*

But if a guy didn't stay alert, trouble could sneak up on him.

He walked down the dock, let himself out of the gated entryway and onto the sidewalk, heading toward the Galleon Resort. He kept a room on hold here for exactly these purposes—well, not *these* purposes—but nostalgia had him keeping the place.

It had been one of his first investments, his first dip into the millionaire mindset.

He worked his way toward the Galleon, then walked through the lobby with its trophy fish on the walls, the beige tiles, the rattan furniture, and stopped at the front desk. A woman named Wanda greeted him. *Blonde hair, pretty.*

"I have a garage. Penthouse suite." He was reaching for his ID when Henry came out of the back, his hand outstretched.

"Declan. I didn't know you were stopping by." A tall mid-fifties Dutchman, Henry had just about been ready to close shop after Hurricane Irma when Declan had seen the potential.

"Just for a few hours. Came to pick up some friends. I should have called ahead."

"Always glad to see you." Henry grinned.

"Sorry I'm not staying. However, I'm going to pick up my scooter."

Henry gestured to a porter, put a hand on his shoulder, and sent him to fetch it.

"I read your last report—sounds like you've recovered since Covid."

"Doing better. We probably need a facelift, though." Henry gestured to the island-themed decor. "Everyone wants the modern rustic style."

"You stick with your plan, Henry. People like to get away, feel like they're in a tropical setting."

The porter arrived with the scooter, a Piaggio Beverly, white with a brown leather seat, freshly washed. "Thanks for taking care of her."

Declan pulled out, headed down Front Street, then worked his way over to Greene and finally onto Lazy Way, which of course felt just right, the wind in his hair, the sun on his skin. He'd grab a table at the Half Shell, facing the wharf, and hopefully Austen would be back by sundown.

He passed a fifty-foot catamaran at the dock, then Schooner Wharf Bar, and headed out to William, through a side street, and over to Margaret Street.

Music lifted from the Half Shell Raw Bar as he pulled into the lot, found a space, and got out.

The scents of raw fish and the wharf settled as he walked inside, past nets, buoys, and ropes hanging on the walls, fresh fish in ice on display, probably caught that morning. The raw bar ran across one wall, facing the harbor, metal-mesh-gloved shuckers behind the bar, busy with their knives.

He found a picnic table on the terrace, the walls covered by license plates from the fifty states. A wooden fishing trawler hung between two pylons. His stomach growled. Nothing like fresh-shucked oysters, a bucket of steamed clams, and deep-fried shrimp to bring a guy back to his roots.

Those days when he was stationed in San Diego, his rare get-aways to Seaport Village. He could almost hear his mom's laughter, see the pride in her eyes when he'd treated her to her first surf and turf. Oh, he'd had dreams.

The memory pinched a little, and he exhaled, smiling up at a waitress who handed him a menu, water. He ordered a plate of oysters.

His gaze hung on the harbor, the afternoon sun sending shadows into the water. Dive boats and other vessels motored in from their afternoon excursions.

"Declan!"

Elise Hunter. He got up, gave her a kiss on either cheek, and then held out his hand to Hunter.

"Thank you so much for picking us up," Elise said and sat on the opposite bench. "With all the storms that came through the last few days, we thought you might be delayed."

"I have an excellent captain," he said, leaning back as the waitress brought the oysters. "But I think we'll wait until tomorrow to leave, just so we don't get caught in anything in the dark."

Hunter ordered for himself and Elise.

"Oh, the sea at night is terrifying," Elise said. "I keep wondering if I should have just braved the float plane." She took a sip of water.

"I think we'll be just fine on Dec's yacht, honey," Hunter said and pointed out to the *Invictus* at the end of the dock.

Declan followed his gesture and stilled. Set down his oyster uneaten.

Steinbeck Kingston stood on the dock, talking and gesturing with another man, still aboard a dive boat, docking at one of the piers.

Declan stared at him a moment longer to confirm—*yes*. Definitely his former bodyguard, now dressed in shorts and flip-flops, a T-shirt, his glasses perched backward on the top of his head, that pensive look on his face.

Whatever he was saying, it seemed to have galvanized the other man, who was nodding.

They started to walk down the dock—

"I'll be right back."

Declan blamed the sense of unfinished business, the crazy impulse that something had gone down between himself and Steinbeck and . . .

Shoot. He simply didn't have that many real friends. And sure,

Stein couldn't exactly be a friend—frankly, that was the problem. Anyone who got close enough to be a real friend was on his payroll.

Still. "Steinbeck!" He'd left the restaurant, walking out to the dock, and maybe it looked desperate, but—"Stein!"

The man turned, and it seemed Declan's appearance shook him because he stopped and took in a breath as if bracing himself. *What?* The coincidence of meeting Steinbeck felt almost providential, but . . . well, maybe Stein had come to the Keys because of Austen.

Not unlike Declan, so . . .

Stein's mouth tightened, his hands in his pockets, and the strangest sense that he wanted to run or maybe . . . *hit him? . . .* snaked through Declan. Because the narrow-eyed look on Steinbeck's face, the fact that he didn't extend his hand to Declan, felt off.

Which only put a burr in Declan. "What's going on? I've called a dozen times, texted more. You okay?"

Steinbeck glanced at the man standing a little away from him. Looked back at Declan. "Yeah, I'm good."

A beat. "I was worried after . . . after you were shot."

"Thanks for your help getting me home."

Declan nodded, frowned. Another beat. "Is . . . did I do something to offend—"

"No. Listen, I gotta go. Austen's . . ." He closed his mouth.

Something about the way Stein looked past him to the harbor, then sighed, made Declan's gut clench. "What about Austen? Is she okay?" He looked to the other man. He wore an Ocean Adventure Divers T-shirt, so probably part of a local dive operation. *Oh no.* "Is she injured?"

"She's missing," said the man. He held out his hand. "You're Declan Stone?"

Declan met his grip.

"People around here know you," the man said. "Hawthorne Marshall. People call me Hawkeye."

Right. "Yeah. What's going on with Austen?" He looked back to Stein.

Stein blew out a breath, met Declan's gaze. "She put out for the DR two days ago to do some diving."

It took a second. "Alone?"

Stein nodded. "And . . . her PLB just went off."

Personal Locator Beacon. "Is she in trouble?"

"Dunno. I can't get ahold of her boat. It's not responding, and no one seems to be able to locate it." Stein swallowed, ran a hand across his mouth. Shook his head. "So, yeah. I think—"

"The DR, you said?"

"Yeah. Lots of squalls down there right now, so maybe . . . could be her communication got knocked out. Maybe that's why she turned on the PLB."

Declan glanced at the yacht. Seemed they'd finished refueling. He turned back to Stein. "Did you alert the Coast Guard?"

"In the Dominican Republic? I was just on my way to do that." He glanced at Hawkeye. "We're taking out his boat, heading down there."

"Come with me," Declan said. "I can—"

"No." Stein blew out a breath. "But I guess two boats are better than one. I'll send you her PLB signature." And for the first time, Stein seemed to be the man Declan knew. "I'll keep you informed."

"I'll find her, Stein. I will."

Stein's mouth tightened. He nodded. Then he held out his hand.

Huh. Declan shook it.

"I'm trusting you," Stein said, his gaze hard on Declan.

Declan suddenly felt like he was back at boot camp on his way to do push-ups without knowing why.

No, worse. He was back in Afghanistan, the horror coiling around him as—

"Keep me updated," Stein said. Then he and Hawkeye took off toward the parking lot.

Declan jogged back to the bar. Motioned to the waitress as he pulled out his credit card. She came over, and he handed her the card.

"We need a takeout box."

Then he looked at the Jamesons. "We're leaving port. Right now."

Hey, Austen. Stay alive. I will find you.

• ————————— •

She'd taken cover in the lions' den. Because rash decisions led to lethal mistakes.

At least for now, Emberly was safe. *Ish*—safe*ish*. What was the penalty for stowing away in international waters? Walking the plank? Thirty lashes?

But what choice did she have with the Petrov Bratva on her tail?

So maybe, yes, it had been a bad idea to stick around the island of Mariposa for the last two months, trying to get a bead on exactly what the Russians on the other side of the mountain were up to.

Maybe she shouldn't have alerted them to her presence by stealing a four-wheeler back a couple months ago when she'd escaped the mine with Steinbeck. But hello, the former SEAL, her nemesis-slash-fellow-survivor had been bleeding out. So yes, into a Russian mining camp she went, liberated a four-wheeler, tore out of camp, threw Stein on the back, and hightailed it to town.

Sometimes in her sleep, she still saw herself dumping Stein off at the doorstep of the Mariposa clinic. Wishing that, just once, it didn't have to end that way with them.

But her life didn't have room for a happily ever after, so . . .

She'd done what she had to in order to keep Stein alive. Then she'd hidden out, having missed her getaway flight from the island.

Apparently her chopper reservation had been commandeered by someone flying a bunch of injured people to nearby St. Kitts.

Declan Stone, pretending to be a hero instead of the mastermind of this colossal mess.

One did not get in bed with the Russian mob and survive. Unless one was part of their evil echelon.

Oh, she wanted to take him down, destroy his empire. Just because a guy gave millions away to a charitable organization—or many—that didn't make him a hero.

Or even a good guy.

But the last place she'd thought she'd end up was on his very yacht. She'd had few choices—as in, *none*—when one of the Russian thugs tracked her down in Mariposa.

So she'd liberated a uniform from the catering crew stocking the yacht, then walked aboard, introduced herself to Chef Camille as Declan's new hire *(What? He didn't tell you?)*, had netted herself a ticket out of Dodge.

Her great escape meant a week on a luxury yacht, which might not have been so bad if she weren't a scullery rat and a cabin maid.

"Declan has guests tonight, so I'll need you to serve, along with Jermaine." The words came from Chef Camille, Declan's fancy chef from France, who had no problem filling up the sink with a thousand pots as she created Declan's gourmet dinner.

A dinner she'd be AWOL for. But Emberly just smiled, nodded, and kept scrubbing one of Camille's dirty pots, her apron wet, her short dark hair in a net, her hands parched as she counted the hours until her shift ended and she escaped off the *Invictus* and into Key West.

Okay, she didn't hate her choice of transportation, even with her lack of options. Big enough to hide in with its three stories and numerous lounge areas, the boat also had a Jacuzzi, a couple of Jet Skis on the swim deck, and a fire-table lounge area on the top sky deck.

Built for luxury for sure, bought with his dirty terrorist millions.

At least Emberly had her own cubby in the crew quarters, a bunk that came equipped with a light and a locked compartment, and a curtain for privacy. Still, she shared the hallway with some kid named Tyrone, the skinny deckhand; and Jermaine, a former Navy corpsman from Puerto Rico; and the engineer, Raphael, who kept to himself and spent his off-shift hours reading. Ivek, the big Swede, and Teresa, the captain, had their own cabins, and Chef Camille slept in a cabin off the kitchen.

Not a bad crew, and Chef Camille was focused and maybe a little exacting, but more bossy than unkind.

Today they would come ashore, and as soon as she got off this boat, she'd vanish into the crowds of America, deliver Declan's precious Axiom hard drive, which she'd liberated from his safe before the terrible landslide, then pop up to see her sister Nimue in Melbourne Beach.

Catch her breath. Because she'd been chasing Declan and his evil plans for the better part of six months, and frankly, she needed to shake off the residue of this op.

No, shake off the residue of Steinbeck Kingston, and the fact that he still haunted her dreams.

She'd left him to die, again. He would probably murder her . . . if he'd lived.

Please, let him have lived. She probably shouldn't care so much, except . . .

Well, except he had long ago gotten under her skin and maybe a little into her heart, and she lost her brains a little around him, total kryptonite for a Black Swan like herself. The way he made her feel when he looked at her with those blue eyes just . . .

Healed her, perhaps. Made her see a different life. A different future.

Naw. He was pure temptation, chocolate on the top shelf that she could never, never have.

"Here's the last pan," Camille said, and set a baking tray on the counter. "Then wash up and take a break. Declan is due back in a few hours with his guests."

And . . . she'd be long gone by then.

She dumped the tray into the sink, scrubbed at the residue, once in a while looking out the window to the port where they'd docked. The sun hung low on the horizon, painting the sailboats a deep amber. Camille had cracked the window, releasing the humidity from the kitchen, and now the salty air swept in, beckoned.

Someday Emberly would retire, find a beach, live in safety. Anonymity.

With Nimue, of course. Because she'd made promises to her sister—to herself—that she couldn't break.

She finished the pan, then dried it and slid it into the cabinet, cleaned the granite countertops and sink. Camille had hung up her jacket and hat, clearly taking her own advice, and now Emberly untied her apron.

Stepping into the cool of the hallway, she saw that Camille's door was shut, as was the captain's. Teresa was on the bridge for sure.

They wouldn't even miss her until they'd left port.

She opened up her bunk and grabbed her folded clothing. She didn't have any personal belongings, really, just her uniform along with the clothes she'd arrived with.

She changed clothes in the bathroom, folded her uniform, put it on her bunk, then donned her cap, tucking her hair up under it. She'd need to score a phone, but she'd worry about that once her feet hit land.

The gangway was out, but as she came along the edge, she spotted Declan heading back to the boat. Behind him followed a couple, well dressed, toting suitcases. Jermaine carried a couple bags as well.

Declan's guests.

Two hours early.

"Where are you going, Belle?"

The name Jermaine used—her alias—didn't register, not right away, because . . . well, because even as Declan marched down the dock to where his yacht moored at the end, she spotted a man standing on shore across the small harbor. He wore a black T-shirt, sunglasses, shorts, and was helping load water and gear into a forty-foot dive boat.

His gait, the sun-kissed hair, the way he moved, his body lean and strong . . . And then he stood up.

And as if he possessed a radar, looked at Declan's boat.

At *her*.

No, no, not at her. Her heart slammed into her ribs, lodged there, and she stepped back, turned away, even as Declan and his entourage walked up the gangway.

"Get us moving as fast as you can, Ivek."

Of course, Declan didn't even look at her as he headed up the stairs to the bridge. Because she was a no one. A staff person.

Not Ashley, who'd nearly run him over in Barcelona. And certainly not one of the catering crew that had attended the Kingston family wedding.

And he hadn't even been in the room when she became the mysterious woman who danced with Steinbeck at the reception of said wedding.

So no, he didn't spare her a glance.

But Ivek did. "We're casting off. Shore leave's been canceled."

She looked at him, caught her breath. "No, I—"

But Raphael and Tyrone were already pulling in the gangway. And sure, she could force her way off—even take a dive into the drink—but then she'd attract attention.

Steinbeck might see her.

And unlike Declan, he knew *exactly* who she was.

She ducked into the shadows, watching Steinbeck through her sunglasses as Teresa backed the yacht away from the dock.

He'd returned to loading his boat.

Maybe it wasn't him. Probably.

Aw, shoot.

She knew Steinbeck Kingston when she saw him. And with that realization, she caught her breath and held in a strange swell of emotion.

He'd *lived*.

Maybe that information was enough.

They pulled away from the harbor, cutting a small wake as they headed out to sea.

"You're needed in the galley," Jermaine said as he walked past her toward the salon. "We have guests."

Right. "Yes, sir."

But first chance she got, she was off this boat.

And maybe Steinbeck Kingston would haunt her no more.

THREE

JUST STAY AFLOAT.

Austen spat out seawater, refusing to give in to the urge to gulp it down. Good way to die of dehydration—by drinking salty water. She wore her mask—the only way to protect herself from the waves—and occasionally she'd duck her head under the rim of water to check for any predators.

At least her BCD stayed filled, acting as a life preserver, and she had hung on to her tank, hoping the steel might reflect sunlight, the empty aluminum also buoyant in the water.

Someone flying overhead might spot her.

But after more than twenty-four hours in the water . . . yeah, she might need to adjust her expectations. With the sun dropping toward the horizon, she might be in for another overnight at sea. Fantastic.

Last night, something had bumped her. But in the darkness, she hadn't been able to see what, although she'd turned on her dive light and searched the vastness, trying not to let the endless gulf beneath her take hold of her bones.

The current had grabbed her, flushed her away from the DR out toward the open sea.

Atlantic Ocean, here she came.

Okay, that might be too morbid.

Don't. Give. Up. What was it Stein used to say—the only easy day was yesterday?

Oh, she longed for yesterday. Any day, really, when she was safely on land. Or on her boat.

Her poor boat. Where the *Fancy Free* might be . . .

"I love this!" Margo walked into her brain, ran her hand along the teak rail of the fishing boat, all sanded and gleaming. "You got this for a hundred bucks?"

It was a hot, sunny day, the boat still on the hard in a boatyard north of Key West, the scent of varnish and sawdust rising from the deck.

Margo reached for one of the bottles of lemonade in the dinged-up cooler and sat beside Austen on an overturned bucket, her long dark hair tied back, in a pair of cutoff shorts and a tie-dyed sleeveless T-shirt. "I see only one problem with your suggestion that I move in."

If Austen remembered right, she had waged a small defense of her accommodation—free rent, and they could dive right from their "home," not to mention the free slip she'd gotten for working at the Galleon.

"No, silly. I mean the fact that the boat isn't *in the water*."

Right. "Two weeks and we have a date with the boat hoist."

Margo had leaned over, tipped the neck of her bottle to Austen's.

Austen would blame her parched throat for the memory of the lemonade, cool and sharp in her mouth. That and the fresh shrimp Margo had brought from town.

They'd made a picnic, right there on the deck, amidst all her hopes and Margo's dreams. "You know, *free* means you can expand your tie-dying operation."

Margo had slid to the deck, sitting cross-legged, peeling shrimp, dunking it into homemade cocktail sauce. "You're missing the point. *Free* means we can hunt for the wreck of the *San Miguel* anytime we want." She'd winked. "We're so close, I can feel it."

Austen had closed her eyes. *No more.*

"Someday, Tennie, I'm going to find it. The statue of Santa María de la Paz."

It had felt like such a dream, but Margo had believed, so she had too.

A hum sounded, and Austen opened her eyes, looked up.

A plane, commercial, too far overhead to see her, but she waved anyway, desperately, her throat filling.

She'd tried to swim earlier, but the storm and the ocean current had fought her, and by nightfall, the shivering had taken over. More fear than cold, maybe.

The plane left a trail of white in the sky. Probably headed to one of the larger airports—the DR, or even Puerto Rico.

Mariposa?

Aw. Now Declan strolled in, even as the waves tossed her, the current stirring up around her. *"Declan, you are a surprising man."*

The words had sort of rolled out of her, her emotions caught up in the moonlight, the music, the fact that he'd pulled her into a dance that felt a little more than polite.

As if . . .

But he'd worn an almost pained expression, and *oh*, she'd just . . .

Well, he was simply a nice guy. A really nice guy. Sure, he occasionally seemed to look at her with something of interest. And they'd worked well together after the landslide, but then again, he'd been in charge and she'd only been trying to help . . .

"He's a criminal, Austen."

Yeah, no. She just didn't buy it. Then again, maybe she was being naive. She had a history of trusting the wrong people, so . . .

Oh, if she got out of this, Stein was going to murder her.

"You're amazingly brave, Austen. I thought you were going to die down there."

Aw, Declan was back, and this time handing her a towel as she climbed onto the boat after the near tragedy during their dive event. He'd seemed shaken, and for a second, she'd thought . . . well, that he might have been worried about *her.* Maybe, but his new codirector had nearly run out of air at the bottom, so . . .

See. She saw what she wanted to see.

Besides, the last—very last—thing she wanted was to fall for a man who turned out to be a criminal.

Again.

No, better to keep moving, keep relationships from getting in the way.

A bump from below, something hitting her legs. She stopped kicking, realizing she'd made motion in the water. Pulling on her mask, she ducked her head down.

Just an endless, bottomless deep blue. Plankton stirring in the water.

Maybe she'd imagined it. She kept her face in the water, barely moving as she turned.

Still nothing—

Another bump, this time against her tank, and it spun her in the water.

The shark darted away, its tail nearly hitting her. A great white, and he wasn't the only one. In the murky distance, she made out more sharks.

A hammerhead swam below, deeper in the depths with more sharks—a couple tiger sharks and some scalloped hammerheads. And at least two great whites.

Oh no. She'd drifted into a migratory path.

If she deflated her BCD, she'd sit lower in the water, be able to face the shark, keep her eyes on him should he circle back. But then she'd lose her air, and her tank had already edged into the red. Although, given time, she could manually blow it back up.

She spotted the shark in the water, circling her, as if still curious. At least sixteen feet long, it wore scars on its dorsal fin, so it could be a female. A hook trailed from its mouth, so also a survivor.

The animal was too big for Austen to push away, but Austen could dodge the shark if she stayed alert. Unfortunately, twenty-six hours of floating didn't bode well for her reflexes.

Still. She lifted her air hose and deflated her vest. As she replaced her regulator, her weights sank her in the water until she settled just below the surface.

There. Her killer, circling, some twenty feet away. Austen stayed upright in the water, not splashing, not moving.

Go away, Big Bertha.

She hung there, watching, as the shark came closer, circled again. She stayed with the animal, watching—

It darted in.

Stay calm—

Whatever. She caught Bertha's nose, pushed, moving over it, away. Nearly surfaced.

Letting out more air, she sank five feet from the surface, her eyes on the animal.

Her air-gauge needle sank deeper into the red.

The shark skirted away, into the murky water, and Austen lost Bertha in the haze.

She turned, just in case any of the others wanted a taste.

"They're more afraid of you than you are of them."

Ha. Sure.

She stayed submerged, her breathing in her ears, her heartbeat a hammer against her chest. Minutes passed. Her oxygen hit the bottom of the red, and her watch started to beep.

Yes, yes, she knew—

The attack came from behind, first a bump, then a terrible wrenching, her body tossed in the water.

Bertha had hold of her tank.

She turned and punched the shark, just like Hunter had said, and yeah, exactly what her training told her not to do, but panic hit her bones, filled her body, and she had nothing else.

The hit landed in the soft flesh of Bertha's snout, and the shark jerked away, darting into the depths.

Her tank had saved her. Which meant—yeah, no blood. But any remaining air whooshed out, and now water rushed in.

Dragging her down.

No—no—

She took a last breath—the final trapped air in her BCD—and unsnapped her vest, the waistband. Pressure cracked her ears, and she equalized even as she kicked hard, fighting the pull to the bottom.

Stay calm!

Shrugging off one side, then the other, the vest finally fell away.

She swam for the surface.

The warmth trapped between her vest and her dive skin vanished, cool water chilling her to the bone as she surfaced into the fading sunlight.

Her dive light hung attached to her vest, fading into the depths.

Along with . . . *Oh no.*

Her PLB. Whether it had worked or not, she didn't know, but why hadn't she put it in her dive pockets? She'd secured it into her BCD pocket and . . .

Now it sat at the bottom of the ocean. *Perfect.*

So it was a choice—get eaten or drown.

She couldn't lie on her back, not if she didn't want to resemble a seal or a dolphin, but she couldn't tread water indefinitely.

At least she'd ditched her weight belt. Maybe she should shuck her dive shorts too, heavy as they were on her legs.

Wait. She reached into her pocket and—*yes, thank you*—found her inflatable safety marker curled inside. She'd taken it out when she put her PLB into the Velcro pocket.

Thank You, Jesus. She pulled it out, unrolled it, and opened the valve.

No shark tried to kill her as she inflated the bright orange "sausage." Six feet tall, it stuck out of the water like a flag. And if she wanted, she could float on it.

She tucked it under her arms, stopped kicking, stopped moving, and prayed.

More.

Prayed *more* because she'd kept herself from weeping last night by mentally singing every hymn she knew, reciting the Lord's Prayer, and finally settling on the twenty-third psalm over and over.

And over.

"Yea, though I walk through the valley—ocean—of the shadow of death, I will fear no evil!"

The sunset dragged a finger across the waves. Maybe she'd scared Bertha off, because no more bumps hit her from below, but now the ocean had turned wild, and in the distance, another squall hovered over the horizon from the west.

So, this would be another fun night. As long as her sausage didn't spring a leak and she didn't drift into some dead animal or succumb to the temptation to slurp up any of the ocean water—

Maybe she should just let go, sink to the bottom.

And right then, Margo's face, her eyes, found Austen's and drilled into her soul. *"Don't give up!"*

She put her head down, tried not to sob.

And somehow, in the swirl of confused ocean, she heard it. A horn.

A *boat* horn.

She looked up but didn't see anything, the shadows deep, the waves tossing her. Maybe they couldn't see her, either—

Grabbing her sausage, she held it in the air, kicking hard to stay afloat. *Please, see me. See me.*

Another horn, then two more.

A flare arched over the water, turning it ablaze with light.

She wanted to weep when she spotted the boat, sleek, white, the setting sun turning it to flame, cruising through the water toward her.

A *yacht.* Large, with three stories, at least a hundred feet long, with a coms tower and deckhands shouting. One of them threw her a life ring and she swam toward it.

Please let Bertha be long gone—

Then, a motor. Someone had launched the rescue boat in the stern, and now it sped through the waves, a man in the bow, leaning over as if to pluck her from the water.

Dark hair, white shirt, tall, broad shoulders, holding onto the sides of the boat.

Declan?

He wore such a dark, fierce look—it thrummed through her and stole her up even before he reached out for her.

His hands gripped her arms.

The man hauled her from the ocean like she was weightless.

Except he fell back then, still clutching her to himself, collapsing onto the bottom of the boat.

She just sank into his chest, gripping his shirt, shaking.

"I got you," he said, his voice cutting through the roar of the engine, the terrible screaming inside. "I *got* you."

She didn't care what Stein said.

Criminal or not, her heart might already be a goner.

●————————————●

A miracle.

That's what Declan decided to call the providence of plucking Austen from the sea just at the edge of sundown, the night hot on his tail.

His brain kept that moment when he'd seen the inflated orange pike protruding from the water. Then the look on her face when she'd spotted him—*surprise . . . joy?*

"When we lost your PLB signal, I thought . . ." He shook his head and gave her a grim look. They sat in the sky lounge, in the upper level of his yacht, her showered and wrapped in a thick bathrobe, wearing a pair of yoga pants and a T-shirt that Elise had loaned her.

Jermaine had also given her a once-over. A former military corpsman, the man suggested that Austen suffered from dehydration and exhaustion.

Definitely, although she'd bounced back, it seemed, her auburn hair wet and falling in waves around her face. She sat curled on the sofa, holding a mug of hot lemon water, sipping it slowly, her green eyes betraying her hours in the sea. Tired and a little traumatized.

And he really just wanted to go back to that moment when he'd pulled her from the water and she fell into his arms.

And hung on.

Oh, she'd just sunk into him, her body trembling.

He'd held her, maybe for too long, but relief did that to a man, flushed away all of his walls, made him hang on, pull her close, and briefly let a part of his heart free.

She'd pushed herself away when they pulled up to the yacht, then managed to climb out of the dinghy on her own power, and by the time Declan joined her on the deck, she'd come back to herself.

So, note to self—don't read too much into that moment.

Ivek had grabbed a towel and flung it over her shoulders, and Elise and Hunter also stood in the stern. He could thank Hunter for spotting the glint on the horizon, still so far away. It had vanished, but that plus the fading location of the PLB signal had sent them in the right direction.

Elise had brought her to the salon, where Jermaine had checked her over, then showed her to a stateroom.

Declan had stayed for a briefing from Captain Teresa. Pretty woman. Capable. He'd hired her only a month ago after his previous captain had gone no-show on him. She came with references from other yacht owners, and he'd been in a bit of a rush. But she seemed loyal and trustworthy.

"The engines have been running at peak for hours. We need to check the oil for any signs of degradation or contamination. And the cooling systems need to be examined to see if we have any leaks or blockages."

"What about the hull and the prop?"

"Yes. I've sent our engineer to check for any stress cracks or abrasions that could have developed."

"Where are we on fuel?"

"Low, sir, but if we take our time getting to Mariposa, we'll make it."

"Do whatever you need to do. I'd rather get there late than not at all."

"Very good, sir." She walked away.

For a second, Stein's expression as he stood on the pier thrummed at Declan.

"Captain?"

Teresa had reached the salon door. Turned back.

"Did you radio the other search boat that we found her?"

"Yes, sir, right away. I also informed the Dominican Coast Guard."

"Thank you."

She nodded and left.

Jermaine arrived not long later with an update on dinner, and Declan asked to have it served in the sky lounge on the uppermost tier in the stern. A squall had passed over earlier, but the stars had come out, and maybe . . .

Aw, c'mon, Dec. The woman had just been traumatized. The last thing she'd want was a romantic dinner. "Ask Camille to keep it simple. Burgers, french fries, a salad."

Elise and Hunter came in then, said they were exhausted and were getting sandwiches from the galley and retiring.

He might never be able to sleep again, despite twenty-four plus hours of pacing as they raced down to her location, watching the PLB signal, praying it didn't vanish.

And then it did.

Now, as they sat in the sky lounge, the trauma over, he took a breath and looked at Austen. "What happened?"

"I got attacked by a shark."

He stared at her.

"The shark got my tank, and it filled with water, was dragging me down, so I had to ditch it. The PLB was in the pocket of my BCD." She'd pulled her legs up under the bathrobe. "Good thing I still had my safety sausage."

"Hunter saw the sun on your tank a couple miles out—or thought he did. It matched up with your PLB, and then . . ." He blew out a breath. "I'm so glad you're okay."

Understatement, but things had sort of reverted to a reasonable distance between them.

"You hungry?"

"I could eat a whale."

He chuckled. *Okay then.* "I asked Camille to make us burgers."

"How did you know I was lost?" She set her hot lemon water down and combed back her hair with her fingers, then braided it into a thick rope. She wore a hair band on her wrist and affixed it to the end.

"I ran into Stein in Key West when I was picking up the James-ons."

"Oh, right." She made a face. "I should probably tell him I'm okay."

"Already done," he said.

"Thanks."

"How did—"

"I end up in the middle of the Caribbean, miles from shore, like a buoy?"

"Yes."

"I was diving. Alone." She held up a hand. "Save it. Stein will already murder me."

"He did seem . . . angry when I saw him." *Huh.* Maybe that accounted for the great chill. But Stein had been ghosting him before that, so . . . "How is he, by the way? He almost seemed like he didn't want to talk to me."

She swallowed. Then, "Um, I guess he's fine. Healing. I don't know, Declan." Then she looked away and sighed. Frowned.

Huh. That felt a little weird. As if a squall had blown in between them.

"So, you were diving and then what?"

She met his eyes with a wry twist to her face. "I came up, and my boat had floated away." She wrinkled her nose, as in *oops!* Maybe he'd imagined the tension. "I thought I'd secured the anchor, but . . . I can't believe it. I came up from my dive and the boat had just . . . vanished."

"I'll have my captain put out a BOLO for it—see if any ships have spotted it."

"It's like having my home swept away in a hurricane. Everything I have is in that trawler, so . . ." She sighed. "But she's survived worse, I guess. I bought her for a hundred dollars after Hurricane Irma. Fixed her up myself."

"We'll find her, Austen." He didn't know why he said that, but the urge to reassure her, to reach out and touch her hand, just swept over him.

Jermaine came into the salon. "Dinner is in the sky lounge, sir."

Declan stood up. "Our chef is French. Her fries are amazing." And then he held out his hand. More of a reflex than purposeful, but she took it and got up.

She looked at him, an emotion in her eyes that he couldn't place. "I can't believe you found me. I just . . ." She swallowed and her eyes filled. "Thank you for looking."

"Of course." His chest tightened a little, and he squeezed her hand. *You mean something to me.*

Just hold your horses, man. He offered a smile and gestured to the stairs to the sky lounge.

The squall had cleared the clouds from the sky, the night canopy a wash of brilliant white light, the moon shining on the water. Jermaine had set the shiny teak table with dinner, candlelight, and jazz playing on the speakers.

Good man.

The gas fire table was also lit, the flames contained inside glass walls, surrounded by a deep-cushioned sectional sofa.

"This is amazing, Declan." She walked to the table, stared into the darkness. Took a breath, turned. "It's a gorgeous boat."

He pulled out one of the padded dining chairs for her. "Thanks. I always wanted a boat. We lived by Medicine Lake when I was growing up, and sometimes my mom and I would go down and watch the boats or swim. I always thought it would be fun." He sat down opposite her. "I guess my vision enlarged a little."

Jermaine came out carrying a tray and set it down on the table. He set plates in front of them. "Burgers á la Camille."

The fries glistened, still hot. Austen picked one up. "These smell amazing."

"Camille is a Michelin-rated chef. Wanted to live in the Caribbean. She has a place in St. Kitts but works for me when I take the boat out."

Austen reached for the ketchup bottle, doctoring her burger.

Now that she'd doused her burger, he didn't have the heart to tell her that Camille had probably made it perfectly.

"I didn't realize you grew up in the Minneapolis area." She recapped the bottle.

"Absolutely. In a neighborhood called New Hope. It's on the northwest side of the city."

She frowned. "Really? I thought . . . I don't know. I guess I don't know how to say this—"

"That I came from family money? No." He cut his burger in half. "I graduated without cash for college, joined the Marines, then went to school on the GI Bill. Sort of." He picked up his burger. The juices dripped off it, and suddenly his stomach came to life. "I actually dropped out halfway through and got involved in my tech company. It was called MapGrid Solutions—helped companies enhance their visibility on digital maps with photos and detailed promotional offers and updates."

"Wow."

"We sold it a couple years later for millions." He put the burger down. "First time I realized that I liked negotiating and strategizing as much as inventing things."

She'd gobbled down her burger. "I didn't realize I was so hungry."

"After twenty-four hours at sea?" He stared out into the blackness, back at her. "You must have been terrified."

She picked up a french fry. "I just . . . I can't think about it." She smiled, but it looked forced.

Right.

"I just kept praying, saying the twenty-third psalm, and believing that God would send someone." She pointed the fry at him.

Heat poured through him, landed in his soul. Her beautiful gaze found his, and again he heard, "You're a surprising man, Declan."

Surprising good, he hoped. So many ways that could go, really . . .

Teresa came out of the bridge, walked over to the table. "Sir, we're looking at a clogged fuel filter. Raphael is going to change it, but it'll take a bit."

"Tuck the *Invictus* in for the night, Teresa, and we'll start off tomorrow."

After Teresa had walked away, Austen leaned back in her chair, her meal finished. "Off to where?"

Oh. "I would like to say Key West, but the Jamesons need to get to Mariposa for a court date."

"They told me when we went diving last week. Jamal and Kemar's adoption."

"Yes. But as soon as we reach the island, I can arrange a flight for you. I hope you . . . uh . . . don't mind sticking around for a few days."

He couldn't read her eyes, the way she considered him. "Where did you get the name *Invictus*?"

Oh. He frowned at her sudden change in topic. "Actually, I named her after my mother. She was a single mom. The word means resilience, strength, even an indomitable spirit. Especially in tough times. That was my mom. She never got to see the boat— but I think she would have loved it." He'd finished his meal, and Jermaine appeared to take his plate. "She passed when I was serving in Afghanistan."

She cocked her head as if taking in that information. Then, "I'm sorry about your mom."

"It was sudden. Heart attack. I took leave, sold the house . . ." He sighed. "Probably returned to duty too quickly, but I . . ." He picked up his water. "I needed something to distract me. Her passing didn't really set in until I came home, but . . ."

By then, other terrible things had consumed him.

"But?"

"Oh. But by then I was focused on college, and anyway . . ." And now his throat had thickened. How had they ended up stumbling around his past?

"I get it," she said. "Sometimes we need distractions when life derails us." She offered him a tight-lipped smile, then took a drink of water.

Huh.

He so wanted to get to the bottom of *that*, thank you.

"I'm sorry we can't get you back right away. I suppose I could drop you in Santo Domingo, but I'd really . . ." *Like to make sure you're safe.* "I really think you should stay and enjoy the boat. Camille's amazing food. And it'll just be a few days."

She considered him, saying nothing.

He nearly leaped on his phone when it vibrated on the table. He picked it up. "I need to take this." Getting up, he walked over to the flickering fire.

"Zeus. What's up?"

"A bit of trouble, sir. The *Pinta* has fallen off the radar."

He stared out into the darkness, spotted lights. Maybe a cruise ship. Or a tanker. "Does she have the pearl?"

"No. That's with the *Santa Maria*. But we fear that perhaps the Petrovs have figured out our game, maybe tracked her."

He stilled. "You think the Russians took her?" *Oh,* probably he should keep his voice down. "Have you gotten ahold of anyone?"

"No, sir. I sent a team to their position. But I wanted to alert you."

"Where is"—he cast his voice lower—"the shipment?"

"Still a few days to the warehouse. They took a circuitous route, as suggested."

"Good." Out of the corner of his eye, movement. He glanced over and Austen had taken a seat on the sofa, staring into the fire, the flames in her gaze.

"Keep me posted," he said and hung up.

He sat down. "You okay?"

"Yes." Then she took a breath and nodded. "I think I will take you up on your offer to stick around, Declan. I think maybe . . . I'd like to get to know you better."

She met his gaze, something solemn in hers. Beautiful, her hair dry and coppery in the fire's reflection, tanned skin against the white bathrobe, and a strange intensity in her green eyes.

"You're a surprising man, Declan."

He pocketed his phone.

And as much as he wanted to cheer, he had the strangest sense that this might get . . . well, tricky.

So maybe he'd keep all the big surprises to himself.

FOUR

AUSTEN JUST COULDN'T WRAP HER BRAIN around the ludicrous idea that Declan might be a criminal. And she didn't want to. Maybe she wanted to believe that he was exactly the man he seemed to be as he sat on the sofa beside her, the stars soft in the night sky, the waves lapping against the boat. A kind, generous, determined man she could count on.

The rush of heat that had crested over her as she clung to him on the boat had washed away, leaving a residue of disbelief. Gratefulness.

According to Elise, when she'd loaned her clothing, Declan had pushed the yacht to its full capacity, running it at thirty knots for over twenty-four hours, using all the fuel reserves on board. Hadn't even slept as he tracked her PLB signal. Had everyone on deck searching for her after her monitor vanished.

"He definitely cares about you," Elise had said, leaving Austen in her stateroom.

And what a stateroom. Queen bed, private head, Italian tile, with a sitting area and port windows that overlooked the blue ocean, now dark and pinpricked with light.

Austen had washed off the salt of the sea, stripping off her wetsuit and warming her body. Had pulled on the yoga pants and T-shirt, wrapped herself in the bathrobe, and decided that maybe Stein didn't know what he was talking about.

Criminal? Whatever.

Then, this dinner. Simple, and yet perfect. She sat across from Declan, watching the wind comb his dark hair, trying to understand what might be behind those blue eyes.

And then he'd changed the subject. Offered to drop her off in the DR, and maybe—probably—that was a good idea, given her brother's inevitable frantic search. But according to Declan, he'd updated her brother, so . . .

So maybe she'd just stick around and . . . what? Sleuth through his private papers? Listen in on his phone calls?

And then he actually received a phone call, and she didn't intend to eavesdrop, except he deliberately turned away from her and cut his voice low and . . .

Aw. See? Stein had put stuff in her head, and now everything Declan did seemed suspect.

Which wasn't fair, and even as he spoke on the phone, she knew she had to prove it to Steinbeck. He was simply wrong.

Yes, by the time she got off this boat, she intended to prove that Declan was every bit the hero he seemed to be, right down to his core.

And maybe in the meantime she'd enjoy some of Camille's French cooking and . . .

Okay, Declan's company.

It wasn't torture to sit out by his fire table, on a padded sofa, watching the stars float by, a balmy ocean wind caressing her skin. Even less torture to sit across from Declan, his back to the wake, the firelight warming his handsome face. A thin layer of dark whiskers added a ruggedness to his otherwise polished aura, and she could trace out the Marine in him.

The guy who wouldn't give up looking for her.

So maybe the swell of affection hadn't completely dissipated.

"Everything okay?" she asked, taking a sip of hot cocoa. It touched her bones, heated her, and the ordeal in the ocean faded to a distant nightmare.

"Yes. Just a business call." He leaned back, his arms spread across the sofa, and crossed his leg, his ankle on his knee.

"It's late for a business call." Why did she ask that? Felt too . . . invasive.

But he shrugged. "I'm working on a project, and the guy in charge wanted to update me. So, you never told me what you were looking for during your dive."

Was it suspicious that he'd changed the subject? *Maybe not.*

"I was looking for wreck debris from an old Spanish galleon that went down off the northern coast of the DR. It went down in the early 1500s, so the wreck's been scattered all over the shoal. People are still finding silver coins, copper dishware, and even sometimes gold ingots."

"Did you find anything?"

"A copper mug. But not what I was actually looking for." She took a sip of the cocoa and watched as one brow went up in question.

"I'm trying to find a black marble statue of Santa María de la Paz. It was on the way to Santo Domingo when the boat went down. It was a gift to a monastery."

"And you think it's down there."

"It's what my college roommate, Margo, thought. Her father was a treasure hunter off the coast of Florida, and after he died, she took up his hunt." She looked past him into the darkness, the moonlight tipping the waves. "After she died too, I just . . ." She swallowed. "It seemed like the right thing to do."

"How'd she die?" He spoke softly, a small frown on his face.

Her mouth pinched, and she drew in a long breath. "A diving accident."

And for a second, she was back on Alvaro's boat, watching Margo collapse, her body shutting down right there in the aft deck, Alvaro shouting, Austen dripping wet, helpless. "She got DCS after her equipment failed and she did a fast ascent from sixty feet down."

"The bends."

"Yeah. We needed financing for our search, so Margo hooked us up with a guy named Alvaro Cortez. He was a rabid collector of wreck artifacts and financed a trip to the Silver Bank to search for the statue. Even gave us DPVs—diver propulsion vehicles."

"I've seen those."

She finished her cocoa, sat cross-legged on the sofa, the bathrobe tucked over her. "We shouldn't have dived that day. The current was too strong. But we had the DPVs, so we thought we'd be fine . . ."

A moment passed, and another as she tried to shake out of the grip of watching—

"Our DPV batteries died. Dead in the water, a hundred feet down. And the current had really carried us out. We had to ditch the DPVs and swim back, and that's when Margo realized that she'd drained too much of her air—more than I had. The seal on her tank had malfunctioned, and we had to buddy breathe. Except, with all the exertion of swimming, I'd drained more air than usual too." She met his eyes, fierce, rapt, horrified. "By the time we got to our deco stop, my air had nearly drained out."

She ran a finger under her eye, caught a tear.

He swallowed, then uncrossed his legs and leaned toward her. "You don't have to—"

"I do. I've never really . . . Even Margo's brother Mo doesn't know the details. Doesn't know that she looked at my low O2, dropped her emergency octo, and quick ascended to the surface."

"She did that to save your air."

Austen nodded. "Worst seven minutes of my life—the deco stop at sixty feet and the safety stop at fifteen. By the time I got aboard the boat, they had her on the deck, and she'd gone into a sort of paralytic state, her brain fighting the air pocket. Cortez called in a chopper evac from Key West, but they . . . by the time they got her into a deco chamber, she was brain dead."

She'd said it without curling into a ball, and that was an improvement. Still, her eyes, already chapped by the salty ocean, throbbed, raw.

And that's when Declan got up and came over to sit by her.

Oh no.

But *yes,* because he sat next to her, then put his arms around her and pulled her to himself, and just like before when he'd yanked her from the water, she let herself lean in.

A beautiful, transitory moment when the grief couldn't wash her out to sea.

"You dive to honor her," he said quietly. "I get that."

She pushed away then, looked at him. He wore a softness in his gaze. "You do?"

"I did mention that my boat was sort of named after my mother, right?" He smiled.

See? A guy who talked about his mother in such a way couldn't be an underworld criminal.

"Did Cortez take any responsibility for his faulty equipment?"

"No. He said it was an accident, but I would have never gone down in that current if he hadn't guaranteed that the DPVs were safe."

Declan smelled good, the scent of the sea on his skin, and kept his arm on the sofa behind her. Close. Protective.

"I never trusted him. He seemed too driven by the treasure." She didn't meet Declan's eyes when she said it, in case it felt too pointed.

But Declan wasn't like that. *Really.* He would never put his agenda over someone's safety.

"When did she die?"

"Four years ago. And yes, I know that terrible accidents while diving happen, but—"

"But she died to save you."

She looked at him then and gave a tight nod, her throat thick.

"There's no time limit on grief, Austen." A strand of her hair had come loose in the wind, and he caught it and tucked it behind her ear.

Sweet. Gentle.

"He's a criminal, Austen."

No. No, he wasn't. Still, maybe she should just *settle down.*

"I was doing just fine until I moved back to the Keys two years ago. I sort of dodged the grief for the first couple years—moved away to Hawaii and studied shark behavior with the Hawaiian shark research institute."

"So, something safe and comforting."

A beat, then she smiled.

He did too.

"Yeah. Well, like you said, it was a distraction."

He gave her a grim nod.

"That's when I started looking for the statue again. I don't think I'll ever find it, but . . ." She sighed.

"It gives you purpose."

She met his gaze, then nodded. "It keeps me moving forward. I keep thinking that finding it might give closure."

"Or redemption."

She raised an eyebrow.

"Because you blame yourself."

She shrugged.

He said nothing. Around them, the night breeze stirred up the ocean smells, salty, briny, the fire flickering.

"You're not to blame for other people's choices."

"Maybe. I try not to think about it. Or talk about it."

"She made a choice, Austen. Although I get it—that's the hardest part, right? Letting go of the things you can't control to find peace in the outcome."

She couldn't look away, his words, his gaze, riveting her.

He touched his fingers to her cheek. "My mother used to say that every day is a new day of grace." He drew in a breath. "I think that's how you start healing."

And that just sealed it, didn't it? A criminal didn't talk about grace. Or mercy. Or redemption.

"Sometimes, telling our story is what we need to do to set ourselves free." He seemed to consider her for a moment, then his gaze flickered down to her lips.

Her heart hammered against her chest.

"Austen," he said quietly, his voice husky. "Can I—"

Yes.

"Not on your life!"

The words jolted through her, and she jerked, turned. *What— Stein?*

He looked like some modern-day pirate, minus the cutlass but wearing flip-flops, shorts, and a black T-shirt, striding toward them with such fury in his eyes that it froze her to the spot.

Declan had found his feet, however. "Steinbeck."

Stein ignored him and his outstretched hand and marched over to her. "Do you not listen to *anything* I say?"

That shook her to life. "Seriously?" She stood up.

His mouth closed, tightened. Then he pulled her into a hug so tight it nearly cut off her breathing. And he was trembling a little, maybe from rage, but possibly from relief.

Oh.

"Are you okay?" His voice lowered, roughened by emotion.

"Yeah."

Then he stepped back, met her eyes, the words from days before in his gaze. *"Do not trust Declan. Don't even talk to him again."*

She wanted to argue with him, but not here in front of Declan. Mostly because she couldn't bear for Declan to hear Stein's accusation.

He didn't deserve to be so disrespected.

"How'd you find me?" Except, just then, Hawkeye came up the stairs. He appeared tired as he gave her a tight smile.

"He made us find Declan's boat."

"I needed to see for myself that she was okay," Stein said, his stare hard on Declan.

Oh, for Pete's sake. "Stein, Declan saved my life. If he hadn't found me, I would have been eaten by sharks or drowned." *In other words, back off, bro.*

Stein nodded and held out his hand to Declan. "Thank you."

Declan shook it. "Of course." He still wore a frown, however.

And Stein's jaw was so tight he might crack some molars.

Yes, she'd need to get Stein alone, talk him off the Declan-is-a-criminal ledge.

"I'll get Austen back to the Keys," Stein said and turned to her. "Let's go."

She looked at Hawkeye, back at Stein, and . . .

She shook her head. Just impulse, but . . . *no.*

And it wasn't about trying to dig around Declan's past, but . . .

That near kiss. The desire that had formed inside her still pulsed.

She hadn't dreamed up that spark between them. The way her body tingled as he stood so close to her, his aura radiating out to her.

"I'm staying."

———•———

Declan didn't know what had gone down between Austen and

Stein in the sky lounge when her superhero brother appeared out of the night, but he attributed it to some twin connection. Or maybe competing strong personalities. Because as the two stared at each other, they couldn't be more alike.

Determined, courageous, and stubborn.

Declan hadn't quite known what to do when Austen dragged Stein away for some private conversation. She'd bade Declan good night, and there went his opportunity to continue what he'd started, or at least had *wanted* to start, as they sat by the fire table under the stars.

When she'd told him about Margo's accident, he couldn't help but pull her into his arms, and of course that had just ignited all of his desires to protect her and hold her and keep her safe. It hadn't helped that only hours earlier, he'd pulled her from the ocean.

Maybe he'd imagined her going strangely cold during his phone call. Because then Austen had smiled at him and said, "I will take you up on your offer to stick around." And suggested that she'd like to get to know him better. And when she'd looked up at him with those big green eyes, yes, he'd been a goner.

So he would have kissed her and kissed her well, and maybe ignited the start of something beautiful if Stein hadn't shown up, obviously simmering. Declan didn't have a clue what he'd done to make Stein so angry, but clearly they had an overdue conversation in front of them.

He'd found Stein later, after Austen retired, standing at the stern of the boat, watching his friend Hawkeye tie his forty-foot fishing trawler to Declan's yacht. Declan had stood in the quiet, the night wind blowing against his linen shirt.

Declan had wanted to ask "Did I somehow wrong you?" But before he could get the words out, Stein turned to him.

"Declan, I can't thank you enough for what you did to find Austen. I'm truly grateful. Is it possible for me to bunk here on the yacht tonight? To be clear, I'll be talking Austen into coming back with me to the Keys tomorrow, but it's getting late."

Declan had understood that. And maybe a little sleep would do them all good. "Sure," he'd said. "I have an extra stateroom."

Of course, Jermaine had appeared out of nowhere and directed Stein to the right stateroom.

Now as Declan lay in his bed, staring outside through the port window, he was still trying to sort out the mix of emotions and the fact that he'd actually found Austen in the middle of the vast sea.

Thank You, God.

And he didn't know where that thought came from, because frankly, God hadn't shown up for him in, well, years.

So maybe it was a dormant habit.

Very dormant.

And if he was honest, he knew he didn't deserve God showing up, not really.

"Grace, son. And mercy. We don't realize it, but they surround us every day." His mother's voice, of course.

Yes, well, she believed because it was all she had.

Still, Declan could admit gratefulness the next morning when he got up and the sun shone bright and warm. As he sat in the sky lounge with a bowl of fruit and a mug of coffee, the dawn cresting upon the waters, his mother's verses from Lamentations came into his head: *"His mercies are new every morning; great is his faithfulness."* He didn't really deserve any of it, but he wasn't going to shrug away the morning mercies.

Movement on the steps, and he looked up to see Elise and Hunter joining him on the deck. Elise wore a yellow sundress, and Hunter, attired in shorts and a T-shirt, pulled out a chair for her.

"I see there's another boat attached to us," Hunter said as he sat down. Belle, one of the new stewards, came over and poured him coffee.

"Yes," Declan said. "Austen's brother Steinbeck showed up last night with his friend Hawkeye from the Keys."

"I remember Stein from the island," Elise said. "How is he? Wasn't he shot?"

"I never did get to the bottom of that." Declan had had his hands full trying to deal with the landslide and three missing kids. When Stein had shown up, shot, Declan had simply arranged for a med flight out. So yeah, he had questions, and he hoped that Stein had answers. But maybe it took a back burner to convincing Stein that Austen was safe. Here. With him.

"How soon do you think it will be until we're underway?" Elise asked as Belle returned with cups of coffee for her and Hunter.

"Thank you," Elise said. She pointed to Declan's fruit. "Could I get a bowl of fruit too?"

"Yes, ma'am," Belle said. She turned to Hunter. "Anything for you, sir?"

"Just some eggs and bacon."

Belle nodded and walked away.

"My captain said that we should be ready to leave this morning," Declan said.

"Is Austen going with us?" Elise asked.

"No, actually, she's not." This voice came from Stein, who had come up the stairs and walked over to the table.

Declan looked at him and raised an eyebrow. This would be an interesting morning.

A night's sleep still hadn't wiped the scowl from Stein's face, but maybe he hadn't slept well.

"She needs to get back to Key West and maybe get checked out by a real doctor, and we need to start looking for her boat," Steinbeck said as he sat down.

Declan nodded. "I'm happy to look for her boat after we drop the Jamesons off in Mariposa," he said.

Steinbeck said nothing as Belle set a cup of black coffee in front of him. She turned quickly and walked away.

"Anything for breakfast, Steinbeck?" Declan added, glancing at her already heading down the galley steps.

Odd.

Steinbeck shook his head. "Thank you."

Declan couldn't help it: "Last night, Austen said she was staying."

Steinbeck's mouth made a grim line. And again Declan wanted to ask "What is your problem, dude? How did I wrong you?" But maybe not here at the table under the bright blue sky with the Jamesons within earshot. Because he had a strange feeling that this wasn't just something superficial—a misspoken word or a neglectful action.

And then it hit him. How *did* Stein get shot? He knew Stein had gone missing during the landslide after going back to Declan's house. Stein had met with security and had even gone down to the vault to check on it. And then he'd disappeared. So yeah, they needed a conversation, and soon.

"What a gorgeous day."

He looked over and saw Austen climbing up the steps. She still wore last night's yoga pants and T-shirt, the bathrobe around her as if she might still be cold. But her auburn hair had been let down and hung wavy down her back, turning a shiny copper in the sunlight, sort of like a mermaid with luminous green eyes.

Once again he was back to last night, sitting on the sofa, the desire to kiss her, to be in her life, filling his chest.

"Good morning," he said, which felt lame compared to what he really wanted to say, which was "Please stay with me on this boat." Or even "Please stay with me." Period, full stop.

And that sounded sappy even in his head, so instead, he spotted Jermaine entering the deck and said, "Jermaine, would you mind getting Austen a cup of coffee? How do you take it, Austen?"

"Like candy," Steinbeck said, "with sugar and cream."

Austen looked at him. "Actually, black will be just fine."

Oh, the sparks had already begun by the shake of Steinbeck's head. Austen went around and sat in the chair at the other end of the table, looking at her brother, and Declan felt like he was in the middle of a family stare-off.

"Shouldn't you and I be heading back to Key West about now?" Stein said.

Declan arched an eyebrow, looked at her, then at Stein. *Okay.* Maybe he'd have a quick talk with Stein before breakfast blew up.

"Stein, a word? Please." Declan got up. Stein glanced at Austen, then gave him an odd look but nodded.

Declan took the stairs down two flights to the main deck and walked out to the lounge in the bow of the boat. Steinbeck followed him.

Declan turned, all lightness gone. "What's your deal?"

Steinbeck took the words like a punch, reeled back just slightly, and then rounded on him. "What do you mean, *what's my deal?* She's my sister, and I want to take her back to the Keys with me."

"I think that's probably up to her, don't you?"

Stein stared at him, ground his jaw.

It was like negotiating with a grizzly. "What is your beef with me, Stein? I thought we were friends."

A beat. Another. Just the sound of the boats lapping in the water as the waves moved under them. And then, "What do you know about the Petrov Bratva?"

Declan frowned. "What do you think I know?"

"My mind is in a thousand different places, but I want to give you the benefit of the doubt."

"Do you? Because it feels like you've already made a judgment about me. Does this have something to do with how you got shot?"

A flinch, then, "The fact is that you told me that you hadn't sold your AI program to the Department of Defense. You said it on the way to the conference in Barcelona. But I met my cousin Colt there, and he specifically said that you had."

Declan frowned.

"And no, I didn't want to believe him. Because I trusted you, Declan. And then I got caught in the landslide—under your vault—" Something flashed in his eyes—*memory? panic?* "Somehow I found my way out on the other side of the mountain, and that's where I watched a couple Russians who were part of a mining crew blow up the mountain."

"They were the ones that shot you." Not really a question, because it felt like the only answer, but Stein nodded.

"I did a little research when I got back to the States and discovered that they were part of the Bratva, the Russian mob. What are they doing in Mariposa?"

Great. Declan wrapped his hand behind his neck. "All right, here's the truth. Yes, the DOD has my AI program. But it's just for testing purposes, so they can see if it works on some of their drone equipment. I did not let them—I did not *license* them to deploy it on any cyber soldiers, so that wasn't a lie."

"I hope that's the truth, because we're going full-on Terminator, and you're the director of Skynet." Stein didn't smile, so that wasn't a joke.

"Calm down, Stein. I'm a patriot, and when the DOD came to me and asked for help, of course I was going to do what I could for my country."

Stein's eyebrow went up.

"Including trying to keep dangerous material out of the Russians' hands. You've heard the saying 'Keep your friends close and your enemies closer'?" He held up his hand. "They asked if they could come in and mine sulfite from the mountain, which, as you know, is a prime source of sulfur. I thought the money would help with the repairs for the island. And I was watching them because

I knew they were lying. They were truly mining something called obsidite. It's a mineral that helps—"

"I know what it is," Stein said. "And I know that in the wrong hands, coupled with your technology, it could create a cyber soldier that would be a threat to the entire world."

"Exactly. That's why I intercepted the shipment." And now he was treading on bigger secrets, the kind that might get him into trouble, especially since Stein didn't work for him anymore. And technically, the entire operation was top secret, so there was that. But Stein had been a SEAL, so once upon a time, he'd had clearance. Which meant he could keep a secret and was trustworthy, right? And they had had a friendship once, or at least some semblance of it.

"Let's just say that I have a plan to keep the obsidite out of the Russians' hands. A plan that's working."

"But then it's in *your* hands." Stein met Declan's eyes, a darkness in his own.

A beat. Declan frowned. "What do you think I'm going to do with it? Sell it to the highest bidder?"

Stein's gaze didn't waver. "You said it, not me."

"Were you shot in the head too? Stein, I am not a *terrorist*. I'm not going to contribute to someone attacking America. I promise."

Steinbeck just stared at him, his jaw tight.

"Really? Come on. You know me. You worked with me for five months."

Stein seemed to consider that, his chest rising and falling. "What happens when the Russians find out that you've stolen their obsidite?"

"They won't," Declan said. "I have a plan." His voice softened. "And I would really like Austen to stay if she feels welcome. Your sister is . . . she is . . . I'd like to get to know her better. I think that there's something between us, and if it's possible—"

"No," Stein said.

Declan raised an eyebrow. "I don't think she needs your permission to stay on this boat with me."

Steinbeck's mouth tightened.

"No, I don't." Austen walked up behind Steinbeck. She glanced at her brother. "Hawkeye's looking for you. He wants to leave." Then she glanced at Declan, back at Steinbeck. "But I'm staying."

Steinbeck cocked his head. "No, I think you need to—"

"I don't care what you think, Steinbeck. I do appreciate you looking for me. Of course I do. If you hadn't, then I'd still be out in the ocean. But you're just going to have to let go a little bit and let me live my own life." She crossed her arms.

So this was something between the two of them. And Declan wanted to let them sort it out, but not if it meant her being pushed into something she didn't want to do. So, "Steinbeck, I will make sure she gets to the island safely. I'll have Doctor Julia look her over. And then we'll look for her boat. I promise you I will get her back to Key West in one piece."

Now Austen looked at Declan with a sort of raised eyebrow. "Oh goodie. I feel like I'm eight years old and you guys are fighting over who gets to babysit me. I'm perfectly capable of taking care of myself." She pinned her gaze back on Stein. "And making my own decisions. I'm staying."

Then she turned to Declan. "Which means I'm going to need a tour." She held out her hand.

Oh, interesting. He took it.

"I'll see you back in the Keys, Stein. Don't worry about me, I'm in good hands." Then she looked up at Declan and smiled.

His entire body just about exploded.

Well. Well.

Hawkeye had come down the stairs too. "Ready to go?" He held a croissant sandwich wrapped in a napkin in one hand and a cup of coffee in a to-go cup in the other.

Austen let go of Declan's hand, stepped up to Stein, and gave him a hug. Steinbeck stiffened, then put his arms around his sister and whispered something into her ear.

Probably something along the lines of "Watch out for the terrorist." Declan shook his head. Yes, he wanted Stein off his boat.

She finally let him go and turned back to Declan. "Was that a spa I saw on the lower deck?"

"Absolutely," said Declan, glancing again at Stein. Stein met his gaze, and Declan caught a warning in it. *Whatever.*

Honestly, the fact that Stein thought he could be involved in something, well, terroristic sort of snagged him. He wanted to add a "You're fired" to their conversation, but Stein already didn't work for him anymore, so there was that.

But as they walked away, a coal burned inside him at the man's betrayal. Declan had trusted him. Let him into his life.

Declan followed Austen along the back of the boat to the big lounge area in the stern. She stopped, watching Hawkeye and Steinbeck cast off.

"Sorry about that," she said. "Steinbeck and I have always had a sort of toe-to-toe relationship. Of course I love him dearly. He's a great brother and he's my twin. But that's also the problem. He was born two minutes before me, so that makes him my *older* brother, and he has let that go straight to his head. That and the fact that I've always been a little independent drives him crazy."

She looked at Declan, gave him a wry smile and a shrug. "Not that he's a guy that we shouldn't worry about. He was wounded three years ago in Poland in an explosion. Nearly lost his ability to walk, and let's not forget he was shot just a couple months ago, so there's been plenty of floor pacing over Stein."

"I think you guys are probably a lot alike," Declan said quietly. "I don't have a sibling." The words pinched, but he pressed on. "But I certainly wouldn't mind one who did everything he could to show up to help me." He offered a smile and she met it.

"I guess so," she said.

Hawkeye's boat motored away, Steinbeck at the rail.

Austen turned. "So tell me about the yacht." Then she reached out and took his hand again. "This is going to be a fabulous two days."

Yes. Yes, it was.

FIVE

S HE DIDN'T WANT TO RETURN TO HER NORMAL life, thank you. In fact, she'd dived headfirst into this life of luxury. She'd eaten a lobster roll with an avocado and citrus salad for lunch—on a china plate, no less—courtesy of the galley and Declan's Michelin-rated chef.

In fact, the *Invictus* hosted a staff of seven, serving *four* people, which felt a little excessive. But then again, it probably took a small army to run a boat this size.

"Any more lemon water?" The question came from the petite, dark-haired female steward named Belle, who materialized from the shadows the moment Austen drained her glass and set it on the table beside the lounger.

"Yes, please." For a homeless woman, Austen wasn't suffering, although her missing boat loomed in the back of her mind. She'd given the *Fancy Free*'s identification number, call sign, and description to the captain, and Teresa had agreed to pass along the information to the vessel-tracking services and the local Coast Guard.

So far, *nada*.

Oh boy.

Elise lay on the lounge chair next to her, her body tanned, wearing a cute swimsuit dress. Austen wore the utilitarian swim shorts and top she'd worn under her wetsuit so at least she didn't have to borrow undergarments.

But good thing she and Elise were the same size; otherwise, she might have had to spend the next few days in a bathrobe.

Also, she wasn't exactly suffering, was she?

Maybe she was Cinderella.

And Declan was what? Her handsome prince? She glanced at him, sitting in the hot tub, talking with Hunter. He'd taken off his shirt, and the man definitely worked out—strong shoulders, muscled arms. He wore a pair of Ray-Bans, like a modern-day movie star, Hollywood written all over him.

Clearly the sun had gotten to her, started to sizzle all the feelings inside.

Declan's grand tour of the boat hadn't helped. The way that, after she'd taken his hand—mostly to get him way from Steinbeck—he hadn't let go.

He'd shown her around the three decks—starting with the opulent salon and dining area on the main deck, then the aft-deck lounging areas, the inside foredeck with large wraparound sofa, and even the second-deck theater and gym.

Hence the washboard abs.

They sat in the spa lounge on the second level, overlooking the deck below, the blue skies cloudless, and frankly, she could sink into sleep right here under the glorious sun.

A perfect day, and she simply didn't have to think about yesterday.

Or about Stein's words to her as he left the boat. *"If you need me, just shout."* What, he'd follow the boat, appear at her first shout? Her brother could be a little overzealous.

Declan rose from the Jacuzzi, water dripping off him, and climbed out, grabbing a towel. He dried his hair, then wrapped the towel over his shoulders, settling onto the lounge chair beside her. "Not a bad way to travel."

"I'll manage," she said, smiling.

He smiled back. Wow, he was handsome when he smiled. And when he didn't smile. And when he scowled . . .

Just, always.

Good thing Steinbeck hadn't stuck around. In fact—"What went down between you and Stein?" She'd walked up with the two men staring at each other like they might be trying to reduce one another to ash.

Usually Steinbeck won any fight, so the fact that Declan had held his own . . .

But the man *had* been a Marine.

"Just a disagreement," Declan said. He leaned back on the lounge chair, and Jermaine came over, set a glass beside him.

"Would you see if Camille has any tapas? And I'd love some of her homemade hummus."

Jermaine left and Austen glanced over at Declan. "Hummus?"

"So good. And she makes her own pita bread, so . . ." He put his arms up behind his head.

Only then did she spot the tattoo on the underside of his arm. *Semper Fidelis,* in script.

She pointed to the tat. "You get that while you were in the Marines?"

He glanced at it, then shook his head. "I got it when I was eighteen, right out of high school."

"Before you joined up? That was prophetic."

"No, I was always going to be a Marine." He lowered his arms, sat up, and reached for his glass. "My dad was a Marine."

"He must have been proud when you joined up."

He glanced at her, and a memory niggled. *Wait*—he'd said he was raised by a single mom.

"He died in the Gulf War when I was three."

"Oh, I'm sorry, Declan."

He shrugged. "He was serving his country. I wanted to be like him. It was rough on my mom, though." He set down the glass. "Especially when I went to Afghanistan."

"Oh, that must have been terrible for her."

Hunter had gotten out of the Jacuzzi, dried off, and sat in the lounger beside Elise. "Yeah, Declan was still wet behind the ears when he deployed. I'll never forget him showing up in A-Stan. Scared to death. Determined not to show it."

Declan stared at him. "I wasn't scared."

"Sheesh, you checked your gear so much I thought you had OCD."

His mouth opened, then closed. "I like to be ready."

"Indeed. This is the guy who took language lessons. Learned Pashto."

"Not well," Declan said, his mouth pinching.

"Between that and volunteering for too many recon missions, I thought I had an overachiever on my hands."

Declan looked at him then. Silence passed between them.

"I didn't know you were in the military," Austen said to Hunter.

"Yeah. I was with an MSOB group."

"A Marine Special Operations Battalion," Declan said quietly.

"We were part of Marine Corps Forces Special Operations Command. We focused on direct action, special reconnaissance, and foreign internal defense. And Declan was one of my grunts."

"Infantry," Declan said. "We did the hard work." He smiled, finally.

Hunter scoffed, shook his head, but grinned. "Someone has to dig ditches."

She looked at Declan. "That's what you did?"

He slid his sunglasses down his nose. "Hardly. We worked out of a COP—a Combat Outpost—with the MSOB team in the

Hindu Kush mountains, setting up observation posts and doing long-range reconnaissance missions. Did you see *Lone Survivor*?"

"Yeah. SEAL team, right?"

"Yes. A long-range reconnaissance and surveillance team that got caught deep in Afghan country. We were that—small teams charged with gathering information to pass on to the big dogs, like Hunter here."

"Usually those teams worked far behind enemy lines. Sometimes the goal was to set up ambushes or sniper nests. And they'd use friendlies to help hide us and gather information," Hunter added.

Declan sighed, replaced his sunglasses, and looked at her. "Hence the Pashto. Helped to have passable knowledge."

"They let you do that on your first deployment?"

"We were at a small FOB—a Forward Operating Base, and we were Marines," he said. "*Semper Fi*."

Belle arrived with a glass of lemon water for Hunter. "Thank you." He took a sip. "I'm not sure why someone needs a Jacuzzi in the Caribbean, but I'm not complaining." He set his glass down. "These guys were our eyes and ears. And they were trained for recon, so we relied on them. And our contacts in the villages."

Declan nodded but looked away.

And again, the weird silence, just the sound of the boat motor, the splash of the waves, parted by the bow, streaming out into the wake in a frothy trail.

"How dangerous was that?" she asked quietly. "I heard the Taliban would execute anyone who worked with Americans. Even translators."

"It was dangerous," Declan said quietly. "War is dangerous." He stood up. "I'm going to check on the hummus."

She watched as he walked away, not sure what had just happened.

After he'd gone down the stairs, she turned to Hunter. "What was that about?"

Hunter met her eyes. "Declan is a good man. But he has . . . things that haunt him. Mistakes. War always inflicts wounds, and some of them never heal."

Oh.

Hunter glanced at his wife, back at Austen. "Something happened down range. It's not classified, but it's not my story to tell either."

Right.

More silence, and maybe that was her cue.

"He's a criminal, Austen."

No, he wasn't, but he had secrets. Maybe she didn't have a right to pry.

"Sometimes, telling our story is what we need to do to set ourselves free."

She got up. Hunter glanced at her, nodded.

Descending to the first-deck level, she headed toward the galley. The aroma of fresh bread drifted out of the space, and she knocked on the doorframe before entering.

Windows along the aft wall let in the afternoon light, shining on the three stainless refrigerator/freezer units. Black granite countertops bordered the room, with a six-burner range under a stainless-steel hood along one wall and an expansive middle island where a woman in a chef's jacket held a tray of croissants in her mitted hands.

She set it down and pulled off the mitts.

"You must be Chef Camille."

Short brown hair under a chef's hat, petite, a no-games aura about her. She looked up at Austen. "Yes, ma'am. May I help you?"

"I'm looking for Declan. He said he was checking on the hummus."

Chef Camille frowned. "I just sent that up with Belle."

"I didn't see her—"

"She took the galley stairs." She pointed to a set of stairs on the opposite side of the room. "They go up inside the boat."

So that the guests don't see the waitstaff?

"Thank you," Austen said and left the galley. She debated, then headed to the bow.

Bingo. She found him standing at the rail in front. He'd put on a T-shirt, and the wind plastered it to his body, raked his dark hair.

She stepped up beside him. "How's the hummus?"

He glanced at her, drew in a breath. "I just . . ."

"I'm kidding. But I do care."

He put his hand on hers, kept looking out to the horizon.

Silence, just the motors churning up the water.

"I got pretty good at Pashto."

She glanced at him but couldn't read his eyes behind the Ray-Bans.

"You were right about the Taliban. They would execute anyone they found working with us. But so many of the locals hated the fear and oppression they lived under . . ." He drew in a breath, swallowed. Let it out. "We had informants all over the Hindu Kush area."

He removed his hand from hers, gripping the railing. "Our COP was located in the eastern part of the region, very strategic. We had mountains on all sides for surveillance. Just down the road, maybe five clicks, was the village of Kushan Deh. They supplied us with fresh produce, and in return, we protected them. We had a translator who lived in the village. His name was Samiullah Rahimi, and I made friends with his son, Farid. Cute kid—about eight years old at the time. Big brown eyes, a crazy smile. He'd come to the base with his dad sometimes, delivering food or information, and we'd kick around a soccer ball."

He swallowed again.

"Hunter and his MSOB group got word of a potential Taliban

visit to the village and knew that some high-level Taliban leader would be with them, so he and his team deployed to capture the HVT—high value target. We were tasked with backup and possible engagement."

He shook his head. "It went south almost immediately. It was dark out and the villagers had fled to their homes, but a few of the local men had stayed to fight the Taliban, so it was a mess. We didn't know who was from the village and who was Taliban. Sami was trying to get to us to help identify the insurgents, but . . ."

Declan closed his eyes. "It was . . . chaos. And in that chaos, Sami was killed."

She wanted to put her hand on his then, but he pressed his hand to his mouth as if reliving that moment.

He gripped the railing. "Friendly fire." He looked at her. "Me. I didn't recognize him in the darkness, and I panicked. I thought he was Taliban."

Now she did touch his hand, wrapped her fingers around his on the railing. "How could you know?"

He nodded. "That's what the inquiry decided too." He glanced at her then, and even in the fading sunlight, his expression betrayed an inner haunting. "I destroyed their lives."

She had nothing.

"And the Taliban took the village. So there was nothing I could do. They executed the men and did terrible things to the women— even killed a few of them too. It wasn't long after that that the brass shut down the COP and moved us to a larger FOB." He glanced at her. "I lost track of Farid, although I kept asking about him even after my tour ended."

He turned his back to the sea, leaned against the rail, crossing his arms over his chest. "He finally landed on the radar with a refugee group that fled the area. His mother had died a few years earlier, and he ended up at an NGO in Kabul. In a fluke of fate, which I'd call providence, one of our translators reached out to me after Farid asked for me."

"When was this?"

"About ten years ago. I had just sold MapGrid Solutions and was looking at where else I wanted to go. I ended up heading back to Afghanistan and wrangling through the legal work to sponsor him and bring him to America as an orphan refugee. One of my former Marine buddies took him in as a foster child."

"Wow."

"I just . . . I couldn't live with my mistake." He glanced at her. "He's now in college at MIT. So smart. Has a girlfriend." He offered a grim smile. "But I'll never get out of my head that moment when I realized I'd shattered his world."

Oh, Dec.

Guilt. *That* was his terrible secret. She stepped in front of him and reached for his hands. Met his gaze. "It was a mistake. And you made it right. You need to forgive yourself."

One side of his mouth tweaked up. "Trying."

"Maybe you need to swim with the sharks." She winked. "The potential of being eaten sort of shakes away the voices."

He laughed, something small, warm. Then his blue eyes met hers.

Oh. His gaze heated through her. "You're good for me, Austen," he said softly. "I wanted to tell you before, but . . ."

She raised an eyebrow.

"Hiring you made it complicated."

She swallowed, studying his face. "I don't . . . I don't work for you anymore."

He tucked a strand of hair behind her ear, let his hand rest there, cradling her face. "No. No, you don't."

He took a step toward her, and she didn't move, just lifted her head.

His eyes searched hers, landing on her lips.

And this time Stein wasn't here to stop her. "Yes," she whispered. He bent to kiss her—

A scream erupted into the air, and then—

Gunshots?

Staccato pinged the air, a succession of shots.

More screaming.

Declan had already jerked away from her, turned, and pushed her behind him.

Then he froze as a man appeared around the side of the boat. He wore a pair of faded jeans and a dark T-shirt and held a handgun.

And just like that, she was in a movie, pirates taking over their ship.

"Down! Get down!" An accented voice, a snarl at the end.

Declan put up his hands, knelt on one knee. "What's going on?"

Then another man appeared, also holding a gun, this one on a strap that hung over his shoulder. He walked right over to Declan.

Cuffed him with his fist.

Declan didn't go down. Just put his hand out to correct his balance.

The next punch, Declan stopped with his hand. And he might have jumped to his feet and punched back if Pirate One hadn't shot into the air and shouted, "Stop!"

Then he walked over and grabbed Austen by the arm, yanked her away from Declan. Put the gun to her head, the barrel grinding into her scalp.

"Don't move or I kill her."

Okay, she took it back. She very, very much wanted off this yacht and back to her normal, boring life.

———————————•————————•———————————

Just breathe.

Think.

He could solve this.

Declan kneeled in front of his hot tub, his hands zip-tied in front of him, his jaw throbbing even as he gritted it, watching the pirates—yes, that's what he was calling them—handcuff not only his guests but his staff too.

Captain Teresa, Chef Camille, Jermaine, Ivek, Raphael, Tyrone—the deckhand, who couldn't be more than eighteen and was scared to death, given the look on his face.

Hunter sat next to Elise on the lounger, sporting a darkening bruised eye. Apparently he'd received the same welcome as Declan.

Austen sat beside him, near the hot tub, her hands also secured, wearing her bathrobe, her expression fierce, almost angry.

A vast difference from the look in her eyes earlier, after he'd told her about Farid. Compassion. Maybe even desire? He'd definitely heard a *yes* whisper out of her.

He couldn't catch a break.

"What do they want?" Austen asked, her voice low.

"I don't know," Declan said. "Money? Ransom?"

"You think they're pirates?"

He'd spent some time studying them. There were five total, so it seemed that maybe he, Hunter, Ivek, Tyrone, and even Jermaine might have overpowered them en masse, except they weren't the ones with guns. So probably not.

The guys were thugs, really, more than pirates, with faded jeans, T-shirts, and grimy ball hats, and built like men who threw their weight around.

Maybe miners?

And then it clicked. The Petrov Bratva. They'd figured out his shell game.

Aw. These weren't just any thugs. They were *Russian Mafia.*

Declan met eyes with Hunter and then Ivek.

Someone had to get free and get to the weapons locker.

The one with the handgun, who'd threatened Austen—Declan

would call him Sergei—came up to him, grabbed his shirt, and hauled him to his feet. Pushed him against the hot tub. "Where is she?"

He swallowed. "Where is *who*?"

The man hit him, and he jerked, off-balance, rounded back. Declan might have kicked him, but the man pointed his gun at Austen. Blood burned Declan's mouth. "I don't know what you're talking about."

Sergei motioned to one of his comrades, the big one—Declan mentally dubbed him Igor—who walked over to Declan and grabbed him by the throat, his meaty hand squeezing off Declan's air.

He grabbed the man's wrists, fighting him despite his tethered hands.

"Stop! Stop!" Austen, who'd gotten to her feet, kicked at the man. "Stop!"

Declan finally tore the man's grip from his neck. "I. Don't. Know!"

Sergei gestured to another man—equally as big (Boris)—who came over and grabbed Declan's arms. Turned him to face the hot tub.

Oh boy. Declan took a deep breath.

A hand viced his neck and plunged him face-first into the tub. *Don't struggle.*

He'd learned a few things about controlling his fear during Marine boot camp. And after, in Afghanistan. Panic set in when fear took hold, kept a man from thinking clearly. Struggling would only sap his breath.

He waited, refused to struggle.

The man yanked him out long before his lungs begged for air. Declan shook off the water, screams from Austen and Elise rising around him.

"Tell us where she is!"

Water trekked down his face into his shirt. "I don't know."

"Fine," Sergei said, walked over and hauled young Tyrone up.

"What are you doing?" This from Elise. She'd jumped up, which made Hunter rise beside her. He stepped in front of his wife when Boris came at her.

"Leave me alone!" Tyrone struggled in Sergei's grip as Sergei hauled him to the side of the boat.

Igor joined them.

"Stop! *Stop!*" Austen, and Elise, and even Camille.

Sergei looked at Declan, held a gun to Tyrone's spine.

Cold flushed through him. "I don't know—but I can find out! Let me call—"

Igor picked up Tyrone's feet and, as if he weighed nothing, pitched the boy out over the edge of the boat.

Sergei stepped up behind him and fired.

Elise's knees buckled, and Declan wanted to retch.

Then Sergei turned. "Who's next?"

Declan held up his hands. "I swear I'm telling you the truth. I don't know who you're talking about—but I can find her—I just need to make a call—"

Sergei strode toward him, handgun up. Set it against Declan's forehead.

And Declan heard his gunnery sergeant yelling in his brain. *"First to fight! Engage and persist."*

A.k.a., grab the gun.

He needed both hands free, really, but if he did go for the gun, then what? Elise would get shot, maybe one of his crew?

Austen.

The thought clenched his gut, tightened his chest. He kept his voice low. "Listen. I want to do what you ask. No one, especially me, wants anyone to die."

Don't think about Tyrone.

"So help me help you. Let me use the radio in the pilothouse. I'll contact my man in charge, and he'll get that location."

Sergei considered him for a long moment.

"C'mon, dude. Just . . . let me make a call. I will find out where she is."

Sergei glanced at Igor, who walked over to Elise and Hunter.

"Not on your life, man," Hunter said, not moving from his position in front of his wife. Igor hit him, but Hunter barely flinched, breathing hard, blood running from his mouth.

"Stop!" Declan shouted. Then he leveled a look at Sergei. "You hurt anyone else and you get *nothing* from me."

Sergei's eyes tightened around the edges.

Declan swept any hint of bluff out of his gaze. Yes, he'd give them the password to his vault, empty his bank account to keep them from hurting Elise or his crew or, most importantly, Austen.

No one moved, the sun hot on the deck as the boat rocked ever so slightly.

Then Sergei stepped back and barked at Igor, Boris, and the other comrades, Thugs One and Two. "Get them downstairs into the salon and lock it down." He looked at Declan. "You. To the bridge."

Declan glanced at Austen, who met his gaze, tight-lipped, her green eyes still fierce. "I'll be okay. Just . . . do what they say."

Boris grabbed her arm, but she yanked it out of his grip. "I can walk."

Declan braced himself. But Boris didn't react, just let her follow Elise and Hunter and his crew down the stairs. Thugs One and Two followed, Igor leading the way.

And then it was just Declan and Sergei.

"Let's go," Sergei said and gestured toward the pilothouse.

Captain Teresa had left the boat at idle, the motors still running. A large sofa stretched across the back, for those times when he joined Teresa in the bridge, watching her work.

Two captain's chairs sat before the expansive console with the navigation screens and security camera that overlooked the foredeck and the stern. It also held the communications center and the steering helm. Now Declan walked over to the Sailor SSB radio and keyed open the mic.

Zeus would wonder why he was calling on the satellite phone instead of his cell, so that might help. Not that he had a small army to repel the pirates, but he did have resources.

Mostly, he just needed to get everyone off the boat—alive.

"Mariposa Base, this is Declan on the *Invictus*. Over."

Static, and his gut tightened. What if the Bratva had already raided his house on Mariposa—

"This is Mariposa Base, go ahead Declan. Over." Zeus's voice.

"I need the current GPS coordinates for the *Niña*. Just verifying position."

"Copy. One moment, I'll pull up the latest communication."

He glanced at Sergei. "He'll send them over EDCIS."

"No tricks."

Declan held up his hands.

Zeus came back on the line. "Coordinates sent. Over."

"Thanks for the quick response. How's the weather over there? Over."

"Blue skies. But reports are there's a weather front moving in. We're watching it. You? Over."

He didn't look at Sergei. "Storm on the horizon, sailing right into it."

And just to prove he wasn't lying—although he hoped Zeus picked up his meaning—he pointed at the radar. Fuzz on the screen showed an incoming squall.

"Anything to worry about?"

"Not at this time. Just keep an eye on the front. *Invictus* out."

"Safe travels. Mariposa Base out."

Declan hung up, then went over to the electronic chart where Zeus had sent the coordinates and zoomed in on the *Niña*.

She sat in waters east of Haiti, on her way to the Caymans.

Sergei swore and Declan stepped back, hands up. He turned to Declan. "Where is she docking?"

"I don't—"

Another cuff. This one jerked him back, bounced him off the console.

And that was just it.

He ran at Sergei, slapped the gun away with both hands, then grabbed his throat in his hands. Slammed him up against the console, stepped up to him, holding tight. "You don't get to hijack my boat, kill my people—"

A blinding pain exploded in the back of his head, his knees buckled, and he hit the floor.

Instinct made him put his hands over his head to protect himself as Igor stood over him, holding the butt of his semiautomatic, an HK G3 probably pulled off a NATO soldier fighting on some Russian battle line and sold in the black market.

And why that thought swept through Declan's head, he didn't know. Just—*yeah,* it left a mark on him. Gray dots speckled before his eyes, his head spinning.

Igor grabbed him up just in time for Sergei to add his fury. His punch hardly registered, however.

Still, Declan tasted fresh blood as Igor hauled him out of the captain's roost, nearly pushed him down the two flights of stairs, then flung him headlong into the salon.

His blood probably wrecked the white carpet. His bell had certainly been rung, because the world tilted even as Igor grabbed Captain Teresa and forced her out of the room.

Probably back to the helm to chase down the *Niña*.

Too bad they were tracking an empty ship.

Declan had about thirty-six hours before things got really ugly.

Hands found him, helped him up, and he focused on Austen, her eyes reddened, her jaw tight. "Are you okay?"

He nodded.

She shook her head.

"We'll figure a way out of this. I promise."

He'd gotten them into this. He'd get them out.

●————————————●

The moment the body dropped into the water, Steinbeck knew his gut had been right.

He set down his binoculars and sat hard at the helm of Hawkeye's dinghy.

It didn't look like Austen, but he couldn't be sure, could he?

He should probably turn around, get back into radio range of Hawkeye's boat, but he'd lose precious time, not to mention the opportunity to sneak on board and end whatever had gone down on Declan's yacht.

The twelve-foot boat listed in the gentle water. No way he'd have taken the dinghy off Hawkeye's boat if the sea had been running angry. *Well, maybe* . . .

Aw, he should have never left. He didn't care what Austen said— he shouldn't have let Declan's explanation soften his resolve. Even if he had dropped his cell phone into Austen's bathrobe pocket, in case she needed him.

It hadn't been enough, because the minute he'd stood at the rail of Hawkeye's boat, watching the yacht disappear, his gut had clenched, something niggling at him.

Hawkeye had noticed. "What's eating you?"

Maybe it had been the way he stood, the wind flapping his shirt, his jaw tight. The external version of the knot in his chest. "I don't know," he'd said, and he wasn't lying. Just, "Something doesn't feel right."

Hawkeye had sat in the high captain's seat, glanced over at him through his aviator sunglasses, his hair curling out from under his backward gimme cap. He'd worn a sleeveless shirt, the name Ocean Adventure Divers on the front, and a pair of shorts and flip-flops.

Not unlike how Steinbeck had looked a year ago, working as a dive instructor in St. Lucia. An easier, simpler life, albeit aimless.

It felt years away now. Declan Stone had changed that. Given him back a taste of the life he'd lost.

Oh, how he wanted Phoenix to be wrong, but his conversation with the operative two months ago as they were fighting for their lives just wouldn't leave him.

"Declan Stone is a terrorist, Stein. I've seen the proof."

And then, of course, she'd spent the better part of five hours laying out that proof.

Declan had eliminated all of that with one sentence: "I'm a patriot, and when the DOD came to me and asked for help, of course I was going to do what I could for my country." Except, he seemed to have good reasons for everything, didn't he?

"Stein? Really, what's going on?"

Austen seems to trust Declan.

Stein had glanced at Hawkeye. "I dunno. Something doesn't feel right."

"Aw, man, she'll be fine."

"I know." He'd walked over to the cooler and pulled out a cold bottle of water. "It's just that she always has a way of . . ."

"Standing up to you?" Hawkeye had grinned. "You and the rest of the world. Sea creatures and men alike."

Stein had glanced at Hawkeye. Once upon a time, the Hawk had had a crush on his sister, had asked her out. She'd shut him down. And maybe Stein would never have known about it, but he'd walked in on the tail end of the conversation a couple years ago while visiting her. He'd felt kind of bad for the Hawk, but it wasn't personal.

She had her reasons.

He'd slid into the co-captain's chair. "I guess. I just worry about her. Even more than about Boo."

"Is it the twin connection?"

He'd taken a sip of water. "Maybe." Even though they were fraternal, they seemed to think alike. React alike. In truth, that's what scared him. "I can't help but think Austen is walking right into trouble, refusing to see danger."

Hawkeye had glanced at him. "Danger? You mean falling for some billionaire? Yeah, you should warn her off." He'd grinned.

Stein hadn't.

"Listen. Your sister literally swims with sharks. I think she's got this."

"Yeah, probably." He'd taken another drink. The fist in his gut hadn't loosened, however. Something had nudged at him, a slow burn in the back of his head. He just couldn't—

Wait.

He'd stood up, turned to stare out the back as if he could see the yacht, probably fifty miles away by now. "Phoenix."

"What?" Hawkeye had said.

Aw. He'd drained the water, dropped the bottle into a recycling bucket near the helm. "We need to go back."

Hawkeye had frowned. "Why?"

"Because"—and even to his own ears, his explanation had sounded crazy—"I think there's an assassin on Declan's yacht."

Hawkeye had pulled his glasses down. "What?" He'd pushed them back up with his finger. "Did you see his security? That Swede looked like Thor's younger brother."

"Yeah, I did. But she's . . . sneaky and . . ." He'd run a hand across his mouth. "I don't know why she's there, but she's trouble. And if Phoenix is on the boat, then there is something going down."

Hawkeye had slowed, the boat settling in the water. "Dude. Listen. I'm half a tank away from dry—I don't have the fuel to turn around and make it back to harbor. We'll land in Turks and Caicos and you can call the Coast Guard."

"I gotta get back on that boat, Hawk."

Hawkeye had scrubbed his hands down his face. Sighed. "I'm sorry, Stein. It's a no go. I can't turn into a bobber in the water."

Stein had walked to the back of the boat. "I'll take the tender." He'd pointed to the twelve-foot dinghy that hung off the back. "You have extra gas?"

Hawkeye had put the boat into neutral. "Yeah. A couple cans."

"Will it get me to the yacht?"

"Yes, but . . . Steinbeck, the sea is calm now. If a storm rolls in, you're in trouble."

He'd looked up at the cloudless sky. "I'll chance it." Then, "Do you have a lifeboat, if something happens?"

"Of course." He'd pointed to a box attached to the end of the boat, then sighed. "Take the EPIRB. If you have trouble, at least it can send help."

Which was how Steinbeck had ended up at the helm of the tender, cutting through the water, beads of spray landing on his skin as the sun dipped toward the horizon.

He'd also taken the binoculars and called up the GPS coordinates from the phone he'd given Austen.

She hadn't called. Hadn't pinged the emergency button. So maybe he was overreacting. No, most definitely he was overreacting.

But he very, *very* clearly remembered now the server who'd appeared on the deck delivering orange juice and clearing the table. Short dark hair, wearing a white uniform, her eyes averted.

Maybe she'd seen him too. But he'd been so absorbed in Austen and her stubbornness . . .

Clearly, he was losing his edge.

He'd stopped a half mile out, searched for the *Invictus* on the horizon, and spotted her.

A speed boat was tied up to the stern, and when a gunshot had reverberated across the water, he'd wanted to hit something.

He'd spotted a group of attackers on the spa-lounge level just as they dumped a body over the edge, firing into the water after it.

Now, he scanned the stern as the attackers forced their captives down the stairs.

He nearly groaned, part relief, part fury, when he spotted Austen, her hands tied, descending to the main level.

Alive, for now.

He didn't see Declan among them, however.

Or Phoenix. He couldn't, just couldn't believe she might be one of the pirates. Instead, knowing Phoenix, she'd resisted capture. And despite their history, he had to put the binoculars down, grab his knees. Blow out a few breaths.

Okay. Think.

Turn around, get help.

Or get on that boat.

He glanced at the fading sunlight. An hour to sunset, max.

Okay then.

There was only one choice.

SIX

EMBERLY HAD NEVER WANTED OFF A BOAT more in her life. The only good news was that she'd been away from the galley when the pirates-slash-Russian-attackers had stormed onto the boat and invaded the lower deck, grabbing Camille and then subduing Jermaine and the rest of the crew. She'd been conveniently in the head.

Which was where she'd stayed as she heard the shouts and even the gunshots.

Yeah, if it wasn't Steinbeck showing up out of nowhere to blow her cover, then of course it would be marauding Russians. Probably hunting for *her*.

In fact, she'd heard them saying things like "Where is she?" as they worked Declan over. She'd gotten a good view of that trauma as she'd climbed up the interior stairway to get the lay of the land. Five captors, all of them armed with H&Ks. She didn't recognize any of them, but they definitely had a Slavic accent to their tones. Big men, they weren't messing around when they asked Declan to find her.

Of course, Declan didn't have the faintest idea who they were really looking for. He'd talked them into leading him to the pilothouse.

She couldn't imagine why, really, but he was crafty. Or in cahoots—and didn't want his passengers to realize his true affiliation.

She'd sneaked back down to the galley and tried to gather her thoughts on what she should do. She couldn't let them find her, but then again, she also couldn't, in good conscience, let innocents be gunned down.

She should have gotten off in Key West. She wanted to bang her head against something hard for not just pushing past Ivek with an "I'm out of here." Especially when, forty-eight hours later, who should appear on the ship but Steinbeck. And looking good too.

She'd plunked coffee down in front of him before she'd realized her mistake and hustled away, her head down. But she'd nabbed a good look at him. Tanned, his dark-blond hair highlighted with gold from the sun. Muscled and fit, looking healthy, so clearly he'd recuperated from his bullet wound, just like she'd suspected back in Key West. Yes, fully recuperated and back to his bossy self, demanding that his sister get off the boat.

Who knew that Austen was such a fighter? She'd done a good job of standing up to Steinbeck. Emberly had to admit the woman had chutzpah. She'd listened to their conversation from a distance, and then, when Steinbeck pulled Declan aside, she'd listened to that conversation too. The one where he'd denied being a terrorist.

Yeah, whatever, whatever. She didn't believe a word of what Declan had told Steinbeck, and she hoped Steinbeck didn't either. She hadn't known what to think when he decided to leave the ship. She'd wanted to jump off with him and say, "Take me back to the mainland," but then again, any proximity to Steinbeck could only lead to trouble.

She'd barely extricated herself last time from the magnetic pull of his blue eyes and the way he and she seemed to be a good team.

She worked alone, thank you. So she'd watched him disembark and resolved not to think of him again.

Instead, she kept turning Declan's explanations over and over in her mind. Even though, sure, some of it could be plausible, she'd been watching this man for nearly eight months, and he had secrets. Secrets she already knew about, and maybe others too.

But someone had clearly forgotten to send the Russian team a memo letting them know that Declan was on their side. Or maybe it was just a show. Still, he'd looked pretty roughed up when she left him on the bridge.

An hour later, the sun had nearly sunk into the ocean, casting a bloodred glow across the waters. The Russians had moved everyone down to the salon, including Declan.

Emberly had hidden inside the galley, and the door remained locked from the inside, so for now, she was safe.

The time had given her space to plan. In darkness, she could get the crew and the passengers off the ship and onto the Russian boat, where they could take off and leave the Russians behind on the yacht.

If she could figure out a way to distract the guards.

There were flares in the hallway storage area—those could make a small distraction—but how to get all of the people out of the salon?

What she needed was something spectacular at the yacht's bow that would draw the guards and allow her to leave the galley through the stairs and hustle people out to the boat.

And she needed a weapon.

Camille's set of deluxe kitchen knives probably wouldn't do the trick. As Emberly was searching for the flares, she found the weapons locker. Locked, of course, but inside it held two shotguns, a couple of handguns, and *hello, mama,* a Sig Sauer P226. She spent about ten minutes getting the gun case open, grabbed the

Sig Sauer, and found ammo. *Bam.* It might be a crazy, desperate idea, but she couldn't just let the Russians shoot them.

Not when it was her fault that they'd attacked.

She'd worked out the plan in her head. She would fire off the flares in the bow, scurry back through the galley, then through the stairs to the salon, and dispatch any of the remaining guards. By that time, hopefully, the captives would be on their feet, and they'd all escape. It could turn into chaos. *Probably* chaos. And maybe people would get hurt, but if all went right, they'd escape on the other boat.

Which could move much faster over open water than a hundred-twenty-foot yacht.

She just needed the cover of darkness.

And of course, in the quiet of the hour as shadows fell through the windows, memory stirred. Krakow three years ago, at the tail end of an op where she'd been trying to liberate a Ukrainian man named Luis. She'd gotten tangled up with Steinbeck and made the crazy decision to drag him to her safe house, where they could regroup.

In truth, she'd been buying time, hoping that she could figure out how to get Luis away from Steinbeck's grip, because the SEAL wanted him too. But she and Steinbeck had formed a sort of alliance, and that night, after they'd sneaked out to make contact with his team, they'd returned to the flat, checked on Luis, who was locked in his room, and let night fall around them.

Maybe she'd let down her guard too much, but when Steinbeck had come into the room with a bowl of ramen noodles, set it down in front of her, and picked up his own ramen noodles and a pair of chopsticks, it had felt like they were a couple of—well, maybe frenemies having dinner.

"You never told me where you were from, Phoenix," he'd said.

She'd looked at him and laughed. "No, I didn't. Where are you from?"

"Originally Minnesota. My family runs an inn. It's a Victorian house that used to be owned by my great-great-grandfather. He also built two other houses for his sons and a carriage house. I grew up in the carriage house while my parents rented out the other homes to guests. It's called the King's Inn."

At that moment, she hadn't wanted to tell him about her past. The one that included a mom who'd tried but couldn't get off drugs, sleeping in cars, makeshift homes, and abandoned buildings, and how she and her sister Nimue had pledged to never, ever, ever live like that when they got older.

At least one of them had kept that promise.

So when Steinbeck had looked at her and said, "Okay, now you," she'd simply shrugged and said, "Yeah, something like that."

He'd studied her with those blue eyes, and she'd felt weirdly naked. She didn't normally care what people thought about her, but he'd grown on her, gotten under her skin over the last thirty-six hours. So *fine,* she'd put down her ramen noodles. "Okay, that's not entirely true. Single mom. We moved around a lot."

"We?"

Oh, he had a devastating smile. "I have a sister too. She's a few years younger than me. Really smart. She's into computers and hacking."

"She a Black Swan too?"

Oh, that's right, she had told him about her organization—the fact that she worked for the clandestine international all-female group that helped stop terrorism around the world. "No," she'd said, "She has a job working for a company that does white-hat hacking. From home. In her pajamas. She lives in Florida, has a normal life."

"I'm not sure what that looks like." Stein had finished his soup and set it down. "I've never thought about leaving the teams."

"What made you want to be a SEAL?" she'd asked as she finished her ramen.

He'd also brought out a couple of cold Fanta drinks and uncapped them. She reached for hers.

"My grandfather was in the Navy and spoke highly of the spec ops team. When I got older, I just wanted to test myself and see if I could make it." He'd picked up his Fanta. "I did. The fact is that I like being on a team, working with people that have a mutual mission. We have each other's backs, and it reminds me a lot of my family."

"What, you have stubborn, tough, and a little bit arrogant siblings?" She'd laughed then, and he'd responded with a chuckle. A deep sound that had tunneled right into her skin and bones.

"Yeah, actually, I do. That includes my two sisters, Austen and Boo. My three brothers are just as, what did you say?—stubborn, tough, and . . ."

"Arrogant."

"Right." He'd leaned back and put his ankle up on his knee. "So, is your sister like you?"

"Like me?"

"Um, sassy, smart, and maybe a little bit pretty?"

Oh. She hadn't had words, so she'd looked out the window, and her reflection had looked back at her. Short dark hair, big gray-green eyes. Fit, yes, but petite. Unremarkable. Hence, she excelled at blending in.

"Let me amend that," he'd said. "Let's try surprising."

She could accept *surprising*. She'd looked at him. "No. She's not like me. She's steady, solid, and incredibly smart."

"Incredibly smart. I *did* say smart."

"Right, okay." She'd smiled.

He'd smiled back. "Where does she live?"

"She's down in Florida. Has a little house on the east coast, in a place called Melbourne Beach."

She'd looked away again. She'd known she should schedule a

trip to visit Nim after they got all this sorted. *About that*—"Have you heard from your team yet?"

"Yeah. I'm supposed to meet them at a coffee shop tomorrow. I'll bring Luis down to the shop and they'll pick us up there." He'd raised an eyebrow. "In broad daylight, so no funny business."

Aw. "You can't think I'm gonna let you take him."

He'd held up a hand. "No, of course not. You come with us. You get all the information you need out of him, and then he's ours."

"Or you get the information you need out of him, and he's all *mine*." She hadn't smiled as she'd met his eyes.

"I should have added stubborn," he'd said quietly.

She'd stared at him and he'd stared back, and suddenly the kiss they'd shared in the alleyway just a few hours earlier had risen between them. She could still taste his lips on hers and feel his body closing in as he'd pressed his hands on the wall behind her. It had been a quick kiss, of course—just to hide them from the police that had walked by. But he'd put enough into it to make it look real, and for that moment, maybe . . . maybe she'd wanted it to be.

Which was super crazy—then and later and especially now, as she shook the memories away in the galley of the yacht.

Darkness bathed the kitchen, the only sound the motor's hum as the yacht churned through the waters. At the top of the stairs, she eased the galley door open.

Two guards sat in the salon, their guns trained on the captives. Declan sat on one of the sofas next to Austen. He held a towel to his nose and sported a fairly brutal black eye. *Yeah, well,* that's what he got for being a terrorist.

Okay, maybe that wasn't fair. Or even accurate. But she found it hard to echo compassion for the man, given his evil global plot. Still, nobody else deserved to suffer, especially since the Russians wouldn't be here if they weren't tracking Emberly. So . . . it was now or never.

She sneaked back down the stairs to the front of the galley. The forward stairs wound up from the galley all the way to the bridge, with an exit to the bow lounge area. Slinging the bag with the flares over her shoulder and hanging the Sig Sauer across her body, she eased up the stairs and opened the door to the bow. She crept out into the lounge area.

The area at the very front, beyond the bow lounge, held all the buoys and bumpers and ropes and coils needed to dock the ship.

She crouched by the built-in sofa, took off the bag, and pulled out a flare gun. She loaded a flare and was about to fire when a hand snaked around her mouth. Another hand grabbed the gun and then yanked her hard against a sopping-wet body.

"Stop." A voice low in her ear.

She jerked, elbowed him hard in the ribs. He released her, and she turned.

Even in the dim light as the moon rose over the ocean and the stars prickled overhead, she could make him out. A very wet, very fierce, very grim-faced Steinbeck. And then he smiled. "I thought that was you."

The smile had the effect of the flare gun, a spark, and light exploding through her entire body. *What? Aw, no, no!*

"Shoot," she said. "I thought you didn't see me."

"You're very hard to miss," he said, his gaze raking over her and then the flare. "So what's your plan there, Sparky?"

"Distraction, then I get into the salon, take out a couple of the Russians, and hustle everyone onto the Russians' boat before the others can get down from the bridge."

He made a face of approval. "Not bad. I think I could help with that, but I need a sitrep first."

"A sitrep?" How had he even gotten back onto the boat? "How are you even *here*?"

"It took me a little bit to realize that was you, but I knew wherever you were, there was trouble."

And then he smiled again.

Stop smiling. Stop smiling! "All right, I'll tell you on the way."
She scrambled back up the bow, through the door, and down into
the galley, Steinbeck on her tail.

"Where are we going?"

"I'm going to get you a gun."

"I love it when you talk that way."

Oh. She had no hope of getting off this boat unscathed.

Next time she got taken hostage, Austen was definitely not
wearing a swimsuit. Because whereas the sun had baked her skin
and settled her into a comfortable, relaxing morning, the chill of
the AC in the salon turned her bones brittle and sharp. And sure,
she was deflecting, because that seemed easier than focusing on
the two thugs carrying lethal-looking machine guns. Or on the
fact that Declan sat beside her holding a towel to his nose, his
expression brutal and not a little angry. Hunter wore the same
look, and he kept exchanging glances with Declan as if they were
in cahoots, ready to overpower the thugs.

Worse, Steinbeck's word kept circling back. *"Criminal."*

Clearly, she didn't know Declan as well as she'd thought she
did. Because she'd heard the thugs talking to Declan, asking where
he'd stashed something. And that's what criminals did, right? They
took things and hid them from others.

No, *no*, that wasn't right. Declan was a good man. But something just didn't feel right in her gut, and she hated to think that
it was Steinbeck's voice latching on and speaking truth.

She wasn't going there. Right now, all Austen cared about was
surviving. And maybe going to the bathroom, because it had been
a couple hours now, and she'd had a lot of lemon water thanks to
her dehydration yesterday.

"Um," she said into the quiet of the room, "is there any way I could use the ladies' room?"

One of the thugs looked over at her and frowned.

"Me too," Elise said. She glanced at Austen and gave her a quick smile. *Solidarity.*

"There's a bathroom just off the salon," Declan said, lowering the towel from his nose. The blood had stopped. He pointed. "And another down the hall in the stateroom."

One of the men rose, nodded toward the hallway, and pointed at Austen. "Make it fast."

He didn't follow her, but where was she going to go anyway? They'd taken Captain Teresa up to the pilothouse—two of the other thugs had disappeared with her. Another man stood by the stern, guarding their boat. Not a big boat—seemed the same size as her trawler, but rusted and beaten by the waves. Maybe they'd taken out some fishermen to steal it.

Darkness had found its way into her brain even as night fell around them. Blackness filled the portholes, the moon glistening on the water. She moved down the hallway, past the dining-room table, and into one of the staterooms.

Opulence touched every area of this boat. An expansive king-size bed took up most of the room, with white wooden nightstands and a giant mirror along the headboard. The room looked out onto the port side of the boat and contained a small en suite bathroom.

She used it, then stared at herself in the mirror. She didn't look like a person who had survived at sea and was now being held hostage. But then again, she'd never seen herself as a victim.

She didn't typically stand around looking at herself, really. She combed her fingers through her hair, braided it into a long ponytail, then stepped out of the room.

A hand covered her mouth. "Don't scream."

She froze, her heart caught, and a voice bent into her ear. "It's me—Steinbeck."

He let her go and she whirled around. "What the—" Again, he slapped his hand over her mouth and pressed a finger to his lips.

Oops. She peeled off his hand, cut her voice to a whisper. "What on earth are you doing here? I thought you left the boat."

"I did," he growled, his tone low.

"I'm so confused."

"I knew something wasn't right." In the semidarkness, he was a warrior, dangerous and shadowy. She'd always seen him as capable. Now the sight of him, the power of his presence, shook her.

Steinbeck was here.

And sure, he was her brother. But he also looked like a protector, fierce and lethal. So this was how people felt when heroes showed up.

She let out a breath. *Still,* "What, do you have a radar on me? A twin radar?"

"Something like that."

"Wait," she said, her eyes narrowing. "Are you surveilling me? Have you attached some super-sneaky SEAL gadget to me to track my every move?"

"No," he said, "but that's not a bad idea." He grabbed her elbow. "Listen, we're going to get you off this boat. In a few minutes, you're going to hear pops and see fire at the bow. Flares will go off. I want you to make for the trawler tied to the stern."

"What? Who's *we*?" Her mouth gaped. "Oh no, you didn't drag Hawkeye into this, did you?"

"Of course not. I'll explain later. Just do what I tell you to do."

She held up her hands. "If you get killed, I will be so angry."

"Love you too, sis. Stay here until you hear the chaos, and then run for it." He turned away.

She stopped him with a hand on his arm. "No, I can't do that. They're waiting for me back in the salon."

He paused.

"Listen, Declan's in there, and so is the crew. If I don't come back, they're going to come looking for me, and I don't know, maybe find you or whoever your sneaky partner is."

He studied her for a second. "Right. Okay. Get back to the salon. But when the chaos starts, get down. And when you hear the word *run,* you run."

"What are you gonna do?"

He looked at her. "Just do what I say, okay?"

"Aye, aye, captain. You don't have to get snippy."

His eyes widened.

She held up a hand. "I will run when you say run."

"Not me. When somebody—yes, anyone—says run—"

"I will run! I promise."

He put a finger to his lips again, and she nodded, then walked out of the room, through the hallway into the salon. Elise had returned too, and the two thugs stood by the window.

Okay. They just had to get across the deck and down to the swim platform and then leap aboard the trawler. Hopefully, there was a ladder.

Declan was glancing askance at Hunter as if they had some sort of secret communication going. She wanted to lean into him and say, "Don't worry, Steinbeck is here," but that was probably a bad idea. She took his hand and gave him a smile. "It's going to be okay," she said softly.

"Stop talking!" said the thug.

"I'm not talking! I'm just, you know, trying to stay calm—reminding everybody *to stay calm*, okay? I mean, calmness is what we need here. No matter what happens, stay calm."

She got a few eyebrow raises from the crew and the chef.

"Stop babbling," the thug said.

"I don't babble!"

He stepped toward her, but Declan stood up.

Oh.

A moment passed, and clearly, Declan didn't care if he got hit again.

The man stepped back and Declan sat down. Squeezed her hand. Her heart thundered, and maybe her breathing had hitched up just a little.

She shot a look at the sliding doors. *Please don't be locked.* What if the thugs didn't go for Stein's distraction? She spotted a dolphin statue on one of the consoles. It looked made of brass. That could work—she could pick it up and throw it.

"Stay still." Funny, it wasn't her voice but her instructor from Hawaii when he taught her how to face a shark in the water. *"Stay still; keep eye contact; don't run away."* Well, maybe two out of three was the right answer here.

She'd never been great at not running away.

Popping. Then fire lit up the night sky. Flames glistened on the water, bright and sudden.

"Oy!" One of the thugs jumped up and ran to the sliding-glass door. He opened it and stepped out, looking up. Another flare burst into the air, followed by gunshots.

Steinbeck.

The first man ran back in and shouted something in Russian. Then he took off, which just left one against many. Although he *did* have a gun, so there was that.

She glanced at the dolphin statue, trying to decide if she could grab it with a leap, and then the door to the galley broke open. A shot fired, and the thug dropped. She looked over, expecting to see Steinbeck, but no.

Belle, the steward, charged in, wearing her white uniform.

"Run!" Belle shouted.

Hunter had already leaped up, along with Elise, and Declan gripped her hand, heading for the sliding door.

"Get to the boat!" Austen pointed to the swim deck, and Camille, Jermaine, the engineer, and the big blond Swede ran past her. Hunter and Elise came next, Hunter gripping his wife's hand.

Declan pushed her ahead of him. "Go!"

She scrambled down to the deck even as the Swede stood on the swim platform, holding the line, helping people to the ladder. Shots fired from the bow, and Austen turned, searching for Steinbeck. *Oh please, God, don't let him get killed.*

Camille boarded the boat, and then Jermaine, and behind him Raphael. Hunter practically flung his wife up the ladder before leaping for the boat himself. But around the side of the ship charged two of the Russians, including the one who had gone to the stern.

Austen just barely made it to the swim deck before bullets tore through the cushions in the back of the boat. Declan pushed her to the ground, then braced his body over hers.

Belle landed beside them, crouching low, shooting back in intervals.

Someone had started the trawler engine, and Ivek leaped onto the ladder, the rope untied from the yacht.

What? No! "Wait for us!"

"Come on, come on!" Raphael leaned over the edge, arms out. "Hurry up!"

The gunman aimed toward the ship, and whoever piloted the trawler put it into reverse.

"Get on that boat!" Declan practically pushed her toward the sea. The trawler was close enough that she could leap and grab the edge of the ladder.

"Go!" Declan put his hands on her waist as if to toss her. Another shot, and she ignored it and leaped for the boat, hands out for the ladder.

Too far away. She splashed down into the water, the trawler inching away.

"Swim for it!" Declan shouted, and then he, too, dove off the edge of the swim deck.

She started swimming as bullets ripped into the night at the trawler.

The pilot rammed it into high gear. The motor revved, churned up a wake.

From the yacht's bow, more gunfire.

The trawler turned and sped into the darkness.

Declan surfaced. "Stop! Wait!"

More shots, now pinging into the water. Austen grabbed Declan's hand. "Big breath!"

Then she pulled him down, deep under the water. Silence filled her ears, followed by the distant hum of a motor as the trawler thundered away.

Hide.

She kicked and pulled Declan around the side of the yacht. They surfaced in the luminescence of the boat, puddling out the back, and she maneuvered them deeper into the shadows.

Declan treaded water beside her. "We have to get to the life raft," he said. "It's on the swim deck. We can just throw it in the water and it'll inflate."

"I'll do it." She started to swim, but he grabbed her arm.

"No, you stay here. I'll do it."

"For the love! We'll both do it. Let's go." She took off, slicing through the water, the waves choppier in the darkness.

Belle still had a position on the swim deck, shooting.

Then, nothing. Her gun empty.

She stood, her hands up, and just as Austen reached the ladder, one of the Russians advanced on her.

Belle glared at him, and Austen couldn't help it: "No. Don't shoot her! Please don't shoot her!"

Austen scrambled aboard, and yes, Stein would have killed her, but she walked right up to Belle, hands up. "She's just a steward. She has nothing to do with this."

Honestly, Austen didn't know what *this* was really. Belle could have something to do with it, she supposed, but it didn't feel that way. Especially when Declan, his hands up, stepped between them and the gunman.

"Everybody just calm down. I'm still here, and I'm the one you want."

And if Austen had any final question as to whether or not Declan was a criminal, it died as he walked up the stairs and said, "I'll tell you everything you want if you let them go."

⸺ • ⸺

According to his SEAL training, no plan survived first contact with the enemy, but especially one as reckless and probably poorly thought out as Stein's epic failure to recapture the ship. Not that he really wanted to *recapture* the ship, but he would have preferred spending the next two days on Declan's luxurious yacht to being shoved into a smelly fishing trawler.

But since he was currently swimming in the ocean in the darkness, trying to figure out how to get back onto a boat, either option might have been better.

At least he wasn't dead. And as far as he could see, Austen wasn't dead either, nor Declan and Phoenix. No, they all sat under the bright stern deck lights, their hands up. Whoever had helmed the trawler and driven away had probably done the right thing. However, he would be having a small conversation with said person later about *doing unto others*.

Stein just had to wait till everybody went into the salon again, and then he'd reboard the boat. Same way he had earlier, although without having the dinghy to draw alongside it, pulling himself up the prow of the yacht might be a little trickier.

Right now, the yacht sat still in the water, so that was a plus. If he had to, he'd hang on to one of the dive ladders and just let it pull him along until he could board.

He should probably lose the Sig Sauer. It weighed about a billion pounds in the water. But who knew what he'd find once he got back on board? He refused to think about it. So instead, maybe he'd think about Phoenix and the look on her face when he had surprised her.

Feisty. Shocked. But was that a smile? As if she was glad to see him? He didn't know how he felt about that. She *hadn't* left him for dead again in Mariposa—in fact, she'd probably saved his life, although he didn't have the foggiest clue how. So maybe she hadn't been lying when she'd told him that she hadn't wanted him to get hurt three years ago in Krakow. Not just hurt—wrecked. Physically and possibly emotionally, although he hadn't taken a good look at the status of his heart when he'd awakened in a hospital in Germany.

If he was honest, he definitely had feelings for her—the kind of feelings that ranged from wanting to run far and fast from the woman to the desire to sweep her up in his arms. And he had a very clear, slightly dangerous memory of kissing her in an alley in Krakow. And while it had been meant to be a ruse, she had responded—playfully, probably, as part of their cover. Still, she'd *responded* and kissed him back.

Shook him more than a little. So maybe he had meant something to her too.

But that was three years ago and before the Black Swan team had blown up the café where he was supposed to meet his SEAL team, absconding with their target. And before, of course, he'd had to separate from the SEALs altogether thanks to his injury. *So everybody just hold your horses.* There was nothing happening here except him getting his sister off that boat.

The motor started up again, and he started to swim toward the boat. His gaze stayed on the captives. He'd taken out one of the Russians, and maybe Phoenix had rendered one ineffective. But three remained, and two of them brought the three captives back into the salon.

His new plan went like this: Get on the boat. Take out Thug One. Get the hostages off the boat and onto the two Jet Skis that sat attached to the swim deck.

He still had to figure out a way to keep the yacht from chasing them down. That would require a bit of tomfoolery.

He didn't have to *blow up* the yacht. He just had to disable it. The second Russian left, climbing the stairs again for the bridge, which meant it was three hostages to one—no, scratch that, *four* to one—in the salon. He just had to get inside without being seen.

But before he could rescue his sister, the boat needed to be dead in the water.

Pulling himself up the back ladder, Stein crouched and slid onto the swim deck. The Jet Skis sat in the darkness, strapped onto the deck. He unstrapped them. Then he lifted one of the handguns he'd swiped from the weapons locker.

He aimed for a light over the main deck and pulled the trigger. The shot echoed across the water, but *bam*! The light died. He aimed for the other one and took that one out too just as a shout erupted from the bridge.

He sprinted up the stairs and ran down the side of the boat, hugging the darkness.

The thug came out and spotted him.

Stein aimed, but a gunshot from above pinged past him. A miss.

No choice but to get into the galley, so he took the stairs down to the lower level.

Oh boy. He was the king of good plans today, wasn't he? But if he could stop the boat, he could keep them from chasing the escapees down.

He descended to the mechanical room. He didn't know much

about engines, although he'd bent over his grandfather's old Ford a few times. Not quite the same setup as he stood in the massive area with its two bulky engines, generators, watermakers, and so many hydraulic and exhaust lines, it seemed like a jungle.

Shouts came from above.

Move. He spotted a couple of hoses and yanked. Steam and water sprayed out. One engine stopped moving.

More shouts.

The hot, dark engine room would be a terrible place to die. He reached for the other hydraulic hose.

The door banged open. Shots. He ducked behind a large AC unit. More bullets pinged off the engine, and one of them pierced something that sent out steam. *Fantastic.* A voice sounded from behind the shooter—probably something along the lines of "Don't shoot in the engine room, you fool!" But Stein didn't know enough Russian to know for sure.

He took a peek and spied a gunman heading straight for him, another man on his tail.

He aimed for the first, but another gunshot pinged through the room, and yes, he was going to die.

And then Austen would be really, really mad.

He held up his hands. "Stop!"

The gunman came straight up and cuffed him across the face with the butt of his gun. Stein jerked back, head spinning. But he shook it off, turned, and slammed his fist into the man's face.

The man roared, but the guy behind him shouted something, and Stein stepped back, hands up again. The first man was bleeding from the nose, and Steinbeck tasted his own blood filling his mouth. Then the second gunman came up, grabbed the handgun out of the other man's hand, and shoved Stein in front of him, out of the mechanical room.

The remaining engine still hummed, impervious. Not good.

They pushed him into the galley, then up the stairs to the salon.

Austen's eyes widened as he came into the room, and her breath caught. All right, so maybe he looked a little rough. But not as bad as Declan. The guy appeared worked over pretty good—black eye, bloody nose, and he was wincing a little bit. Steinbeck tried not to care.

They led him over to the sofa where Phoenix sat in her now-grimy white uniform. He lowered himself next to her and glanced at her. She rolled her eyes. Yeah, well, they weren't dead yet. And that counted.

The first Russian, the one Stein had hit, came into the room, shouted at the guard, and then pointed his gun at Steinbeck. *Uh-oh.* Steinbeck raised his hands. *Oh, please, not in front of Austen.*

But maybe Big and Angry was just making a point, because he glared at Steinbeck, then stalked out of the salon.

"What happened to you?" Austen said. "I was so worried!"

"Stop talking," said the Russian, but Stein ignored him.

"I went for a little dip."

"Oh brother," Austen said.

"This was not the plan," Phoenix said beside him.

"Really?"

"Stop talking!" The Russian got up, walked over to Steinbeck, and it looked like he was going to hit him again, but Steinbeck held up one hand, met his eyes, and gave a *try me* look.

Whoever these guys were, they weren't mercenaries. Lousy shots and easily intimidated. So that made them who? Maybe Mafia, although the Russian Bratva was one of the toughest, meanest in the world. So if they were Bratva recruits, they seemed low on the ladder. Which meant they could be overpowered, right?

Especially this guy.

Stein glanced at Declan, then at the salon door, back at Declan.

The man's mouth tightened around the edges. Whatever Stein thought about Declan, he'd been a Marine, so he could handle himself.

And Stein's adrenaline was still running hot. Better to attack now while they still had a chance to get away. The longer they settled in, the less momentum played on their side.

Steinbeck looked at Phoenix. She gave him a nod, and then she smiled.

He did not expect the burst of heat inside his chest. The way her smile lit him up. They weren't friends. And maybe not enemies either, but yeah, this woman had gotten way too far into his psyche. Still, she was tough. A partner, for now.

He said quietly, nearly a whisper. "When I go, you go."

She nodded.

"So, Declan, who are these guys anyway?" Stein directed the question to Declan but glanced at the Russian. He had answered his radio, listening to something.

Hopefully not a kill order.

Declan frowned, his voice low. "I don't know. Russian pirates?"

"Oh, please," Austen said, her voice also quiet. "They said they were looking for something, and then they brought you to the bridge. What were they looking for? What do they want, Declan?"

Oh, she sounded mad. As if she'd decided that Declan was a criminal after all.

Steinbeck felt a little sorry for Declan when his eyes widened. *So long, Romeo.*

Then Declan sighed. "In truth, they're looking for a ship. One of my ships. It has cargo on it that they want. They found her coordinates, and they're going after her."

Out of the corner of his eye, he saw Phoenix scowl.

"What kind of cargo?" Austen whispered.

"A superconductor chemical that's mined out of the volcano in Mariposa. It's used with AI and defense technology."

He looked at Stein when he said it, and Stein frowned. This was the second time he'd heard this, and again, it felt like Declan was telling the truth. But Declan had gotten very good at lying over the last six months, so he wasn't sure.

"Stop talking or I hurt her." The Russian walked over to Austen.

Declan held up a hand. "Dude. There's no need for that. We all want the same thing—to get out of here alive." And he reached out to Austen as if to reassure her. She moved her hand away.

Ouch. "You got what you wanted—the coordinates of the cargo ship. Just let us go," Steinbeck said.

The man pointed his gun at Steinbeck. "No."

Go.

"Yes." Steinbeck lunged at him, kicked, and pushed the gun muzzle away with his hand. Then he landed a kick against the guy's knee.

The man jerked. Steinbeck had hold of the gun, so when the shot went off, he directed it to the ceiling. Then he slammed his open hand into the man's jaw, snapping his head back.

Phoenix swept up a handgun that lay on the table behind them. "Let's go!" She flung open the door.

Declan and Austen had gone through the sliding door. Phoenix looked at Steinbeck wrestling for the handgun. "Leave it! Let's go!"

Right. Steinbeck cuffed the man, then ran out into the night, Phoenix behind him. Austen and Declan had hit the swim deck, and Declan struggled with a suitcase life preserver on the side of the boat.

"No. Get on the Jet Skis!" Steinbeck got behind one to push it into the water.

Declan pushed the other one into the sea. It slid into the water just as shots fired behind them.

Stein turned. Phoenix had dropped the gunman onto the deck. But from the bridge came shouts, and in another second, more shots.

Declan reached for Austen. This time she did take his hand and scrambled behind him.

Stein leaped on one of the Jet Skis. "Come on, Phoenix!"

She sprinted from the deck and jumped, landing behind him, like she was a bareback rider. She locked her arms around his waist, squeezed tight, and said, "Move it!"

Hoo-yah. He gunned the engine and they roared off, a plume of water spraying the swim deck. Declan and Austen had already disappeared into the night. He followed their wake, the glimmer of moonlight off the hull of their Jet Ski.

"Just couldn't get enough of me, could you?" Phoenix said over the roar.

Steinbeck looked over his shoulder at her. "Yeah, yeah, that's it." But when he turned back to follow Declan's foamy wake, all he could think was . . .

Yes. Maybe, definitely, yes.

SEVEN

Out of the fire, into the frying pan.
Or the ocean, as the case may be.

"This is crazy stupid," Declan said even as the motor from his Jet Ski ate his words. Austen hung on behind him, her arms around his waist.

And okay, at least they weren't still on the boat.

But they were far away from safety.

He slowed and glanced behind him. Just Steinbeck's light, a pinprick in the darkness, but as far as Declan could tell, no one was following them. Of course not. Because who would be insane enough to drive into the dark, increasingly choppy sea with no land in sight and who knew how much gas? The tank looked nearly empty.

It might get him five miles, max. But who knew how far land might be?

Yeah, the farther they got from the yacht, the more they headed into trouble. Which was why he slowed the Jet Ski and waited for Steinbeck to catch up.

In that space of time, he tried to reel back what had just happened. First, his steward had materialized as Wonder Woman and started shooting, taking out one of the Russian captors. And then Steinbeck had barreled into the salon, also guns blazing, and everything had turned to bedlam.

For a second there, it had looked like Steinbeck's epic plan had crashed and burned. The fact that it ended with them in the ocean, Declan on a Jet Ski with Austen behind him holding on, seemed like a crazy miracle. *Or disaster.* And as Steinbeck came up and shut his engine down, Declan couldn't stop himself.

"Of all the stupid escape plans, this has to be the stupidest. What were you thinking? Seriously!"

Steinbeck just looked at him, and Declan couldn't really read his expression thanks to the darkness, but there was enough moonlight for him to grasp Steinbeck's open-mouthed shock.

"What? I got you off the boat, didn't I?"

"Yeah, off the boat and in the middle of nowhere. Where do you think we're going to go?"

"My compass says that we're heading due south. I figure we'll run into land at some point."

"You *hope* we'll run into land. We could be headed out to sea." He shook his head. "Maybe you should have taken one more second to think through this crazy plan."

"It wasn't a plan!" Steinbeck shook his head, looked at Austen. "You okay?"

"Yeah." She looked at the woman behind Steinbeck. "Are you okay, Belle?"

"Her name's not Belle," Steinbeck snapped. "It's Phoenix. And it's probably not even that, is it?" He glanced back at the woman.

"What are you talking about?" Declan said.

Steinbeck turned to him. "Really? I can't believe you didn't recognize Ashley. The girl nearly killed you in Barcelona."

What? Declan looked at the woman but couldn't make her out of the darkness. *Still.* "That was you?"

"We need to keep moving," she said now. The girl he'd met in Barcelona had a small accent. This one spoke with a flat Midwestern tone.

He didn't want to make a big deal about it, but the fact that Steinbeck thought he was a terrorist suggested that maybe he didn't have the best of gut instincts.

Speaking of gut instincts—"We should go back to the boat."

"Were you paying attention back there?" Steinbeck said.

Declan held up a hand. "I'm not suggesting we stick around once we get there. But we need better transport than these skis. Like the tender."

"What tender?" Stein asked.

"The tender that's stored in the swim-deck garage. It slides right out into the water."

"Well, forgive me for not understanding the schematics of your boat, Declan," Steinbeck said. "You forgot that little briefing in the tour of your floating estate and all your toys."

"Hey. I'm not the bad guy here."

"Seriously," said Belle, or Ashley or Phoenix—*whatever her name was*. "Yes, actually, you are."

"Not—I—" He stopped. "Forget it. This is not the time to explain what is going down on that boat. All I know is that we're out here in the middle of nowhere with a half tank of gas in a couple of skis that are going to be nothing more than floaties on the current in about an hour."

"Oh, no, we'll be in the water sooner than that," Austen said.

In the moonlight, he could barely make out her face, but her eyes were luminous and wide.

"What are you talking about?"

"We're sinking." She lifted her foot from the side of the Jet Ski. "The water is rising around us as we sit here."

That's when Steinbeck scooted his ski over. "Yep. Your hull looks Swiss cheesed. You're definitely going down."

"I feel like I've done this before," Austen said.

Silence. Waves rocked the boat, and Declan turned back to see the yacht's lights shining over the surface of the water.

"How far is land?" Phoenix said. "We have a nearly full tank. That'll get us a hundred miles. The DR can't be that far."

"We've been heading east," Declan said. "We'll land in Haiti. Or we could go north and hit Turks and Caicos. It's only a hundred miles between them and Haiti." He shook his head. "But if you put four on your ski, we'll be lucky to make it fifty miles."

"Okay, listen," Steinbeck said. "I had to get you off the ship—and fast—but I agree that I didn't think this all the way through. We *do* need transportation." He looked over at Declan. "Where's that tender again?"

"Why don't we just take back the yacht?" Phoenix said. "Come on, Steinbeck—there are four of us. I know Declan knows how to handle a weapon, and I'm sure Austen can figure it out."

"Have you lost your mind? No, I'm not gonna let my sister get killed. Stop talking. You don't get a say in this."

"What vote did I miss that put you in charge?" Phoenix said.

Declan looked at her. Maybe she *was* Ashley. Which meant what? *How did she—*

"I can handle a gun," Austen said. "Hello—Dad took me hunting too."

"Big difference, sis—"

"It doesn't have to be a firefight," Declan said. "We sneak onto the beach deck and—"

"Stop!" Steinbeck said. "Declan. Have you asked yourself how the Russians knew where you were?"

Declan went silent, his mind sifting through ideas. Maybe they'd gotten ahold of Zeus back at his compound in Mariposa . . . But he'd talked to Zeus, and no, that didn't make sense.

"Captain Teresa," Phoenix-Belle-Ashley said quietly.

Stein nodded. "It had to be an inside job. Somebody who could give them coordinates. Where is your captain from?"

"Portugal," Declan said.

"When did you hire her?" Steinbeck asked.

"Just recently."

"You do know that Portugal is a hotbed for Russian mobsters—" Phoenix-Belle-Ashley started.

"Oh, for Pete's sake," Declan said. "The entire world is a hotbed for Russian mobsters."

"Yeah, but she was the one at the helm, so my bet is on her," Austen said. He glanced at her, and she wore a frown.

Weird how she wouldn't take his hand in the salon. *Wait—she didn't think—*

"Here's what we're going to do," Steinbeck said. "Phoenix and I will go back to the boat, grab the tender, tow it out, then we'll all go on our happy, merry way."

Declan shook his head. "Are you just making this up as you go? That's a terrible idea."

"Absolutely," Steinbeck said, "and *why?*"

"Because we're going to sink. Have you ever tried to find someone in the ocean in the dead of night?"

Austen lifted her hand. "I, for one, do not recommend. Zero stars."

Declan wanted to smile, but she didn't seem to be kidding, so, "Stein—you and I will go back to the boat while the ladies limp back with the Jet Ski."

"No. I'm not staying out here on a sinking Jet Ski!" Phoenix-Belle-Ashley said.

"Me either," Austen said. "Why would you suggest that?"

He said nothing. A beat went by, then Austen turned to him. "Because we're women?"

He cocked his head. "Listen—"

"You listen," Austen said. "We'll all go back as far as we can on our ski, then transfer to yours. Steinbeck, you do some sketchy SEAL stuff while Belle and I stay with the Jet Ski and Declan gets the tender."

"Sketchy SEAL stuff?" Steinbeck said.

"Whatever it is you do."

"And I'll make sure that no one kills Declan—or Steinbeck— while they're getting the tender," Phoenix-Belle-Ashley said.

Steinbeck turned, looked at her. "And we're going to trust you?"

"Good point. Get off and we can part ways."

Steinbeck pressed his hand to his forehead. "Fine. Sorry."

She sighed, looked at Declan. "For the record, I wasn't trying to kill you—"

Declan held up a hand. "Fine. Whatever. We need her, Stein."

"Okay, we go back together," Steinbeck said. He looked over at Declan. "I'll think of something between here and there."

"I can't wait." But the guy *had* gotten him off the boat. It just irked Declan that somehow *he'd* turned into the bad guy, at least in Steinbeck's eyes.

And maybe Austen's.

And, of course, Miss Clandestine's on the back of Steinbeck's ski.

So, yes, everyone's.

Declan glanced at Austen. "We're going to be okay."

"Oh, I'm having the time of my life." But she gave him a thin smile.

He didn't know what to think as he took off, Steinbeck following behind.

They kept their lights off, using the light from the yacht to guide them. Austen held on as they slammed over waves, down into troughs. The water sprayed around him, chilling his bare skin.

How could Teresa have betrayed him? But the explanation from Austen and Phoenix made sense. He'd add that to his list of epic mistakes, along with trying to divert the obsidite from the Bratva, because that had been a super-great idea. And as long as he was cataloging mistakes, maybe he should go even further back and list the mistake where he'd believed the government when they'd said they'd watch his back.

So in the end, this wasn't on Steinbeck but on him, and he planned to get them out of this. No matter what it took.

Declan stopped a hundred yards from the yacht, which was still moving in the water, although barely.

Steinbeck pulled up beside him.

"So, what's the plan?" Water sloshed over Declan's ankles, and the ski struggled to stay afloat.

"Austen, you climb on behind Phoenix. Declan, I'm coming over," Stein said. "I'll drive you close and let you off, and then I'll do some sketchy stuff." He glanced at Austen and added a brief smile. "I'll create a distraction, and you work on getting that tender out."

"What kind of distraction?" Declan asked.

"Just pay attention." Stein looked at Austen. "And you stay alive. If they start shooting, put the Jet Ski between you and the shooter—but even better, get out of range completely."

"Steinbeck—"

"I'll be back, sis." He looked at Phoenix then. "Don't even think about ditching us."

Her mouth opened. "Where am I going to go?"

He shook his head, gave a small snort.

Interesting.

They changed places and Steinbeck took the helm. "Ready?"

"Go." Declan held on to the bench as Steinbeck puttered through the darkness, all the way to the swim deck. He pulled up and Declan rolled off into the shadows.

"Get that tender out no matter what happens." Then Steinbeck gave him a thumbs-up, and for a second, it hinted at a friendship Declan had thought they had.

Stein sped off into the darkness.

Declan ran over to the garage, where his tender sat under the main deck. He punched in the key code, and the garage door opened. The tender sat inside on rollers. He unhooked the security straps, and the tender started to roll out.

He pulled it, then got behind it and pushed.

An explosion thundered into the darkness. He looked up and the sky lit with flames.

Hello, distraction.

Gunshots, then shouting sounded from the bridge, and Declan kept his eyes on the tender. The six-seater speedboat should have enough gas to get them the one hundred miles to shore. Which shore, he didn't know, but the boat had GPS and hopefully extra fuel.

Operation Escape the Yacht accomplished.

Almost.

The tender slipped into the water, and he jumped onto the back deck, letting the boat float out to sea.

Gunshots pinged the water beside him, and Declan rolled down behind the bench, then crept up to the captain's seat. The key hung from the ignition and he turned it. The motor gurgled and spat. Died. More shouts erupted behind him, and he spotted one of the remaining gunmen running down the stairs.

He turned back to the ignition. "Come on, baby. Help a guy out." It spat, choked, and then caught. Gas fumes clouded the night. He gunned it. The boat's wheel nearly shot out of his grip, but he kept hold and righted it, then headed out into the darkness where he'd last seen Austen and Phoenix-Ashley—*whoever.*

From the yacht, gunshots still rang out.

Glancing back, he spotted flames in the ocean. Steinbeck had somehow set the sinking Jet Ski on fire.

Had probably taken off the fuel line, used the spark plugs to ignite it. *Smart.*

He turned around. Searched the night for the other Jet Ski. He spotted it, a winking light in the darkness. He motored toward it, shots still echoing from the yacht, but he kept his light off, the other guiding him.

Pulling up beside it, he'd barely throttled down when Austen pulled herself onto the back of the boat. "Where's Steinbeck?"

He shook his head.

"He's in the water!" Phoenix said. She turned her Jet Ski, stood up.

A fist formed in his gut.

"In ten minutes, turn your light on," Phoenix said, and shot off toward the yacht.

Austen sat on the side, her expression unreadable in the darkness.

"You okay?"

"Too early to tell," she said. "But I think I'm over the three-hour tour."

The what?

"*Gilligan's Island?*"

Right. "Who am I?"

"The professor."

"And you?"

"Mary Ann."

He laughed, and it released the knot in his chest. "You sure you're not Ginger?"

"Yes. And I'm diving overboard if you suggest I'm Mrs. Howell."

He turned the boat around, searching for Phoenix's Jet Ski. "The professor, huh?"

"You always have everything figured out."

He gave out a sound that held nothing of agreement. "I wish."

"Really?"

"Trust me. I spend most of my time trying to stay one step ahead of my mistakes. There they are." He pointed to a white hull just outside the light of the yacht. Flicking on his light, he let it shine for a moment, then turned it off.

In the flash, he spotted Steinbeck seated behind Phoenix, the two of them slicing through the water.

As if they belonged together. Interesting.

Phoenix pulled up, and Steinbeck climbed onto the boat. Then he threw her a line. "C'mon!"

But she just looked at him.

A beat. Two.

"Phoenix—"

She gunned it, jetting into the darkness.

What—what?

"Phoenix!"

Steinbeck stood there, his expression unreadable as he watched her disappear.

"Where is she going?" Austen said.

Steinbeck shook his head. "I didn't see this ending like that."

Declan either. But he was tired of being blindsided. And betrayed. "Let's find out," he said.

And took off after her.

———————————•———————————

All she wanted was her boat. And maybe a warm bed.

Okay, dinner too. A pizza, with lots of pepperoni and mushrooms.

Mostly, Austen just wanted off this danger train.

She sat on the bench of the boat, Steinbeck now manning the wheel as he followed Phoenix or Belle or whatever her name was west into the moonlight.

They'd slowed in the darkness and the churning sea and hadn't been able to catch Belle, losing her now and again in the swell. Somehow, they'd managed to stay on her tail, despite the darkness.

Declan sat next to her on the bench, looking a little undone and beat up by the events of the last few hours. His face still bore the bruises, but now he also wore a hint of dark whiskers, and it turned him into a rogue. Fact was, she felt a little bit like she'd been kidnapped and set into some action-adventure movie where everywhere she turned, she was running.

Literally, not metaphorically, so that was a change. "At least I'm not in the ocean," she said mostly to herself, but Declan cocked his head at her.

"I'm just saying, it could be worse." She turned her attention to Belle. "Where do you think she's going?"

"She's trying to get away from me," Steinbeck said.

"Why you?"

Austen's brother had been standing as he drove, and now he sat down on the back of the seat, his feet on the cushion. Austen guessed they'd eaten about an hour since they'd left the yacht, which put the night nearly at midnight. No wonder she wanted to lie down and sleep. She simply wanted to stop thinking about the escape from the yacht, and even before that, about being taken hostage, and even before *that*, about seeing Declan get beat up.

She'd also like to erase the sight of Steinbeck leaping off a boat with bullets flying around him. And the terrible clench in her gut when Belle had gone off into the darkness to find him.

Yes, Austen really just wanted her boat and her very quiet, normal life back. Especially since she was no closer to landing on a decision about Declan. She didn't know what to think, and his words on the yacht about double-crossing the Bratva didn't help. But it made sense why they'd come after him. And that made him a good guy, right?

The stars scattered above them, the moonlight rippling on the water. "'Whom do I have in heaven but you?'" she said quietly. "'For you know my coming and my going. You are my strength and my shield, and you I will trust.'"

Declan looked over at her.

"It's a bunch of verses from the Psalms, in the Bible. Talking about how we can't hide from God, no matter where we are."

Declan looked away, and it seemed she'd hit a nerve.

"Declan?"

He sighed. "Do you ever wonder if you've walked outside of God's favor? Done something to set yourself at odds with Him?"

"We set ourselves at odds with God all the time. Whenever we take control of our own lives and say, 'Thanks, but I'm in charge now.'"

She glanced at the boat in the distance. "There's a verse in James that talks about how doubting God's love, his faithfulness, is like being a wave tossed by the sea, driven by the wind. Out of control, no mooring."

Steinbeck hit a wave hard, and she grabbed the edge of the boat.

"Doubt keeps us from having a firm foundation when the world erupts into chaos."

Silence, but he nodded.

Declan moved to sit next to her. "I'm sorry I got you into this. I thought I was outsmarting them. Clearly, I didn't count on them coming after me. Or you."

Sweet. She didn't know what to say except, "It's not your fault."

"It is *totally* his fault," Steinbeck said, looking over at her. "Completely, one hundred percent his fault. We would not be out here fleeing from the Russian mob and chasing down a spy if it wasn't for him."

"She's a *spy*?" Declan said.

"She's a Black Swan," Steinbeck said. "She works for an all-women clandestine international agency that helps thwart terrorists around the world." He stared at Declan for a beat before turning away.

Terrorists? Steinbeck had called him a criminal, not a *terrorist*. She looked at Declan. "Is that true? Are you a—"

"No," he said, glaring at Steinbeck. "It is *not* true."

"When you create something that could put America in danger and blow up the entire world," Steinbeck growled, "it's called terrorism."

"Listen," Declan said, "I can't control how people use the technology I give them."

"Then maybe you shouldn't have made it in the first place."

Declan held up his hand, clearly schooling his voice. "It's also used for self-driving cars for people with disabilities and for robot dogs that can serve as security and even assist the vision impaired, and frankly, it could be used in nanotech to target and destroy cancer cells. I'm working on all sorts of adaptations to this AI program, so let's not start calling people names."

Steinbeck's jaw tightened.

But what Declan said made sense. The word *terrorist* felt like a reach.

"I don't understand. Why does he think you're a terrorist?" Austen said.

Declan sighed. "Because my technology can be used to create supersoldiers. And obsidite is the vehicle that makes that processing happen."

"And you stole the program."

"I rerouted it into a more secure, out-of-the-Russian-Mafia's-hands location."

"But you have it."

"I have a backup copy." He scrubbed his hands down his face.

Austen wanted to reach out and take his hand. But whatever this man was into, she just didn't know if she possessed enough bandwidth for it. She liked her simple, although currently homeless, life. "You live a complicated life, Declan."

He looked over at her, grimaced. "Yes, I do, I guess." He straightened. "All we have to do is get back to land. I have people, and we can fix this."

Steinbeck looked at him. "Are you kidding me? How are you going to fix this?"

Declan drew in a breath, clearly fighting a retort. She could almost see the Marine in him, stoic, unmovable. "I'm going to find my ship and make sure the cargo is destroyed."

What? "Didn't you say you were using it for medical advances and a cancer cure and helping people find healing? Those seem like pretty good uses." She turned to him. "You can't control whether bad people take your good program and use it to do evil."

Steinbeck stood with one knee on the seat, not looking back.

"No," Declan said. "But it is my responsibility to do whatever I can to make sure that evil doesn't win."

"Evil doesn't win." Austen wished Steinbeck would turn, because she wanted to say, *See? Good guy. Not a terrorist.*

Maybe Steinbeck heard her twin-ESP, because he shook his head, glanced at Declan. "What about all the deals you made with the Chinese and the North Koreans and the Russians in Barcelona?"

"What deals?"

"Don't lie to me. I have a source who told me that you were thinking of selling the program to one of them."

Declan's mouth opened. Then, quietly: "For medical purposes. I wouldn't think of giving them defense capability."

"But like you said, you can't control how people are going to use it," Steinbeck said. He glanced at Austen and wore his own *see?* expression.

She glared at him as he added, "The road to hell is paved with good intentions."

Declan looked away as Austen flinched.

They drove in silence.

Finally, Declan turned to her. "My mom was a nurse. All I ever wanted to do was help people the way she did."

"That's why you brought Farid to America and why you purchased the orphanage and why you're involved in so many charity organizations," Austen said.

"Yes," he said. "Thanks for noticing."

Then he smiled, and for some reason, all of the chill of the night whooshed out of her, warmth settling into her bones. So what that he was a complicated man? Maybe she could figure out how to do complicated.

"Phoenix is slowing," Steinbeck said as he throttled back. "I think she's out of gas." He looked at the gauge. "We're low too." He looked back at Declan. "Don't your people keep these things topped off?"

"Hunter and Elise spent an entire day on the Jet Skis, and I used the tender to search the ocean for Austen. But we should have extra fuel on board."

He got up and went to the front, then picked up a plastic can and shook his head. For a second, he looked like he might toss it into the sea in fury. He came back, sat on the bench. "Sorry. No one anticipated a run for shore in the tender. We're probably another thirty or forty miles away at least."

"Maybe we'll cross paths with a cruise ship before we run out of gas," Austen said. "I'm in for the all-you-can-eat buffet."

Steinbeck didn't say anything, and Declan's expression remained stoic.

"Really? That was kind of funny."

They'd pulled up beside the Jet Ski, now just floating in the water. Phoenix looked over at Steinbeck. "Couldn't get enough of me, huh?"

"I thought we talked about this ditching-us thing. Just can't get it out of your system, can you?"

Her mouth tightened. She held up her hands as if in surrender. "Are you going to invite me aboard?"

Steinbeck gestured with his head, and she climbed up the back of the boat and onto the seat beside Austen.

"You okay?" Austen asked.

"Super fantastic," Phoenix said. Then she glanced at Steinbeck. "For the record, it's not that I ditched you as much as . . ."

Steinbeck raised an eyebrow.

"Okay, I ditched you."

"Where were you going?" Stein asked.

"I don't know. South? I figured I'd hit land eventually."

Just once, Austen would like an absolute. Steinbeck kept the boat moving south.

"Hey," Phoenix said, "what's the worst that can happen? We end up stranded in the ocean?" She smiled at Austen.

"Not funny."

Phoenix lifted a shoulder. "Trying."

"Steinbeck said you were a spy. Really?"

Phoenix narrowed her eyes at Steinbeck. "Thanks." She turned back to Austen. "I'm not a spy. I'm a problem solver."

"Whatever," Steinbeck growled.

"I don't understand. How did you end up on my boat?" Declan asked.

"It was just a gig to get me off Mariposa."

"What were you doing on Mariposa?"

She made a face. "Oh, just . . . you know . . . saving Steinbeck's life."

"Seriously?" Steinbeck had started for shore, the motor kicking up.

"What do you mean, saving Steinbeck's life?" Austen said. She glanced at her brother. "That's when you were shot."

"Yes," Phoenix said. "He got himself shot and lost a lot of blood, and he had a little hemothorax going, so I sneaked into the Russian Mafia camp and liberated a four-wheeler." She looked at Steinbeck. "A guy could be more grateful."

"A guy might not have gotten shot in the first place if he hadn't followed you into a smuggler's tunnel. If he hadn't caught you stealing from Declan's safe."

"What?" Declan said.

"She stole your AI program," Steinbeck said.

Declan's mouth opened.

"Copied it, thank you." She glared at Steinbeck. "Stein got trapped underground with me. And we might have caused a little ruckus with the Bratva on the way out." She looked at Declan. "Nice friends you have."

"They're not my friends—but why would you steal it?"

"Only a billion reasons, all with dollar signs after them. But mostly so we could create a virus and stop you from destroying the world."

Silence descended over the boat as the motor hummed.

Declan nodded. "Not a terrible idea. It's always good to have a fail-safe."

And again, *see?* A terrorist wouldn't think that they should create a solution for world-ending destruction.

Phoenix's mouth hung open. Then she got up and moved to the side of the tender, near the front captain's seat, leaving Austen and Declan on the bench seat.

Declan turned to Austen. "I really am sorry I got you into this. I was hoping for a nice two-day cruise down to Mariposa." His gaze scanned her face, and he offered a small smile. "I thought it would be a nice way to get to know you better."

"Yeah, there's nothing like being taken hostage and escaping from the Mafia to really get to know somebody," Steinbeck said.

"Stop, Stein," Austen said. "He couldn't know that the Bratva were going to chase him down or that you were going to dive in like some unwanted superhero to save the day."

"Unwanted?"

"Thank you," Declan said as he held up a hand. He turned back to Austen. "I did screw up, Austen. And for that, I'm sorry. Next time I'll be smarter. *More* than one step ahead of them."

She frowned. "How—"

"There's a boat ahead," Steinbeck said, and Declan sat up as the boat came into view. Lights shone along its deck, and in the darkness, the form looked like a small cargo ship, or a large fishing trawler.

"We're down to the *E*," Steinbeck said. "Maybe we can get them to see us."

He flashed his lights. Over the water, a low moan sounded. Then another.

"I guess it's better than the drink," Declan said, but his jaw was tight.

They pulled up next to the boat, and a couple of men leaned over the side. It was a deep-sea fishing trawler. The crew let down a rope ladder.

Phoenix grabbed it as she looked back at Steinbeck. "You sure we don't have enough gas?"

He nodded his head.

Phoenix climbed up first, then shouted down and gestured for Austen.

Austen went hand over hand up the ladder to the top and climbed on deck where a handful of men stood.

Another shout, and she thought maybe Declan was coming up. The boat wasn't as big as Declan's yacht, but a pilothouse rose in the front, and stairs led off the deck, probably down to the crew quarters. Three large hatches were closed with a number of empty nets piled in the middle, the stink of brine lifting from them.

Declan shook hands with one of the sailors, speaking to him in Spanish. He smiled, although it looked a little tight, and nodded while they shared a small conversation.

Then Declan moved over to Austen. He slowly reached out

and took her hand. Then he pulled her away as Steinbeck got on the boat.

Stein walked over to Declan.

Austen watched the captain come out of the pilothouse and down the stairs.

"Do not tell him that you were in the military," Declan said quietly.

Steinbeck frowned. "Okay. Why?"

"Because this ship is on its way to Cuba."

What? Oh brother. The action movie simply continued.

EIGHT

THIS DIDN'T HAVE TO BE COMPLICATED. ALL Declan had to do was get alone with whatever immigration official they met in port and ask to talk to the US embassy. And if it got hairy, he could add a few dollar signs to his request.

At least, that was his plan as he stood in the tiny crew cabin looking out the port window, sweat running down the back of his shirt.

Belle—although maybe he should call her Phoenix, because clearly that was the name Stein knew her as—sat on the lower bunk with Austen, who had her legs pulled up, her arms resting on her knees, her head back against the wall.

Phoenix looked as if she'd like to have another go at her attempt to take him out in Barcelona.

Steinbeck held up a wall near the door, his arms folded, stoic.

The entire place swam with the odor of sweat and hot metal saturated in the brine of the sea.

At least they weren't starving. The captain had had the decency to feed them—a bowl of rice and beans and some hard bread— before locking them in the crew quarters.

Declan had tried to reason with him. *Americans. Lost at sea.* But apparently his rudimentary Spanish wasn't enough to convince the captain, especially since they all came minus any identification. So maybe it was up to a stack of promised greenbacks from Declan to keep them out of Cuban custody.

"How long till we get to port?" Phoenix said.

"My guess is midmorning," Declan answered.

"So we have about four hours to figure out how to get off this boat." Steinbeck frowned.

"Calm down," Declan said. "I have a plan."

"Oh, goody, goody," Steinbeck snapped. "Because your plans are so fantastic."

Declan's mouth gaped. "Listen, Joe Impulsive. I get that it was my fault that my yacht got boarded. I own that. But it's fate that landed us on this fishing boat. One simple conversation with the right authorities should iron this all out."

Steinbeck stared at him. "Are you serious? Because the *minute* they find out that I was with the teams, everything changes. And your background isn't stellar either." He directed that at Phoenix.

"What?" She leaned up. "I'm a ghost. Nobody knows who I am."

"Exactly. You don't think that's going to raise a few red flags?" Steinbeck shook his head. "No, we're all headed for detention at best."

"I'll reason with them," Declan said.

"Money doesn't always trump ideology," said Phoenix. "American–Cuban relations aren't so great right now, and when they figure out who you are, suddenly this won't be a diplomatic event. It will be a *ransom*." Phoenix shook her head and looked at the porthole. "You guys should have just left me floating at sea."

"You shouldn't have taken off!" Steinbeck said, glancing at her.

She held up a hand as if to stiff-arm his words.

Austen sighed and lowered her head into her arms.

"You okay, sis?" Steinbeck asked.

"Yeah," she said and raised her head. "I'm just praying."

Declan looked away. "Not sure God's going to get us out of this one."

She frowned at him. "Of course He is."

He met her gaze. Silence fell between them. Then, "I think it's pretty clear that we're in over our heads here. I mean, we're locked inside a smelly crew berth on our way to a communist country. I feel like maybe God has abandoned us." Or worse, was laughing at them. But he couldn't manage that thought aloud.

"God never abandons us," she said.

Yeah, well, maybe he wore his argument on his face, because Austen sat up and hung her legs over the edge of the cot.

"Do you really believe that? That we can get into so much trouble that God abandons us? That's *exactly* when he shows up."

He shook his head. "Maybe that's true for some people, but . . ." He couldn't look at her. "He didn't show up when my younger brother was hit by a car. I sat in the hospital chapel, listening to my mom pray all the way to the moment when the doctor came in and said that he was gone. He was ten years old. Delivering papers on his route. So the best-case scenario is that God looked away." He met her eyes then. "Or He just didn't care."

She frowned.

"We're in this alone, Austen."

He paused, and no one made a move to respond. He took a breath and ran his hands down his face. "Listen, I know things happen. But everything changed after that. His medical bills swamped my mom, and I tried to help, but she worked herself to an early death. Where was God then?"

More silence. Then, from Austen: "I'm so sorry. And I'm not going to say something stupid like there's a reason for everything. But I do know that in the midst of terrible things, God *does* show up."

He glanced at her.

She met his gaze, raised an eyebrow. "We run out of gas, and at that very moment, we see a boat?"

"A boat on the way to *Cuba*," Declan said. "Maybe it would have been better if we had stayed at sea. Thanks, but I'll rescue myself."

"Then you'll miss the grace of God's provision. Just because you land in the belly of a whale doesn't mean that God isn't in the middle of rescuing you."

Whale? Oh, wait. He'd heard a Bible story about that.

"And what if he *doesn't* rescue us?" Phoenix said. "Just like Declan said."

Declan looked at her, and she didn't meet his eyes but lifted her shoulder in a shrug.

"Then," Austen said, "we're not meant to be rescued in that moment. Or in the way we think. But I can guarantee you that God *does* rescue us. Not always in the way that we want, but definitely according to His great plan for us."

"So His great plan for us includes sitting in a Cuban prison?" Declan said.

She sighed. "Either we trust that God is good and that He has a plan, or we go our own way and try to figure it out ourselves." She glanced at Declan. "Not to throw shade on anyone, but it's possible that if we stop trying so hard to fix things, God will step in." She looked at Stein then. "'God opposes the proud but gives grace to the humble.'"

Stein's mouth tightened.

She offered them all a small smile.

And *oh,* Declan wanted to prove to her that he wasn't the guy Steinbeck and Phoenix said he was. That sure, he'd made some big mistakes, but she could trust him. *Really.*

Austen looked at Steinbeck, then back at Declan. "Everyone thinks that God won't give us more than we can handle. But that's not true. In fact, that thought is absolutely contrary to the nature of God. He puts us in situations that are over our heads because

He wants us to need Him. Paul said that when he was sitting in a prison in the bottom of a ship, during a storm at sea that overwhelmed them to the point where they gave up hope of being saved. In another passage, Paul talks about their troubles in Asia as being so dire, they *despaired of life itself.* That doesn't sound like something they could handle on their own."

Her voice softened. "I know it's terrifying to be in a place where we can't control things. But we have to trust that God is good and He is sovereign. Even in Cuba."

Declan wanted to let her words seep in, find a place in his soul.

"There's land out there," Phoenix said. "Looks like we're coming into port."

Steinbeck stood up. "Now comes the fun."

Austen drew in a breath.

Declan couldn't help it. He moved beside her. "No matter what happens, I will get you out of here. No matter what it takes." He touched her hand. "I promise."

For a moment, she gripped his hand back. "I know." And then she touched her other hand to his face, her eyes sweet and gentle. "And that's what scares me."

He frowned, but the sound of a lock releasing clattered at the door before it squealed open. A couple of sailors stood in the opening.

"The captain wants to see you," one of them said in Spanish. He pointed to Declan.

"What about my friends?"

"Just you."

He turned to Steinbeck. "Sit tight. This will all be over soon."

At least, if he had it his way.

———•———————•———

"Stein. You and I need to get off this ship," Emberly said as Declan stepped out into the hallway.

The door closed and locked behind him.

"Before we get into port." She looked at Steinbeck as she said it, and she probably deserved the wide eyes that he gave her back. Because yes, she *had* tried to ditch him earlier in the ocean. Maybe not her brightest move. *Okay,* she'd blame panic. And she didn't do panic. It never worked out in her favor. So of course he'd tracked her down and she'd climbed aboard the tender without a fight. What was it that Mystique, her Black Swans boss, always said? "Live to fight another day"?

That day was here.

"How do you propose we do that?" Steinbeck said, leaning over her to look out the window.

"I'm not sure yet, but I *do* know we can't go ashore. A background check on you is only going to land you in some dark hole someplace. You'll disappear while they try to pry American secrets out of you."

His mouth twisted. "They're not going to get any."

Yeah. That's what really scared her. Because Steinbeck, at his heart, was a patriot. She'd met that patriot up close and personal three years ago. So *no way, no how* did she want him in the hands of some communist Cubans.

Or Russians.

And maybe she shouldn't care that much, but, *shoot,* she *had* started to care. Hadn't even minded that much when he'd caught up with her in the ocean. The fact that he'd come after her despite her trying to ditch him made her feel, well, maybe not as alone.

Which was why she said *we* and shot the idea across the bow.

"I watched these guys when we came in. They're not armed. They're just a bunch of fishermen who are tired and hungry from being out at sea. They're not going to put up much of a fight. We get off the ship and we go from there."

Steinbeck glanced at his sister and then back at Emberly. "I'm not leaving my sister."

Austen had gone back to sitting with her back to the wall, her legs up. She was watching the two of them, frowning. And then, "I agree with her, Stein," Austen said. "I'm nobody. They're going to run information on me and find out that I'm just a tourist in the wrong place at the wrong time. You, however, are a different story." She put her legs down and leaned forward. "I know you're not active duty anymore, but you still have the SEAL history." She shook her head, looked at Emberly. "You guys get out of here the first chance you get."

Emberly could nearly see the war inside Steinbeck, fighting between reality and responsibility.

She didn't need his help to escape this boat, *thank you.* She was very capable of breaking out of custody and going over the side into the harbor and disappearing in the murky depths. But if she was honest, she'd prefer to do it with him, although she couldn't put her finger on why.

"Listen," she said, "I'm not saying we leave Austen and Declan behind." Although if she'd had her way, she would have left Declan on the yacht with the Russians. She didn't buy for one hot second his explanation about how he got into this mess. But that was a chatty chat for another day, once they disentangled themselves from Cuban custody. "If we're free, we can figure out how to help them better than if we're stuck in a cell with them. Or worse."

She met Stein's eyes. *So blue.* They fixed on her, and for a second she was back in the water, searching for him right after he'd blown up his Jet Ski. She hadn't been sure where he'd gone, but she knew he was swimming hard for the stern of the boat, where they'd parked the tender. So it wasn't too hard to skim along the water in the glow of the ship and spot him. She'd scooted around him, pulled up beside him, and he'd grabbed her hand. She'd wanted to say something quippy like, "Miss me?" But he was winded, and the first question out of his mouth was, "Did they get the tender?" So maybe there was no time for quips.

And then of course, a few minutes later, she'd ditched him. Which again was simply panic. She just couldn't imagine stepping inside the boat and chaining herself to the ragtag misfits who seemed to be going from tragedy to tragedy.

Except she was making this up as she went along too, so here she was, stuck in a smelly, humid sweatbox on her way to an iffy conversation with immigration police, who would pull her up on the screen and find too many different aliases. Or none at all. Either of which would probably land her in the dark cell next to Steinbeck's in the middle of communist Cuba.

So, c'mon, pal—catch up and play along.

Maybe he read her mind. "Right," Steinbeck said. "What are you thinking?"

"This doesn't have to be hard. These fishermen aren't equipped to take us into custody, so unless they dock and invite the immigration officials on board, we're over the side. But"—she glanced at Austen—"we can't take her with us."

"I'm not going with you," Austen said. "Get off this ship any way you can." She looked at Steinbeck. "And don't die." Then she flashed a smile at him. "My guess is that Declan is going to untangle this situation quickly and we'll be on our way in no time."

Emberly couldn't help it. "Seriously? That's what you think? Declan is up there right now making some deal with them. Probably agreeing to hand over some technological secrets in order to get you released. He's not the good guy you think he is. I don't care what he says—he is diabolical and on the wrong side here. Don't let his good looks and charm deceive you."

Austen's mouth opened, and she glanced at Steinbeck, then back. "Excuse me if I misunderstood, but you're the very *last* person I'm going to listen to. One minute you're saving Stein's life, the next you're leaving us in the ocean. I don't know you—but I *do* know Declan. And I don't care what Steinbeck says about him, he *is* a good guy. Did you not hear his explanation?"

Emberly didn't know why Austen's words pinched—she'd been accused of worse. By Steinbeck himself. But, "I heard his lies, yes. And I know him a lot better than you think I do. I've been tracking him since January, looking into his background. I know what he likes for breakfast." She leaned in, lowered her voice. "I know his trail of dead bodies."

Austen's voice pitched low. "His trail of what?"

"Yeah. He killed an unarmed man in Afghanistan, was even charged with a crime, but he somehow bought his way out of it."

Austen folded her arms. "He told me about that. Friendly fire."

"That was the 'official finding,'" Emberly said, finger quoting her words. "But what they didn't tell you was that Samiullah Rahimi was involved in an information-smuggling operation, delivering secret satellite images of artillery and troop positions from Afghanistan to Russia. When he went down, a guy named Dark Horse took over."

Steinbeck glanced at her. "I heard about that. There was a man embedded in Afghanistan who knew Russian and Pashto and smuggled the information through channels to the Russian military. They never caught him." He frowned. "Are you saying that was *Declan*?"

"His mother was Russian. He's fluent." Emberly turned to Austen. "He didn't mention that, did he?" She got off her bunk. "Don't believe all his good deeds."

Silence. Emberly shook her head. "I'm going to say it again. Don't be deceived by his good looks or his money, honey. Rich men only have room for one thing in their heart. Themselves."

Austen's mouth tightened, and Steinbeck looked away.

Well, Emberly hated to be the bearer of bad news, but the fact was that Declan was right about one thing.

God didn't show up for people like him.

They'd come into port, the city of Havana rising in the window. A mix of old and new, with burnt-yellow Spanish-style buildings and the rotunda of the capital rising in the distance, surrounded by newer high-rises with mirrored windows glinting in the sun. Red-roofed tile buildings, towering pine trees blowing in the breeze, and even a stone-walled fortress that overlooked the water.

A medley of communism, cubism, and conquistadors.

The latch screeched as the door opened again.

Emberly got up. "I'm going with or without you, Steinbeck." Then she walked out of the room into the corridor of the ship. Another crewman stood there. They did not look armed, just serious as they led the three up the stairs and onto the deck.

Declan stood with the captain and shook his hand as they walked up. Yeah, he'd probably sold her out in exchange for his freedom.

"All sorted," Declan said. "We're just going to pop into immigration. Then I'll give the US embassy a call and we'll be on the first flight out of here."

Sure they would. Emberly didn't trust him as far as she could throw him, and truthfully, he was a big man.

Out of the corner of her eye, she saw Steinbeck glance at her, his mouth a tight line. Then he looked past her, toward the portside railing.

The boat was still a good fifty yards from the dock. A handful of other fishing vessels were tied up to two piers that jutted out into the bay. An adjacent harbor held larger cargo ships and cranes and acted as the official shipping port.

Which meant that it wouldn't be too hard for her to go overboard and lose herself among the clutter of fishing trawlers and other dockside debris.

She hung back as Austen walked up to Declan. "How'd you do that?"

He frowned at her, then raised his shoulder. "I explained to them that we are just a few travelers lost at sea." And then he smiled.

The smile of a shark. Emberly wasn't waiting around any longer.

She took off, running hard for the side of the ship.

"Stop!"

Oof. A body tackled her and she crashed on the deck. She rolled and pushed away from whoever had tackled her. *One of the crew.* She kicked, landed on his jaw, and he fell back.

She launched to her feet. Steinbeck had taken off after her and now grabbed up the man and flung him away.

Then, "Go, go!"

Okay, so he was in. She headed for the rail and climbed up. The drop looked to be about twenty feet, so not lethal.

There was shouting behind her, and Steinbeck appeared beside her.

"Aw," he said, "this is a bad idea."

"I know." Then she looked at him, grinned, and jumped.

Austen stood frozen next to Declan as Steinbeck leaped off the railing and vanished over the side of the boat.

She glanced at Declan and back to the space where Steinbeck had been. *Don't panic.* He knew what he was doing.

Declan grabbed her hand. Maybe to keep her from running, but her words to him earlier swelled through to her.

"I can guarantee you that God does rescue us. Not always in the way that we want, but definitely according to His great plan for us."

She dearly hoped God had a great plan in all of this.

"Don't worry," the captain said, now in English. "The harbor patrol will find them."

She glanced at the man. Dark hair, dark eyes, burly, grizzle on his chin—salty, seasoned—and with a couple teeth missing as he smiled at her.

It felt a bit like being smiled at by a crocodile.

Oh, c'mon, she wasn't in any real danger. They'd done nothing wrong, and besides, she wanted to believe Declan. In fact, every cell of her body wanted to repel Phoenix's words about him.

"Don't believe all his good deeds."

She didn't know what to believe. Still, she let go of his hand. He looked at her and frowned.

"You'll see," he said quietly.

She nodded, because what was she going to do? Throw herself off the boat? She wasn't a Navy SEAL. And she wasn't . . . well, whatever Phoenix was. And sure, Austen could swim, but diesel fuel and other pollutants saturated the water, and besides, she'd done nothing wrong.

So she didn't follow her brother and his spy gal-pal over the rail.

But an hour later, Austen was rethinking that decision as she sat in the immigration office in the Havana harbor. Detained and questioned by the police. Again. And again. She gave them the truth every time. *We were on a boat. It was taken by pirates. We escaped and ran out of gas in the middle of the ocean. The fishing boat picked us up.*

Same story, over and over and over. In the lobby, through the glass, Declan paced, holding a cell phone and gesturing with his hand. So maybe it wasn't as simple as he'd expected either.

Worse, Phoenix's words simply wouldn't dissipate.

"Don't be deceived by his good looks or his money, honey. Rich men only have room for one thing in their heart. Themselves."

She shivered, feeling a little naked in her swim shorts and top. The office, a small room in a raw cement building, smelled of brine and fish, diesel and cigarette smoke. Her stomach growled, the beans and rice long gone.

A guard, maybe in his early twenties, stood near the door, clearly some dock worker who'd been assigned to watch the Invaders.

She pulled up one knee and rested her chin on it, and prayer just rose from inside her. *"For who is God, but the Lord? And who is a rock, except our God, the God who girds me with strength and makes my way blameless? He makes my feet like hinds' feet, and sets me upon my high places."*

She glanced at Declan, his back to her.

"He sent from on high . . . He drew me out of many waters. He delivered me from my strong enemy, and from those who hated me, for they were too mighty for me. They confronted me in the day of my calamity, but the Lord was my stay. He brought me forth also into a broad place; He rescued me, because He delighted in me."

She closed her eyes and heard her own words to Declan. *"I know it's terrifying to be in a place where we can't control things. But we have to trust that God is good and He is sovereign. Even in Cuba."*

Oh, she wanted to believe that. It sounded good, but frankly, the words pinged inside her, fragile. She didn't like finding herself in over her head any more than Declan did. Except her approach was not to figure out an escape plan but to dodge the whole situation in the first place.

So maybe she should have a little mercy on him.

The door finally opened and the guard moved and Declan walked inside. "You okay?"

She got up. "Yes. Although I'm hungry and I've given the same debrief about twenty times to three different people."

"I know. Took a little longer than I thought it would, but a rep from the US embassy is on the way to pick us up."

She considered him for a long moment and tried to suss out if he was lying to her and what he'd had to do to arrange for their release. But she was an American citizen, so why wouldn't the US embassy come and help them?

"Who were you talking to on the phone?"

"A friend I have in DC. He placed a couple calls and vouched for me. And for you. It's hard when you land in a country without any identification." He smiled.

It seemed honest. "Have they found Steinbeck or Phoenix?"

He shook his head. "Not that I know of." Then he put his hand on her shoulder. "But Steinbeck is going to be just fine."

She wanted to lean into his touch. Wanted to trust him. But all she could do was nod.

"Let's go," he said, his mouth a little tight at the edges, and they headed out of the building into the gravel parking lot.

The afternoon sun waxed hot on her shoulders, and fatigue burned into her bones. She just wanted off this island. And frankly, away from Declan long enough to straighten out her brain. Because the story of Dark Horse, or whatever, still hung inside her too. A man who could finagle his way around international complications and come out on top sounded exactly like Declan.

She almost turned to him and asked if he spoke Russian, but then a car pulled into the gravel drive. Black SUV, dust-covered but with embassy plates.

A man got out of the passenger seat. He wore a suit, glasses, and a short haircut. Very official looking, mid-forties, and he held out his hand. "Tobias Clark. You're Declan Stone?"

Declan shook his hand.

"Never thought I'd meet you in Cuba," Clark said. He turned to Austen. "And you must be Austen Kingston."

She shook his hand. "We're fixing up a new passport for you back at the embassy. We'll get you on a plane to Miami as soon as we can."

Oh. She glanced at Declan, and he gave her a smile.

Phoenix was right about one thing. His good looks did go right to her head. Those dark-gray eyes, the way he held open the door for her and then slipped in beside her in the back seat.

Two cold bottles of water rested in the cup holders, and he grabbed one, opened it, and handed it to her.

"Thanks." She took a sip.

He opened the other one and drank as they drove through the city.

The city bore the marks of Spanish influence, with orange, teal, and burnt-yellow buildings, some with second-story wrought-iron Juliet balconies along with archways and cobblestone courtyards. But the farther they drove from the harbor, along the outskirts of the city, the more the newer, communist-style buildings—white, cement—rose to shadow the city. A few Neo-Renaissance buildings (probably other embassies) suggested a European presence, but the US embassy contained no adornment. Just a plain white building inside an iron fence.

They passed two American guards at the gate, and only then did she realize she'd been holding her breath. *And please.* How much of a criminal could Declan be if the US embassy welcomed him in with open arms? Clearly he couldn't be a terrorist or a smuggler or even a person of interest. Especially since, as they pulled up to the entrance, someone who looked like the embassy director came out to greet them.

Yeah, she should put Phoenix's jaded words right out of her brain.

As Austen was sliding out of the car, she overheard the man introduce himself as Eugene Prescott, and Declan glad-handed him, patting him on the shoulder.

"Phil said you'd take care of us," Declan said, laughing.

Phil? Maybe his DC friend.

Declan turned to Austen and introduced her.

"Gene," the man said as he shook her hand. "It's going to be a little bit before we can get those passports processed. Look for them in the morning. But I secured your lodging at a nearby hotel."

"The lady will need some clothes," Declan said. "Is it possible to get a car and do some shopping? I'll also need to stop at a bank."

Clothes? Shopping? But of course—she was back in Declan's world.

For a second she thought she might rather be in the ocean with Steinbeck. At least there she knew her way around deep water and dangerous fish.

But Declan put his hand on her back, and she headed inside the embassy. She took a bedraggled picture for her new passport photo, so that was lovely. And then the director brought her and Declan into a private receiving area. The American flag hung on the wall, and two gold sofas faced each other with an oval mahogany coffee table between them. Sprays of tropical flowers sat in vases on a couple of credenzas.

"I'll arrange for a car to take you to the hotel," Gene said, then left them there.

And it was just her and Declan standing alone in that air-conditioned, carpeted room of the embassy.

"See, I told you everything would be fine." Declan walked up to her where she stood by the window, staring out at the manicured grounds inside the embassy complex. Palm trees, a few twisty sand oaks, and a garden full of amaryllis and bougainvillea.

She nearly jumped when Declan put his hand on her shoulder. She turned and he withdrew it.

"I don't know why," he said softly, "but I feel like I'm in trouble."

She caught her breath. Closed her eyes. *Oh,* she didn't want to have this conversation, but, "Have you ever heard of . . . Dark Horse?"

She opened her eyes in time to see his mouth open and then close into a tight pinch. "Where did you hear that name?"

"Phoenix, then Steinbeck. He told me a story about—"

"The story is a cover," Declan said. "Not to get into too many specifics, but yes. For a while, because of my connections with

Samiullah Rahimi, I was able to play the role of smuggler. Just long enough to root out the traders inside the base where we were ferreting out the information. I promise you that we did not leak any secrets. It was a sting operation. And I really shouldn't even be telling you that, but I don't like the way you're looking at me, Austen. Please, trust me. I'm not who they say I am."

She wanted so much to believe him. He took a step toward her and took her hand. "Have I done some things that have gone south? Yes. But they've always been because I was trying to do something good. Not evil."

Aw. She had her own mistakes.

The door opened behind them, and a middle-aged woman came in. "The car is ready for you. It will take you to the hotel, and the driver will wait there for your instructions."

"Thank you so much." Declan looked back at Austen and held out his hand.

And heaven help her, she took it. And let herself hold on as he walked her out of the building and into the car.

Because frankly, she was tired of doubting him. He'd done nothing but save her, protect her, and now he was going to feed and clothe her.

What was a girl supposed to do with that?

NINE

'LL BE HONEST, DECLAN. SITTING AT A CAFÉ IN the middle of Havana, eating a pork brisket under the starry sky with Cuban tango music playing, is the very last place I thought I would be when I boarded a ship bound for Cuba last night."

He looked over at Austen, who sat in a yellow sundress, her auburn hair down and flowing, a tan on her skin, her green eyes glowing, a slight smile playing at her lips as she stirred her lemon water. Indeed, it had gone a lot more smoothly than he'd expected.

Sure, he'd suggested a tip to the captain for bringing them safely ashore, and another tip to the immigration official for calling the embassy. Thankfully, a stop at a nearby bank had netted him the cash to fulfill those promises. But in truth, he had his own military background to worry about, and if it hadn't been for the call from his friend Phil, the senator from Florida, to the US embassy, well, maybe he would have followed Steinbeck into the ocean.

Truthfully, Declan was a little worried about Steinbeck and even Phoenix, although he blamed Phoenix for the Dark Horse slip. Steinbeck certainly hadn't known about it until recently, or he would have brought it up earlier. But Phoenix seemed to have all sorts of tidbits of information about him, even if they were wrong.

Right now, all he cared about was the next twenty-four hours—making sure Austen got on a plane to Miami and that his boat, the *Santa Maria* arrived to her destination without altercation. He'd called Zeus and pinpointed the *Niña's* location. She was still in international waters, and Zeus couldn't raise the captain, so that didn't bode well. Possibly the yacht had already reached her, the Russians already boarded her and discovered her cargo bay empty.

But as far as they knew, he'd disappeared at sea, so for now, he and Austen were safe.

Declan nodded to Austen's statement. "I agree. I secretly feared that we'd end up in some state gulag tonight."

"Really?" she said. "You seemed so calm."

"No, I just really know how to hide it well." He smiled.

She didn't. "That's the thing, Declan. You always seem so in control. So calm."

"Me?" he said. "You're the one who's always calm, Austen. You have this aura about you that doesn't seem to be shaken by the events surrounding you. I'm just trying to stay one step ahead of everybody."

The waitstaff had taken their plates after the pulled-pork dinner, and now a waitress delivered slices of key lime pie. Declan was very aware of the driver-slash-security-guard who had driven them to the café and was now standing by the door watching him. But that was fine. It kept them against getting pickpocketed and secured their return to the hotel.

He liked the hotel, even with its outdated, slightly rundown exterior. They'd given him one of the penthouse rooms on the third floor, with a mahogany bed and palm-tree bedding, and a worn green velvet sofa in the sitting room. Austen took the room next door, and he supposed she had a similar setup overlooking the Havana port.

163

Austen picked up her fork. "It's not that I'm calm. It's just that I don't like to sit in trouble. I'd rather just keep moving."

"But trouble is what teaches us how to survive," he said.

She looked away from him at the dance floor, where a few couples were salsa dancing. A mariachi band played on the stage. The outdoor café wasn't full, and he had the sense that it was probably one of the cafés approved for internationals. But the food was good, and frankly, this felt like a date.

The wind tousled Austen's auburn hair, and the twinkle lights above added a little magic to the night. Now if he could just get her to trust him.

"Please tell me you don't believe what Phoenix said about me." He knew it sounded a little too pleading, but he was tired, and Phoenix's words about him stuck like a burr inside him.

"Actually, it's not you, it's me." She sighed. "The fact is, I have a history of trusting the wrong people." She took a bite of her key lime pie and then set down her fork, pushing the pie away.

"When I was in college in Miami, I dated a guy I met in a Christian group on campus. Nice guy, or so I thought. And yeah, he came from money. His family had a place in Boca. He took me up there a few times. We went out on his boat, and he even introduced me to scuba diving. He was two years older than me, and I thought he was the one. His name was Cameron."

Declan didn't like where this was going, wanted to reach out and take her hand, but she was chopping at her pie.

"One night, I was out with some friends, and I don't know how, but we ended up at a local beach club. I guess I was a little sheltered growing up, but I never got into clubbing, so I found myself sitting at a table while my friends danced, watching their drinks. Way out of my element. And then I spotted Cameron. He was dancing with some girl, clearly tipsy or more, and I watched him drag her off the dance floor and crowd her into a corner and kiss her. There was a lot of kissing."

She looked away again, and again he wanted to reach for her hand, but now it felt invasive. "I was really angry, and I don't know—I decided to confront him. His friends were there, and I knew a few of them, and they intercepted me before I got to him. But I shouted his name, and he saw me, and he came over. And that was when I realized I knew the girl. We'd been out on his boat together when I visited his family. Her family lived next door. So of course they knew each other. And from the way she was hanging on him and he on her, probably pretty well."

Her face had turned a shade of pink. "Cameron and I didn't have that kind of relationship because, well, I was and still am a Christian. But I made a complete fool out of myself by bursting into tears and saying, 'What are you doing here with her?' His friends laughed, and he said, 'Upgrading.'"

Oh, Declan really wanted to get his hands on this Cameron fellow.

"I just left. I was humiliated and angry." She looked at him and shook her head. "I realized that I didn't want a man like that. A man who could lie to my face. Later I found out he'd been dating her the *entire time* he'd been dating me. So, yeah, I too easily give up my heart, and I too easily trust." She met his eyes. "At least, I did."

"I promise you, Austen," he said quietly. "I'm not dating anyone. Except maybe you, if you'll let me."

She seemed to be considering his words, her eyes narrowing.

"I can add that not all of our dates are going to be quite this exciting. I tend to lead a rather quiet life."

"Really. With your yacht and your numerous homes and your extensive travel?"

"With my long hours in the office and my occasional solo dinner with steak and a glass of wine. My life isn't as fantastic as you'd think."

She sat back, arms folded.

He sighed, not sure how he'd gotten here. "Actually, it's rather lonely. I'm not unlike you in that sometimes it's hard to find some-one to trust. I thought Steinbeck and I were friends, for example. Guess I got that wrong."

She leaned forward and touched his hand. "I don't think so," she said. "But Steinbeck—well, he's been betrayed too. And he's got an even touchier trust meter." She met his gaze. "He'll come around, Declan. He'll see that you're a good man."

Declan stilled, his chest tight as his breath caught. He didn't know why he needed to hear those words from her, but yes. "Thank you," he said softly. "I am trying."

She nodded, sat back. "And for the record, I really love the dress you bought me. I think it needs a decent twirl on the dance floor, don't you?" She winked.

And something inside him released, set free. He smiled. "Oh, indeed." He got up and held out his hand.

She followed him out to the dance floor and stepped into his arms. "You do know how to salsa, right?"

"Oh, honey," he said. "Hang on and try to keep up."

She laughed, and it was like glitter to an already beautiful night. He cradled her hand, settled his other at her waist, and started to move. They circled the dance floor, him twirling her in and back out again. He did a couple of quick moves and then pulled her back into his arms. She stood maybe six inches shorter than him, and *oh,* she fit perfectly into his embrace.

The song ended and segued into a slower and more sultry beat. She hung her arm around his neck as he pulled her closer to him. The blues rhythm had their bodies tight, moving around the dance floor as one.

"You are a pretty good dancer for being a lonely guy," she said.

"You can blame my mother for that. She would come home from a shift, and it would be late at night, but if she'd had a good day, she'd turn on the radio or put on a Sinatra CD or even country western, and we'd dance."

"Sounds like you two were close."

"Very," he said. Austen smelled so good. She'd showered after they'd arrived at the hotel, clearly, and the scent of her soap rose up, twining around him.

"How old were you when your brother died?" she asked, her head on his chest.

"I was twelve," he said. "We had just gotten a paper route and were trying to help Mom make some extra bucks." He closed his eyes, losing himself in the rhythm, making the story easier. "We were crossing a slick street, right about at dusk, and a car took a corner and didn't see him."

"Oh no." She looked up at him. "That's terrible."

"Yeah. He was right behind me. And then . . . his papers were all over the road and he'd been thrown into the ditch. He died instantly."

She stopped dancing. "I'm so sorry. And your poor mother."

And now he'd wrecked the night. He took her hands. "She never got over losing him. There was always a sadness in her eyes, even though she tried to hide it."

Austen stepped close again, put her arms around his waist, and laid her head on his chest. He settled his cheek against her head, moving with the music again.

So maybe the night wasn't in tatters. "You mentioned your sister getting lost. How old were you when that happened?"

"I was about twelve too," she said, lifting her head to look at him. "She got lost on a camping trip and was gone for three days. My brother Jack helped find her. But it really affected the entire family, especially my grandmother. It was the first time she ever collapsed."

"The first time?"

"Yes, she had cancer and she was in a lot of pain, but she didn't want to tell anyone. When Boo went missing, my mom left me, Stein, Conrad, and Doyle with her. My grandpa took the boys out to work on his sailboat while my dad and mom and Jack hunted for her with the local community. Grandma stayed in the kitchen with me, and we were baking—a common ploy she used to get my mind off things. That's when she collapsed. So one tragedy led to the next, and pretty soon we were at the hospital with her. My mom came to the hospital, and I remember her pacing the floor, praying for Boo and my grandma."

The music stopped and switched to something peppier. Declan took her hand and led her off the floor. "You ready to head back to the hotel?"

"I guess so," she said. The way she said it, though . . .

As they walked toward the door, he handed the server a couple of big bills, then motioned to the driver. He came over, and Declan said, "We're walking back to the hotel." Most likely, the man would follow them in the car.

Declan laced his fingers through Austen's as they headed out into the street. Stars sprinkled the night sky overhead, the heat of the cobblestones rising around them. A few dogs barked, but other than that, the streets were quiet—nothing but the sounds of their feet and the swish of wind in the towering palm trees as they strolled along the street.

"The crazy part of the whole Boo story is that after she was found, my mom was so grateful not just because Boo was found but because Grandma had collapsed."

He glanced down at her. "Really? Why?"

"Because when Grandma collapsed, the doctor found her cancer, and they were able to treat it. She ended up living for five more years, much longer than she would have if they hadn't found it. Her collapse prolonged her life."

She looked over at him. "That was the first time I heard my mom say that sometimes God leads us into a place where we can't fix it so that he will. He lets us get in over our heads."

"Like Paul being shipwrecked."

"Yep. 'Humble yourselves, therefore, under God's mighty hand. Cast all your anxiety on him because he cares for you.'"

"That sounds like a Bible verse," he said.

"It is," she said. "I need to remember that a lot more."

"To be clear, Austen—it's not that I don't believe in God. I do. But somehow, I just can't help but think that I messed up somewhere long ago and He said, 'Declan, you're on your own now.'" He hated how his throat burned at the admission.

She looked up at him. "But you don't have to be."

Wow, he hoped that she was talking about the two of them. He stopped, and when she did too and turned to him, he took her other hand. "Austen, you are good for me. You have a fresh perspective on life, and that's something I desperately need. I know the last forty-eight hours haven't gone quite like we'd planned, but I would really like to get to know you better, and frankly, let you get to know *me* better—preferably in less challenging, pirate-enhanced situations."

She laughed then, and he smiled as he ran his gaze over her face. "Can I . . . ?"

She stepped up to him, closing the gap. "Yes."

So he kissed her, keeping it slow, trying for perfection, cradling her face, angling his mouth to press against hers. She tasted of the sweetness of her smile, smelled of the allure of the night as she returned the kiss, her lips softening, receiving, giving. Oh, the woman was goodness and light, and he just wanted more of her. Maybe she felt that way too, because she wound her arms up around his shoulders and stepped closer. The sense of her rushed over him, and *fine*—he let himself just a little off his rein. And maybe this wasn't the right place for this kind of ardor, but it was a dark street in the middle of sultry Havana, and he didn't care that the chauffeur was watching every second of it.

At least that meant they were probably safe.

He made a sound, deep inside, and felt her relax. He could stay here all night, holding her.

Finally, he lifted his head. "I do know that I don't deserve you," he said softly.

"Oh," she said, "don't be so sure." Then she smiled. "I might be more trouble than I look like I'd be."

He laughed then, and she smiled, and light poured into his soul. For the first time in years, he felt that maybe, yes, everything was going to be just fine.

———————•———————

It wasn't a date. Really, it wasn't. But tell that to her heart as Austen walked hand in hand with Declan through the Plaza Vieja, the stars sprinkling down from overhead. The scent of the sea layered the air, and coconut trees rustled in the scant wind, lifting the heat from the air.

Streetlamps lit the plaza, puddling light on the cobblestones, and a fountain in the center cast mist into the air. Spanish-style buildings from blue to pastel pink ringed the square on each side with ground-floor arched porticos. A number of patrons sat at the cafés and restaurants, drinking coffee or late-night cocktails, while buskers sang folk songs and people dropped coins into upturned hats.

The taste of Declan's kiss still lingered on her lips. Really, through her entire body, the way he'd woven himself into her senses, perfectly, gently, the sense of him overtaking her.

As if he knew she needed time and protection, he had waited for her to step in, to deepen the kiss. And then he'd kissed her with a sort of depth and need that had her bones turning to liquid as she clung to him, needing him right back.

No, she'd never been kissed by anyone the way Declan Stone

kissed her. And now he walked beside her as if he hadn't shattered her defenses and staked a place in her heart.

Oh boy.

Please, let him be a good man. Because she believed it, despite the words of Phoenix and even Steinbeck. And it was more than just *wanting* to believe. His dark-gray eyes possessed an earnestness, and his explanations about their accusations made sense.

It didn't hurt that the man looked like his billionaire self, in a pair of black linen pants and a light-gray linen shirt and leather loafers. Smelling of aftershave and a shower. The Declan Stone who made deals and ruled a kingdom.

"Would you like some coffee?" he asked as they passed a café.

"Oh, I won't sleep for a week if I have coffee at this time of night," she said, "but maybe some ice cream?" She pointed to a gelato shop, and he nodded.

"Good call."

They'd passed their hotel on their way to the square, and he'd suggested the stroll. She felt pretty and even safe with his hand in hers. She'd turned into Cinderella at some tropical ball, the velvety night overhead, the music of romance in her heart.

They stood in front of the gelato shop, peering through the glass at the flavors.

"Pistachio," she said, pointing to the light-green gelato in the bin.

"In a cup?"

"Yes."

He ordered in Spanish, then, "I got chocolate."

"Boring."

"I'm a simple man."

She laughed. "Hardly."

"Well, some things need to be simple in my life. I need to leave room for the more complicated problems."

"Like getting your boat back?"

He sighed. "I hope I'll get my boat back. It means something to me. In my head, I sort of thought if I had a yacht, then the rest would come after that."

"The rest?"

"I don't know. A wife? A family? I saw us taking trips through the Caribbean, the kids jumping into the pool or taking out the Jet Skis."

Us. She didn't let the word land. But . . .

"And your wife? What is she doing all this time?"

He glanced at her. "Swimming with the sharks?"

She raised an eyebrow.

"Kidding," he said and winked.

But her throat had warmed. *Really?* She'd be lying if she didn't admit that the thought had bumped into her a few times yesterday in the sun. *What might it be like to—*

"Maybe she's helping me figure out our next charity." He paid the vendor. "I'm not looking for a trophy wife. I want a partner. Someone who sees life the way I do and wants to do something about it."

"How do you see life?"

He received his gelato and she did hers. They'd both gotten cups, and now he let go of her hand and ate his chocolate with a spoon. "This is good," he said.

She took a bite of her pistachio. "Yes, it is."

They walked over to a table, and he pulled out her chair. She sat down, watching the foot traffic as couples walked by hand in hand.

"I don't know—I guess I see life as a problem I need to solve." He sat opposite her. The night settled over him, his gray eyes hooded, and he embodied a subtle sense of intrigue and confidence. Superman in a suit.

"I look at medical issues or defense issues or communication issues and think, what can I do to fix that? I think it's my mom in me. She was a trauma nurse, always trying to figure out how to think faster on her feet, helping the doctors respond better and quicker to patient problems. She worked very hard, but she also loved her job. Her only vacations were to see me in San Diego, where I was stationed, except for the year she won a cruise. She got it as a prize for being the top nurse at her hospital. We went together. It was an interior cabin and we got seasick because of a storm, but we had a great time. That was right before I shipped out to Afghanistan."

He'd finished his gelato. "She told me that she loved the ocean. I don't know why, but I put it in my head right then that I wanted a boat."

"Sad that she never saw the yacht. It's beautiful."

"Thanks. I used to keep it at a dock near my place north of Miami. But I've been spending more and more time in Mariposa, so I transferred her down to the island, taking her back and forth when I can."

"You have a place in Miami? How many places do you have?"

"Four," he said. "I do a lot of travel, and it's nice to have my own landing pad. I have a condo in Minneapolis, a lake house out near Duck Lake, where your family lives, the house in Boca—north of Miami—and of course, the estate down in Mariposa. And a number of rental units around the US, like in Key West and New York City."

He said it casually, like it was normal to own so many locations, but maybe for him, it was. Maybe it was simply about getting used to a different normal. Could she get used to this normal? Right now, it felt simple. Easy.

But tonight she was in the middle of a fairy tale.

"When we get back to Miami, I'll check on the search for your boat," he said. "Someone's got to have seen it."

"I hope so. Unlike you, I have only one residence—and that's it." She finished off her gelato. "But I do get around in it. So, in a way, I also have many homes."

"I like how you think." He got up to throw their cups in a nearby trash bin. "So, did you always want to be a diver?" He helped her out of her chair and took her hand again.

"Oh, no. That was after my parents took us on a trip to Sea-World. Of course, I grew up around lakes in Minnesota, but there's something about diving in the ocean. They let me take a beginner diving class at the resort in the pool, and I absolutely fell in love with it. It's like flying underwater."

"Yes," he said. "I agree—it's very freeing. Although I had to get over the idea of claustrophobia the first time I did it." He'd laced his fingers through hers, intimate, his hand encompassing and strong.

"Oh, that's normal. One of the biggest things we tell people is that you *can* breathe, so stay calm."

"I just didn't love the idea of not having any options. I only have that air, and if it fails me, then I die."

"Yeah, that's not a great way to look at it." She laughed. "But you're right, you have to learn to trust your equipment." She looked at him. "You don't seem a man easily frightened. Is there anything you're afraid of?"

He considered her a moment, and her question seemed to play in his eyes. "Yes," he said quietly. "I fear getting it wrong, and getting into a mess that I can't untangle myself from." He stopped and turned to her, pushing a strand of her hair behind her ear. "I fear other people getting hurt because I made a bad decision."

She wanted to kiss him again, especially when his gaze roamed her face. She could get lost in those eyes, in the sense of him holding her.

"I fear freezing. Or running. Mostly because I don't know what to do," she said. "Like when Boo went missing and then Grandma collapsed in the kitchen. I thought Grandma was going to die and that it would be all my fault. Thankfully, my brother Conrad came into the house, saw what had happened, and ran to get

Grandfather. But I was just paralyzed—useless—and I hated that about myself."

He was watching her, and she looked away, started to walk again. But he said nothing, his presence easy, quiet. Freeing.

"I *ran* after Margo died. I couldn't stay in the Keys. Everything there reminded me of her. Her brother Mo has a memorial for her every year—a big party to celebrate her life." She shook her head. "I've never gone. I think that's why Steinbeck came down to Key West—because he knew that the anniversary of her death was coming up and he really wanted me to go."

"Really wanted you to go?"

"He thinks I need to face it and forgive myself, but it's too easy to go back to that moment when I'm watching her fast ascend and I'm paralyzed. I can't bear the memory of it, so I just don't go."

He made a sound like understanding, a deep hum in his chest that somehow rumbled into her too.

"What's funny is that I always tell people when they're shark diving to not panic, to stay still. Don't run, because it only alerts the shark to follow. I froze with Grandma, but with Margo, I ran. And now I just . . . I run."

"And the shark is always on your tail."

She looked up, nodded.

He stopped and took her other hand. "Whatever business problem I have, I have two choices. I can either ignore it or I can face it. Facing it helps me figure out how to fix it."

"I don't know how to fix grief." She sighed. "And I didn't know that grief would feel so much like fear."

She felt a little naked standing there, but he just smiled, softness in his gaze.

"I guess the truth is that I don't like being scared. And I don't like being helpless either."

He studied her and then gave a nod. "Join the rest of the world."

Right.

And then he shrugged. "We're not so different."

Oh, she only wished that were true. Because at any moment, the clock would strike midnight and the fairytale would end.

They walked along a shaded corridor and stopped at the entrance to a restaurant. Tables crowded with patrons flowed from the interior into the outdoor area, covered in umbrellas and lit by candlelight. Timba music played from inside.

But Austen's gaze landed on a woman seated at a table at the edge of the crowd. She sat alone, nursing a glass of something dark, and wore a faraway look, as if she were out to sea.

That's when it clicked. "Is that Captain Teresa?" He looked, and she jerked him back. "Don't look!"

"My mistake. I'll use the eyes on the *back* of my head."

She pulled him away from the restaurant, toward a pillar, and moved him around it, putting her back to the pillar. "Okay, stand here, pretend we're talking, but *now* look."

His mouth hitched up as he placed his hand over her shoulder against the pillar, as if he was going to lean in to kiss her, but at the last moment angled his face so he could see the woman. "That's her," he said, his mouth tightening into a grim line.

"Which means your *boat* is here."

"Hmm." His gaze returned to hers. "I think we need to go back to the hotel. I suddenly have a bad feeling about all of this."

"Do you think she followed us?"

"I don't know how she could have, but it does feel suspicious that she's here. And I don't like it." He sighed. "I hate to say good night, but I need to make some calls." He leaned away from her, took her hand again. "I think it's time to get off this island."

"Are we in danger?"

"I don't know yet. My gut says yes." Then he leveled his gaze at her, put his hand on her cheek. "But I'm not going to let anything happen to you, Austen. No matter what."

She met his eyes, barely visible in the darkness, the nearness of him sweeping over her. And then she couldn't stop herself. She lifted up on her tiptoes and kissed him. She thought he might keep it short, given the impending danger, but he tightened his hold around her—his arms around her shoulders, hers circling his waist—and kissed her back. He was safety and strength and decisiveness, and somehow, in his embrace, she was braver.

Not at all wanting to run.

An hour later, in her hotel room, she opened the windows to the small balcony on the third floor. The harbor glittered against the starlight in the distance, a few ships' lights waxing out against the dark water. She hadn't stopped thinking about Steinbeck. But mostly, she thought about Declan, asleep in the adjoining room. It was too soon to say that she was in love with him, but she could—*was* falling for this man. Falling for his charm, his kindness, his ability to stay calm and make decisions—the sense of confidence that he exuded.

A partner. The problem with having a partner was that they could let you down and make decisions that broke your heart.

She changed into a pair of pajama bottoms and a T-shirt she'd picked up at the market. The wind collected the summer night smells and stirred them into her bedroom. With them came a verse, a memory from her grandmother. *"The Lord's unfailing love surrounds the one who trusts in him."*

Maybe Austen didn't have to have all the answers. She just needed to trust. Trust God, and maybe trust Declan.

She climbed into the king-size four-poster bed, watched the fan stir the air, and sank into sleep.

A movement startled her, and she rose a second before a hand clamped over her mouth. She jerked and nearly screamed—

"Shh. It's me—Phoenix. We gotta move."

The light flicked on. Sure enough, the woman who had leaped off the edge of a boat stood beside the bed, dressed in all black, her dark hair tousled, probably from the sea, her gray-green eyes fierce. "Now. There are people coming for you."

"What?" Austen scrambled up, reaching for her clothes.

"No time. Get your shoes on."

"Seriously? I'm leaving in my pajamas?" But maybe it didn't matter, because Phoenix had lit a fire under her with her tone.

"Where's Steinbeck?" The night pressed in around her windows, and she guessed it was well into the wee hours.

"He's fine. He's safe. Come on." Phoenix opened the door and looked out, gesturing for her to follow.

"What about Declan? Are you going to get him?"

"No," Phoenix said, grabbing her hand as they edged out into the hall. "He's already gone."

TEN

'M NOT GOING ANYWHERE WITHOUT AUSTEN."
Declan had said that at least twice as Steinbeck threw his pants at
him in the hotel room and made to sneak out into the corridor.

"I get it. But we need to act as a decoy and get the hounds
away from here. Then Phoenix can grab Austen and meet us at
the airfield."

"Why the airfield?"

"Phoenix, as it turns out, is a pilot."

Of course she was.

"How did you even know where to find us?" Declan said as
Steinbeck opened the door to the stairwell. Darkness seeped up
from the unlit lower floors. Steinbeck flashed on his Maglite and
cast its beam down the steps. Declan headed down, Steinbeck after
him, flicking off the light at the bottom.

"Hold here." He slid outside.

Declan braced his hand against the cement wall and looked up.
He should go back for her. Mostly because her story about Margo
now circled in his head. She'd think he'd abandoned her.

Never.

"I need to go back," he said.

"Dec, you gotta trust me."

Declan stilled, gave Stein a hard look. "Do you trust *me*?"

Stein's jaw tightened. "I think so," he said quietly. "I want to. But mostly I want to get my sister off this island, so let's go."

He reached out as if to make a grab for Declan, but Declan swatted Stein's hand away. "I'm right behind you."

They slipped out into a back alley. Streetlights lit the entrance, but Stein ducked into the shadows, toward the back of the building. They cut through an alleyway, and then again through another narrow passage between houses.

"How did you survive the jump off the boat?" Declan kept his voice low.

"It wasn't a long jump, so that wasn't the problem." He didn't add any more except, "It's a long story. We get out of this, maybe I'll tell you."

Steinbeck led him out into a lonely street, only one streetlight illuminating their path. Then he pointed to an old Russian Lada, a small sedan about the size of a Volkswagen. "Best I could find. Hop in."

"Where are we going?"

"There's an airstrip outside of town that isn't monitored. If we get there, we can get off this island."

"How—"

"I'll tell you later." Steinbeck pulled out.

"How did you know someone was after me?"

Steinbeck wore a pair of jeans and a T-shirt, not what he was wearing when he jumped off the boat, but Declan didn't ask. Except—"Are you wearing flip-flops?"

Stein glanced over. "Didn't want to run through Cuba in my bare feet."

Oh, of course not. Declan shook his head.

"Listen. Phoenix and I've been following you for hours. We saw you outside the embassy when you left and watched you check into the hotel. I wanted to duck in and have dinner with you, but surveillance had a pretty good eye on you. And then they doubled their efforts at the square. We think there's a group of Russians here waiting to grab you. Probably first thing in the morning, but it could be anytime."

"Do you think we were betrayed?"

"After you left, so did your consulate buddy. He headed back to the wharf, where, surprise, surprise, our friends from the yacht pulled up. They met with him, so my guess is that whatever you told him and maybe whatever you paid him, they matched and raised. He sold you out. And it's just a matter of time before your security is called away and you're unprotected."

Stein turned onto a street that headed out of town. "They want that obsidite. And I wouldn't be surprised if they want Austen too. Because if they have to, they'll use my sister to put a little pressure on you." Stein glanced at him. "And I just can't have that."

"Me either." The thought pressed a fist to his gut. Especially after . . .

Well, he'd stood at the window a long time after they'd returned to the hotel, staring at the darkness, thinking about how she'd felt in his arms.

Thinking about his lame joke—

"And your wife? What is she doing all this time?"

"Swimming with the sharks?"

Sort of kidding. Because the longer they'd strolled, her hand in his, the fragrance of her presence loosing the dark knots inside his soul, the more he'd realized that he was falling for her. Probably had been for a while now.

"For the record, I care for her."

Steinbeck nodded. "I figured."

They drove without speaking. Steinbeck finally turned onto

another road that led up a hill into the outskirts of the city. "Just to be clear, if you hurt her—"

"I won't," Declan said.

Steinbeck's jaw tightened.

Declan looked behind them. "I don't think anyone followed us, so I'm not sure your decoy plan worked."

"Phoenix will get her out of the hotel without anyone seeing her."

"You really trust that woman?"

Steinbeck made a low sound deep in his chest. Declan couldn't tell whether it was agreement or not.

They had left the city, driving past coffee and tobacco plantations, and he spotted the airfield in the distance. The moonlight shone off the rounded top of a row of Quonset buildings. A handful of small planes sat tied down, some of them covered with tarps. Darkness hovered over the runway.

Steinbeck pulled up to the far Quonset building. They got out and worked their way around the building to the front, facing the tarmac.

The doors had been rolled open, but the hangar remained empty.

"So now what? We liberate a plane?" Declan asked.

Stein stood in the darkness, scanning the airfield, and even as he spoke, they heard the low drone of a motor behind them and a scooter pulled up. Steinbeck looked back along the Quonset hut. "It's Phoenix and Austen."

Declan wanted to take off in a run toward Austen when he saw her disembark from the back of the bike. He drew in a deep breath. "Okay, let's get outta here."

Phoenix came walking up, Austen with her.

Austen looked at Declan, hurt in her expression. "I thought you left. Phoenix said you'd already gone."

"I'm sorry," he said. "Steinbeck thought we could lead the peo-

ple watching us away. But I think we all got away without incident."
He stepped up to her. "Are you okay?"

She glanced at Steinbeck, then back at him, and nodded.

And he didn't care what Steinbeck thought. Declan put his
arms around her and pulled her against himself. "I'm so sorry I
got you into this," he said quietly. "But I am going to make sure
you get out safely."

"Let's find some wings," Phoenix said. She jogged out toward
one of the untarped planes.

"Come on," Steinbeck said and started off at a jog toward the
plane.

Gunfire ripped out of the darkness. Bullets strafed the plane.

Declan, who had followed Steinbeck, whirled around, grabbed
Austen, and threw her to the ground.

Phoenix dropped too.

"Are you hit?" asked Steinbeck, now crouching, running toward
Phoenix.

Gunfire shredded the plane's wings and body, but Phoenix
rolled away and launched herself behind a nearby cart. *So, still
alive.*

"Run!" Steinbeck shouted as he reached Phoenix. "Come on,
let's go!"

Declan scrambled to his feet, pulling Austen with him. Of
course whoever was shooting caught their movement. Shots pep-
pered their wake.

He stopped behind a nearby truck, parked between them and
the Quonset hut. Steinbeck and Phoenix scuttled in beside them.

Steinbeck looked at Declan, his expression strained. "You need
to get her out of here." Steinbeck picked up what looked like a
tire iron.

"I'm not leaving without you, Steinbeck." *Austen, of course.*

"Look what I found," Phoenix said. She had disengaged the

nozzle of a portable gasoline tank and now clutched the hose. "You guys go. I'll stop them."

"Where are we going to go?" Steinbeck said.

"The yacht," Declan said. "We saw Captain Teresa down in the square. You said you saw it—"

"Yes," Steinbeck said. He looked at Phoenix. "We get to the harbor, then."

Their gazes seemed to catch. A beat, then Phoenix nodded. "Go. I'll take the scooter and be right behind you." Then she stepped out from the truck, spraying gasoline onto the tarmac.

Declan grabbed Austen. Steinbeck rose, his gaze hard on Phoenix, something in his eyes that probably matched Declan's own desperation when Steinbeck had told him he'd have to leave Austen behind.

"You'd better show up," Steinbeck shouted.

Phoenix waved her hand. "Go! I'll be right behind you! I promise!"

Steinbeck let out a growl. "Let's go!"

They took off running. Bullets pinged around them, but they crossed behind the Quonset hut and dove into the Lada, Steinbeck at the wheel.

"Was that—" Austen said, climbing into the back seat.

"Our Russian friends?" Declan said. "Maybe."

"Or it could be local police," Steinbeck said. "I'm not gonna stick around to find out."

As he pulled out, however, Declan saw him angle the rearview mirror, glancing at it as they headed down the dirt road.

"Come on. Come on," he muttered.

They'd reached the gravel when an explosion lit up the night, a plume of orange and red that blew apart the sky.

Austen put her hands over her head, ducking before she looked back. "Oh no, I hope Phoenix got away."

From the look on Steinbeck's face, that was an understatement.

"Should we go back?" Declan turned, searching for her form in the glow.

Steinbeck shook his head. "We need to get to the boat. She'll be there."

They hit the outskirts of town and wove their way through the darkened city streets, losing themselves in the tangle of neighborhoods until they finally reached the harbor. A chain-link fence cordoned off the entire area, locked from the outside. But inside, along the pier, Declan made out the *Invictus*.

Beautiful. White. Hope glistening under the moonlight.

Steinbeck parked in the shadows, and they got out, crouched, surveying the area. "Phoenix and I came through some rusty gates. Down this way," Steinbeck said. "Stay low."

Declan ducked as he followed, Austen right behind him. They reached the fencing some fifty yards away from the opening in an area of shrubbery and overgrown brush. Steinbeck pulled it back and crept in, the chain link broken from the pole.

"We might have given it a little help," Steinbeck said. He held back the fencing, and Austen clambered through. Steinbeck held it open for Declan, searching the parking lot. Then he crawled through after Declan, wearing a grim look. "Let's go."

They ran past metal buildings, fisheries, and crouched behind boxes piled on the pier as they finally worked their way to the dock. The *Invictus* floated at the end. Fishing boats listed in the waves, tied to the pier side by side.

"What if she's being guarded?" Austen said.

"Oh, she's most certainly being guarded," Declan said.

Steinbeck gave a nod. He still carried the tire iron and now glanced at Declan.

"Listen," he said, "I'll get on the boat first—see if I can create a diversion. You get on, get down to the lockers, and arm yourself."

Then he looked at Austen. "And you get someplace safe. Lock yourself in a closet or something. Wait till I come and get you."

"I can help," Austen said.

"You can help by making sure you don't get in the way."

She recoiled. "I won't get in the way—"

Declan took her hand. "He's right. Let us get you out of here."

"Fine," she said. "But neither one of you better die."

Steinbeck gave her a smile. "Oh, I wouldn't dream of it. I know you and your temper."

Her mouth opened, and Declan smiled. But Steinbeck had already moved down the pier, staying low.

Declan followed him, Austen on his tail.

The gangway to the ship touched the dock, so clearly the Russians weren't worried about stowaways or attackers. Steinbeck huddled in the shadows. Moonlight glinted upon the water, and the various trawlers and skiffs tied to the dock bumped against each other.

"I see one guy in the bow," Stein said. "Looks like he's doing rounds. We'll wait till he goes to the backside of the boat and then we'll board. I think we can catch him by surprise."

It felt like they were a team again. Well, he'd never really been a *team* with Steinbeck, but still, it felt good to have Steinbeck back by his side.

"All right, let's go," Steinbeck said, and led the way as they hurried up the gangway. Steinbeck went aboard, then Declan, finally Austen.

Declan grabbed her hand and headed into the salon. It was dark, but he knew his way. He found the galley door, pulled Austen down the galley stairs. "Stay here," he said. "Maybe in one of the crew berths."

Then he headed down the hall to the security area. He keyed in the code, and the lock to the weapons cache opened. He found a Beretta 92XI, grabbed another and returned to Austen.

"Do you know how to handle a gun?"

"We've been over this. Yes."

"Okay, hide, and if anyone shows up that's not me or Stein-beck—"

"To be clear, I'm not killing anybody."

"You may change your mind if they decide to kill *you*."

Her eyes widened. *Oh,* he hadn't meant to scare her. He put his hand behind her neck, leaned in, and kissed her, fast and hard.

Somehow he pulled away. "We'll be back."

Then he headed back up the stairs and into the galley. The boat listed in the water, just the hum of the AC units betraying life. He searched the stern. Nothing. But on the port side, Steinbeck dumped something into the harbor waters.

Oh. Declan didn't want to know, and maybe that was for the best.

Steinbeck came in through the salon doors. "You get up to the bridge. I'll get us off the dock."

"We should wait for Phoenix," Declan said.

A beat. "She'll be here," Steinbeck said. "Let's get moving."

Declan took the outer stairs to the spa deck and then up to the sky lounge and finally onto the bridge. The console lights illuminated the darkness. He'd been up here at least twice while Teresa had taken the boat out of dock, and before that had watched the previous captain of the *Invictus*, a skipper out of Grenada, take the boat out of harbor. So he wasn't a pro, but he could certainly figure out how to drive his own yacht.

Declan fired up both engines, saw them come to life on the monitors. The deck cameras showed Steinbeck pulling the rope from one of the cleats. He tossed the rope onto the boat and then ran down the dock to the other cleat. Declan searched the console, found the reverse and forward throttles for each engine, the compass, the wheel attached to the helm. He could figure this out.

On-screen, Steinbeck threw the other rope onto the boat, then stood on the dock, his hands on his hips, staring out into the darkness.

Declan could almost feel his thoughts. *Come on, Phoenix. Come on.*

Finally Steinbeck scrubbed his hands down his face and turned, ran up the gangway. Then activated the hydraulics and pulled the bridge.

Oh no.

Steinbeck stared again into the darkness, clearly hoping that she would appear. He waited a second, then another, and finally he turned and ran up the stairs to the pilothouse.

Declan already knew what he was going to say when he opened the bridge door.

"Let's go," Steinbeck said. "It won't take them long to figure out what's going on."

"Phoenix?"

Steinbeck shook his head. "I don't know."

"We should wait."

"No, we should go. She can take care of herself." But his jaw tightened as Declan maneuvered the yacht off the dock and out into the shiny black harbor.

Declan didn't blame him at all when Steinbeck walked outside and slammed his fist against the rail.

Then Declan motored them out of the harbor into the dark ocean water, the moonlight glistening on the waves ahead, the yacht gaining speed. Now they just had to get out of Cuban waters.

Steinbeck came in, his expression still strained. He stood with his arms folded, staring into the darkness. Declan glanced at him. "Um . . . maybe someone should go get Austen?"

"Right." He turned to head out the door.

Stopped.

Out of the corner of Declan's eye, he saw Steinbeck put his hands up, take a step back.

Austen appeared in the room, her hands also raised. Behind her, Sergei held a gun to the nape of her neck.

"Ach," he said. "Welcome back."

———————————•———————————

She'd frozen.

Austen wouldn't even call it staying calm. Her body had simply shut down and stopped working when the Russian opened up the door to the crew room and stared at her.

Sure, she'd held a gun, but she didn't lift it, didn't point it at him, *nothing*. She'd just stared, and of course the man had reached out and grabbed the gun, which left her with no recourse except to scream.

Only, even *that* reaction hadn't surfaced.

He'd lunged for her. Then somehow she'd come to life and kicked him, but by that time it was too late. He'd shoved the gun up against her neck and said, "Welcome back."

The same words he'd said to Declan and Steinbeck when he'd used her as hostage fodder to keep them from jumping him, and then as he'd marched them down to a stateroom on the spa deck to lock them inside.

That had been their last chance before the rest of his crew woke. Because apparently, the boat *wasn't* unoccupied. And they'd added a few crew members since their last excursion. So it was a Russian party on a hijacked boat, and she, Declan, and Steinbeck were the unwelcome guests.

Thankfully nobody had gotten hurt, unless she looked at Steinbeck and Declan. She wouldn't call their dark expressions *hurt*. Fierce, angry, frustrated, maybe helpless. Although, she knew both of them enough to know that they weren't actually *helpless*. Regardless of what he'd said in the plaza, Declan might be the least helpless man she'd ever met. He always had a plan, something up his sleeve, and even now as she looked at him, the dawn cresting into the locked stateroom, he seemed to be thinking.

He'd spent most of the last hour pacing the room, occasionally glancing out the massive windows that overlooked the dark sea. She could practically see the steam churning inside his brain as he tried to figure out how to get them out of this.

And note to self. Next time she was taken hostage, she'd prefer *not* to wear her pajamas. That thought conjured up Phoenix pulling her out of bed to drag her up to the airport. Which led to Phoenix setting up a fiery blockade so they could make their escape.

Steinbeck's entire body resembled a coiled rattler, his tail practically buzzing as he sat on the other sofa. She'd never seen him quite so miserable. Okay, maybe when he'd returned from Germany, both of his legs wrapped after having both knees replaced.

This felt different, though.

She knew better than to suggest that maybe it was a good thing that Phoenix hadn't joined them. But then again, why *hadn't* she shown up? That horror sat like a burr deep in her heart.

That and the fact that, well . . . "I'm really, really, really sorry that I didn't shoot him," she said into the quiet.

Both men turned and looked at her, frowned. "Seriously?" Declan said. "First, I'm just glad Sergei didn't kill you. And second, of *course* you shouldn't have shot him. Because if you had, who knows what they would have done with us? You might have saved our lives."

"I completely froze," Austen said.

"You did fine," Steinbeck said quietly.

She did *not* do fine, and she didn't want to admit it but, "I was just in the way. I've been in the way this entire time. If you hadn't had to find me, you would have been safe in port and—"

"Stop," Declan said and walked over to her. Sat on the bed. "Austen. You are not in the way. You're the reason. The light in the middle of the dark ocean."

"Oh brother," Steinbeck said. Then he looked at her. "But yes, you are . . . Well, there's no one like you, sis."

Her eyes filled, and she pulled up a pillow from the bed to hold on to. "What's going to happen now?"

Declan hung a hand behind his neck. "Well, they're tracking my last ship, the *Santa Maria*, so I guess when they find it, they'll take it." He looked at Steinbeck and lifted his shoulders.

Her eyes widened. "And then what? Are they going to kill us?"

"They might not kill Declan right away. After all, he has what they want," Stein said.

"Which is what? His money?"

Declan sighed. "No. It's not about that," he said softly. He looked at both of them. "It's one thing to have a program. Another thing to have the obsidite that can fuel it. But you have to synthesize it, right? You have to know how to turn it into the fuel that will make this resource valuable." He stuck his hands into his pockets. "And I have that."

Silence from Steinbeck as his expression changed. *Horror? No, fury.*

Her voice emerged low. "What do you mean?"

"He means that he was always planning to use it for his own purposes," Steinbeck said, looking at her. "He was never planning to dump it into the ocean and scuttle it." He looked back at Declan. "Were you?"

"No."

Her mouth opened. "So you *were* planning to use it?"

"Not just me," Declan said quietly. "There's a bigger plan in play here. And I can't . . ." He sighed, shook his head. "I'm sorry I got you guys involved in this. This was never my intention. I thought I could outsmart the Petrovs. Clearly I can't. Now I'm in over my head and your lives are at risk." He turned to Austen. "You have to believe me that I am not a terrorist. I am not planning to use this for evil." He reached out to touch her hand, but she pulled away.

"Then what will you use it for?"

His mouth tightened around the edges. "I can't tell you. I'm not . . ." He sighed. "I'm not allowed to."

"What? If you tell me, you'll have to kill me?" She wasn't really kidding. *Seriously?* He'd *lied* to her? After everything?

And Phoenix's words rose inside her. *"Don't be deceived by his good looks or his money, honey. Rich men only have room for one thing in their heart. Themselves."*

"Get away from me," she said. "I can't believe that after everything, you won't tell me what's going on. How do you expect me to trust you?"

His eyes darkened, a fierceness in them. "I expect you to trust the man that you know. The man that I've been to you. That's the man I hope that you'll trust."

Steinbeck shook his head and looked away.

"And now I hope you'll trust me enough to escape this ship."

"What?" Austen said.

"The stateroom is equipped with an escape hatch. In case the boat goes down or flips, there's a hatch under this floor." He pointed to a small square etched into the carpet. "It leads to the walkway on the deck level. You get to the swim deck, deploy the lifeboat. And get off this ship."

Austen stared at him. "No. I'm not leaving you here. You can't be serious."

"Yes, he's serious," Steinbeck said. He stood up, considered him. "How do you propose we accomplish this?"

"I'm going to knock on the door and tell them that I'll lead them to where we're taking the obsidite. The captain of the *Santa Maria* is waiting for final coordinates from me. I will send them and we'll meet it there."

"Where is *there*?" Steinbeck said.

Declan shook his head. "I want you guys off this ship. I want Austen safe."

"And I want you to tell me the truth," Austen said. "I want you to not be this guy that lives a double life. I want you to be the nice guy I met at my sister's wedding, who danced with me and left me wanting to know him more. The same guy who showed up in Key West and asked me to come help him at a charity event he was running. For *orphans*!" Her voice shook, rising a little, but she didn't care. "I want you to be that guy who helped look for a couple of lost kids on Mariposa and even got my brother out of trouble with a bunch of thugs on the island. I want that guy who helped people during the landslide and got dirty and sweaty because he cared about people." She took a breath, her eyes filling. "I want the guy who stopped at nothing to find me in the middle of the ocean just because he cared about doing the *right thing*."

"I *am* doing the right thing!" He recoiled, then schooled his tone. "I *am* doing the right thing. But sometimes doing the right thing requires you to do some, well, some bad stuff to get it done."

"Stuff that gets people killed?"

He paused and looked at her. "Not you." He looked at Steinbeck. "Can you get her off this boat?"

"I'd like to see you try!" Austen said. That sounded tougher than she felt, and probably stupid too, but frankly, she didn't know what to believe. Because in her heart, everything she'd said about Declan, everything she *saw* about him, proved that he was a good man. An honorable man. She couldn't believe that he would do evil things.

But maybe she *didn't* know him. "Was there anything you told me that was true?"

"Everything I told you was true, Austen. Everything. I just left a few parts out."

She nearly lifted her hand to slap him, but even that she couldn't do. Because of course she again simply froze.

"We'll need to do it quickly, before the sun rises," Steinbeck said tightly.

Declan said. "It's about two hours to sunrise, and I figure the current will carry you east. You should be able to hit the Keys or even the Bahamas. Or, more likely, a cruise ship."

"Does the raft have an EPIRB?" Steinbeck asked, rising.

"Yes, it does. All the rafts do. It's in the survival case."

Steinbeck nodded, looked at Austen. "Then yes, I can get her off this boat."

No. Yes. Oh, she couldn't move.

Declan looked at Steinbeck. "Thank you, Steinbeck. I don't deserve ... Well, you are the best bodyguard I've ever had."

"You're a hard man to protect," Steinbeck said quietly, and held out his hand.

Declan considered it for a second, then shook it.

"You're not going to let them find that ship, are you?" Steinbeck said.

Her eyes widened as Declan considered Stein.

Her brother held up a hand. "If, say, a guy was planning some sort of sabotage of your yacht, what would it be?"

Declan glanced out the window, back at Steinbeck. "If a guy knew where the lithium batteries were, in the front bow garage, he might damage them so they'd light on fire. Once they're on fire, nothing can stop them."

"The ship would go down," Steinbeck said.

"It would."

Silence.

Wait—was he—

Declan looked back at Austen, so much in his eyes that she didn't know how to unpack it. Finally, "Stay safe."

What? No. "Declan!"

But he ignored her, walked to the door, and knocked. It opened and he said something in Russian.

And if she hadn't believed it before, all the accusations that Phoenix had leveled at him about being Dark Horse and a Russian contact and a smuggler and a terrorist—all clicked into place.

He was a criminal and a hero.

And she could not love a criminal.

Her eyes filled as Declan stepped out and the door closed behind him.

Steinbeck kept staring at the door.

"What?" she said.

He seemed to be lost in thought, and then he looked at her and shook his head. "Nothing. But he's right. The most important thing to do is get you off this ship." He turned to her. "And as far away from Declan Stone as possible."

It might be a twin thing, but Steinbeck knew *exactly* how Austen felt. A tight clenching in the gut and a sense of fury and despair all wrapped up in a hard ball inside the chest. Yeah, he totally got it as he watched Austen sitting on the bed, her knees pulled up, her forehead braced against them.

He'd spent the last hour, while watching Declan pace, trying to tell himself that yes, Phoenix was just fine. She *hadn't* been captured by some Russians, or worse—killed. She'd somehow gotten away.

And ditched him.

"I'll be right behind you. I promise."

He wanted to hit something because leaving her had been the *right* thing to do. He'd known it in his gut even as he'd told Declan to drive away. And he'd hated it anyway.

Then they'd been taken captive again, and *shoot*, Steinbeck nearly wanted to go over the side of the rail, swim his way back to Havana and find her.

But priorities said he had to stay and rescue Austen. And sure, Austen was plenty capable, even knew how to face down sharks, but terrorists were a different kind of danger, and frankly, he wanted her off this boat ASAP.

But if Declan thought Stein was leaving him behind, he had another thing coming. Stein would get Austen into that life raft, push her out to sea, and then help Declan take down the Russians. Because Declan's story dug deep inside Steinbeck. Declan was hiding something. And it was just outside Steinbeck's reach. There was something bigger afoot, like Declan said, and if Steinbeck thought hard enough, he could figure it out.

Unfortunately, his brain kept circling back to yesterday in the harbor, when he'd gone overboard, splashing into the water in Phoenix's wake.

He'd surfaced in the murky water, his head on a swivel for boats ready to run him over, and made a beeline for the nearest pier. He'd come up again between a couple of fishing trawlers tied to the dock.

But he'd lost Phoenix.

He'd swum toward the dock and hung out there, watching as the fishing boat docked and officials boarded, and had turned into a prune by the time Austen and Declan left the boat under official escort. Working his way closer to shore, he'd watched as they disappeared into the immigration building.

It was during that surveillance that a hand had touched his back. He'd jerked, whirled around, and Phoenix had treaded water, her dark hair plastered to her head, her gray-green eyes shiny.

"I can't believe you came in after me."

He'd wanted to say, "Yeah. Yeah, I did. Because, well, you're just crazy enough to do something that could get yourself killed. Or thrown into prison. And maybe I couldn't bear the thought of that, although I don't know why."

But instead his stupid mouth had said, "Don't get excited, honey. I just wanted to make sure you weren't gonna betray us."

"Oh." Her smile had vanished as her mouth turned into a grim line. "No, Steinbeck, we're in this together. At least until we can get off this island, right?"

Aw, she'd been nicer than he was. So he'd nodded, grunted, and given her a sitrep. They'd sat in the water and watched the immigration center while she talked through possible scenarios. Like getting to the airfield, appropriating a plane, and escaping Cuban air space. Although, he wasn't a pilot, so he hadn't known how she'd planned to accomplish that until she'd said, "I know how to fly."

Which had seeded all sorts of ideas. Then she'd scanned the harbor and pointed out a couple of boats that looked capable of taking them out of the harbor and the ninety miles to Key West.

Meanwhile, a car had pulled up, and someone had gotten out and shaken Declan's hand. Austen had seemed just fine as they'd gotten into the SUV and driven away. And that's when he'd said, "Let's go."

"Where are we going?"

"Wherever that black car is going. It looks like it has embassy plates, so my guess is the US embassy."

"Oh, perfect. Because it's not enough that the Cuban police will find us—we're gonna let the Americans grab hold of us too," she'd said, looking at him. "For you, that's not a problem."

He'd worked his way over to a ladder in the water. "What, are you wanted in America too?"

She'd sighed. "Not exactly. But I don't like people asking questions. And sure, I have contacts that could probably wheedle me out of custody, but . . . I just like to stay below the radar."

He'd landed on the dock, and she came up behind him, still dressed in her whites, which did a great job of outlining her body.

"That should start with us getting a change of clothes," he'd said.

"Will that do?" she'd said as she pointed to a nearby trawler. A pair of pants and a T-shirt hung from the line, small enough to fit her.

"That'll work for you," he'd said.

"Calm down," she'd said. "It looks like a liveaboard. We'll go shopping."

His clothes plastered to his body, he'd hustled down to the trawler. It looked recently docked, so maybe the owners were inside sleeping. Or had gone ashore. She'd hopped onto the deck, walked over to the clothes, and grabbed them. Then she'd stuck her head into the cabin area, motioned to him. He'd sneaked inside too.

Small space, dark. A single bench with a table. Small kitchen. A coffeepot sitting in the sink, a stained, chipped mug next to it. Tackle and nets and fishing rods cluttering the table and bench. Clearly they'd hopped aboard a big-game fishing boat, probably in from that day's charter.

"I found some clothes that might fit you," Phoenix had said. She'd held up a men's Speedo, grinned.

"Oh, you're hilarious," he'd said. But he'd spotted a pair of black cargo pants, held them up. "Maybe a little baggy, but they'll do."

He'd started to slip off his pants, but looked at Phoenix. Circled his finger in the air.

"Oh my, you're precious." She'd rolled her eyes, then headed into the back cabin, shut the door.

He'd changed into the pants and found a black T-shirt as well. He'd left his clothes in exchange and was scanning the harbor from the steps of the boat when she emerged.

Phoenix simply had a way of commanding the room. Sure, she could make herself invisible when she wanted to, but now that he was aware of her, he couldn't imagine not seeing her if she entered his airspace. With her short dark hair, big gray-green eyes, she possessed a fierceness that had once prompted him to call her Mighty Mouse, and he hadn't been wrong. She was smart, fast, tough. But she also could laugh and get under his skin, and for a second, he'd been back in Krakow, kissing her. And then again in Mariposa, only two months ago, right before she'd saved his life. Or gotten him nearly killed, depending on whose side of the story he stood on.

So yeah, she'd gotten inside him just a little bit.

But she could also betray him any second, so maybe he'd needed a good old cold shower.

"Where to?" Phoenix had asked as she joined him on the steps in his memory of their epic day.

He'd hopped onto the pier. He'd also found a pair of flip-flops, which wouldn't go very far in a run, but at least they were something. She'd still had the Converse tennis shoes that she'd worn on the boat.

She'd followed him onto the pier.

"I'm pretty sure the embassy picked them up, so we'll head up there and see if we can scout them out."

"But first we need to get off this dock and out of this harbor without being noticed," she'd said.

Then she'd picked up a cooler that was about the size of her entire body and started to lug it down the pier, as if she were a deckhand.

He'd grabbed one end and nearly tripped. "There's nothing in this."

"Still, you were a little impressed, weren't you?"

"Phoenix, the truth is..." *Shoot,* he hadn't been able to stop himself. "I'm almost always a little impressed by you. Scared, mostly, but still a little impressed."

She'd found a pair of aviators and now put them on. "Of course you are."

He'd shaken his head but grinned.

They'd lugged the cooler to the end of the pier and then set it down near a truck. The place had felt abandoned, although this late in the day, probably most of the fishermen had come in.

The sun had hung halfway down the horizon, and they'd probably had three or four hours of daylight left.

"Over there," Phoenix had said, and he'd followed the gesture she made with her head.

The chain-link fence had unraveled near one of the posts, rusty and probably easily breakable.

"Come on," she'd said, "while nobody's looking." She'd jogged over to the fence and kicked it before he could stop her. Pushing it open, she'd made a space wide enough to scoot through. Then she'd held it back, and he'd ducked and wiggled through as well. It had led out into scrub brush and then to a road that ran along the harbor.

Because he hadn't wanted anyone asking questions, he'd taken her hand and they'd walked out of the harbor together as if they were out for a stroll. She'd seemed to catch on and hadn't pulled away as they'd walked to the street and woven their way through the city.

As they'd come into Old Havana, the crowd had grown. Tourists had walked hand in hand, and people had sat at the cafés that ringed the big center square.

Steinbeck had stood in the shadows under the portico of one of the shops, watching the fountain as it sprayed kaleidoscope drops into the air.

"Stay here," she'd said. He'd turned, but she had slipped out of his grip, already gone. She'd walked down the row of shops, bumped into somebody, held up her hand in apology, kept moving all the way to the end, turned, and strolled around the square. He'd lost sight of her in the shadows across the cobblestone street.

A number of buskers had stood in the square, a couple of them playing guitars, another doing tricks. A few pigeons had darted about.

"Miss me?" she'd said. She'd grinned at him, wearing a gimme cap, then handed him one too. And a pair of shades. "Also, I scored us some cash and a phone." She'd pulled out a burner phone, still in the package.

"Where did you get that?"

"There's a guy selling burner phones across the way there." She'd opened the package, turned it on.

"What are you doing?"

"Trying to figure out a way out of here." She'd held the phone to her ear.

"Who are you calling?"

"My boss," she'd said. "She'll know what to do."

"I'll find the embassy." He'd walked away from her to a street map attached to a wall. It featured the Old Havana area as well as a larger metropolitan map. He spotted the embassy located along the shoreline, about six miles away. So, a little bit of a hike.

"I have a plan," Phoenix had said. He'd turned, found her standing next to him. "Get to the airport, fly out, and my contact will pick us up."

"Where?" he'd asked.

"The Bahamas. A little place called Alice Town on North Bimini Island. All tucked away and quiet, about 250 miles from here. My contact should get us where we need to go."

"The Keys are closer."

She'd given him a tired look.

"Fine. But first we need to get Declan and Austen." He'd pointed to the embassy on the wall map. "The problem is, we have a small window of time. If we don't get there before they leave the embassy, we lose them."

"No problem." She'd indicated a rack of rental bikes. Then she'd pulled out a wallet and produced a card. "I think that Thomas McKnight would just love to take a ride on a rental bike."

Nice. He'd have to find Thomas McKnight and apologize, but, *right now, yes.*

She'd run the card and released the bikes, and he'd gotten on.

"You *do* know how to ride a bike, right?" she'd said.

"Are you kidding? Try to keep up."

"Challenge accepted." She'd grinned.

Aw. He'd gotten on and maneuvered his way through the square and then out to the street, where he'd followed the road along the coastline and through the city toward the embassy. He'd turned into a tourist, glancing back at her as she'd pedaled, grinning at him. And for a second, he'd been in Krakow again, sneaking out of their safe house, working together as they went to the café to meet his team.

Stop. He couldn't go there. Because it would only end up in darkness and pain and fury.

They'd reached the embassy, the tall white building with the long windows and the gate around the perimeter. An American guard had stood at the entrance.

Stein had kept pedaling, found an alleyway, and parked the bike. Then they'd set up shop in a nearby café, and he drank black take-the-roof-off-your-mouth coffee and they watched people come and go.

"Who did you reach out to?" he'd asked.

She'd sat opposite him, the street traffic mirrored in her aviators.

"My boss, Mystique," she'd said. "She has connections. We'll figure out how to hustle Declan and Austen away from their over-lords, sneak up to an airfield, and find some wings."

"You hope."

"According to Mystique, there's a remote airfield with small planes. It won't be the first time I've hijacked a plane."

He'd shaken his head, rolled his eyes. "I don't think I want to know."

"Oh please," she'd said. "Like you never did anything sketchy during your time as a SEAL."

His mouth had pursed and he'd looked away because he didn't like to think about that life anymore.

"You miss it," she'd said.

He'd nodded. "I miss the teams. I miss the teamwork and the

camaraderie. I miss knowing I'm doing something for good. The tip of the spear."

He'd sat up then, seeing Declan and Austen emerge from the embassy. They'd gotten into an SUV, and by the time they'd pulled out, he and Phoenix had retrieved their bikes. They'd followed them through the congested traffic toward Old Havana to an old-style colonial Spanish hotel. There they'd parked while Declan and Austen wandered around Old Havana, shopping like they were on a date or something. Steinbeck had wanted to grab them then, but he'd spotted their tail, and Phoenix had talked him into holding back.

Then they'd nearly gotten caught. Maybe they'd ventured too close, maybe the tail had seen them, but Phoenix had grabbed him and pulled him into the shadows between shops.

"What?" he'd said as he braced an arm over her.

"I think you should kiss me," she'd said.

"Really?" he'd said. "I feel like we've been here before."

"Then we'll know how to do it right," she'd said. And she'd leaned up and put her arms around his neck.

And it had felt like the first time, when he'd kissed her in Krakow. Surprising and sweet, although this time he'd known her better. Known that he'd started to trust her a little, maybe. And he'd wanted her to trust him too. He'd blamed the fatigue and adrenaline of the last few days for the way he'd stepped up, put his arm around her waist, pulled her to himself, and kissed her back. Maybe put a little more oomph into it than necessary. But she'd asked and he'd wanted to deliver.

She'd tasted sweet and smelled of the salty ocean and felt, well, a little too right in his arms for his own good.

Then she'd let him go, palming her hands on his chest. "I see you've upped your game," she'd said quietly. "You've been practicing?"

"It comes naturally." He'd given her a smile and stepped back, grabbed her hand.

Declan and Austen's tail had started moving again, and Stein had kept his hand in Phoenix's again as they followed. They'd stopped at a souvenir shop, and she'd pretended to look at a dress, which he'd suggested might look great on her.

"In your dreams, sailor." But she'd smiled, as if . . .

Stop. Not a date. Surveillance. And she was good, very good, at the pretending game.

When Declan and Austen had gone out for dinner, he and Phoenix had a meal on a terrace as if they were actually on vacation. Ceviche and fresh chips and pulled pork, and they'd drunk a couple of lemonades, lingering until Austen and Declan had finally made their way back in. The tail was still on them, so Stein had suggested separating and using himself and Declan as decoys.

Never in his wildest dreams had he thought that that would be the last time he'd see her.

Now, with the darkness bleeding in through the stateroom windows, with Austen sitting on the bed, her jaw tight, well, whatever sacrifice Phoenix had given, he had to make it worthwhile.

He simply wouldn't think any further than that.

Footsteps finished pounding up the stairs, so Stein got up, held his hand out to his sister. "You ready?"

"Let's get off this stupid boat," she said and got up.

He opened the hatch that Declan had pointed out, and sure enough, below was the lower deck. Austen angled herself through and dropped. He followed.

It was almost too easy to scurry along the side of the boat down to the swim deck and unlatch the lifeboat. He flung it out into the ocean, holding on to the attached rope. As it inflated, he reeled it back in, safe in the darkness of the blown stern lights.

"Get in," he said.

Austen crouched, looking up at the bridge, her expression broken and hollow.

"He's gonna be okay," Stein said.

She looked at him then. "Whatever. I don't care."

Yeah, that's what he'd said about Phoenix too. "Move."

She turned and jumped into the bottom of the life raft. And then he threw the rope in and pushed it off.

"Stein! What do you think you're doing?" She leaned over the edge, trying to paddle back.

"Trust me."

Then he turned and made his way back up the deck. Oh, he hoped his gut was right. Because he'd finally figured out exactly the memory that he needed to latch on to.

And he was betting everything he had on the fact that Declan was exactly who he said he was.

ELEVEN

ET THEM GO," DECLAN SAID QUIETLY, WATCH-
ing as the life raft deployed and then drifted out into the darkness.
"Let them go, and we will finish this."

Sergei looked at him and then barked into his radio. "Leave them."

Declan released a breath. At least Steinbeck and Austen would be safe. His contact would follow their EPIRB and pick them up, even if they only found a smoking hole where the *Invictus* once had been.

He had two hundred miles to figure out how to get to the bow, open up the fender garage, access the lithium batteries, destroy them, and start a fire, exactly the plan he'd outlined for Steinbeck. He hadn't wanted Stein to think he might *really* be a traitor. He didn't know why it mattered so much, but . . .

Okay, it was Austen that he was trying to prove himself to, although he didn't know why. Maybe he should harbor no hope that he might fix anything between them. Maybe his best hope would be that she'd remember him with some warmth, after the truth came out.

Fact was, he probably wouldn't live through this, so any hope beyond this felt futile.

Now the captain plugged in the coordinates Declan had given him and told Declan to sit down on the sofa. Another guard held a handgun on him. He lifted his hands in surrender. "Where am I going to go? There's nothing but ocean around us for fifty miles."

He said it in Russian, and Sergei looked over at him and then at his henchman, a new guy whom Declan decided to call Ivan, and nodded.

"You think we don't remember you?" Sergei said and glanced at Declan.

"What?"

"Alosha. You're on a dozen wanted posters." The chair creaked as Sergei laughed. "I didn't know you were so famous till I got to Cuba."

Oh, that accounted for why the US official had turned on him. It wasn't about the obsidite or even his AI program.

It was about Operation Cybernet.

Declan looked over at Sergei. "That was a long time ago."

"We have a long memory."

Yes, well, Declan did too. The kind that kept his Russian fluent.

Maybe because he'd feared exactly this day, his past coming back to haunt him.

"So after we find the obsidite and the refining facility, I think you will have to return to the motherland for another conversation."

Another conversation. After which, if he wasn't executed, he'd end up in a Siberian gulag, if they still had such things.

Alosha. A play on the name Dark Horse, *loshad*.

He just could not seem to outrun his mistakes or even the consequences of his decisions. His stupid words to Austen played back to him, *"Whatever business problem I have, I have two choices. I can either ignore it or I can face it. Facing it helps me figure out how to fix it.*"

Clearly not. It only dug him deeper.

Well, at least she was alive, and Steinbeck too.

He stared out into the night and uttered a prayer, wanting to believe that God might listen to him. *Please get her safely to shore.* Maybe for her sake, God would.

Although her words still dug into him, ached.

"I want the guy who stopped at nothing to find me in the middle of the ocean just because he cared about doing the right thing."

He was *still* doing the right thing. But helping her had also made him feel like he could step out of the choices he'd made into a new place, a new version of himself.

"Watch him," Sergei said to Ivan, then looked over at Declan. "If he tries to touch the console, shoot him."

Declan held up his hands and rolled his eyes. "I'm just an observer here, man."

Sergei stepped out of the pilothouse, heading down the stairs, probably to the galley.

Ivan, maybe in his early twenties, glanced over at Declan. "What did he mean by all that?"

Declan frowned.

"When he called you Alosha."

"It's an old name," Declan said. "From the Afghan war. I had some Russian friends. We got into a bit of a disagreement." He stared out the window, remembering the early days after Hunter had moved the FOB to a different location. He probably didn't even know about Declan's stint working for counterintelligence.

The door opened.

It happened so fast Declan almost didn't move. Two shots, dimmed by a silencer. It took a full second after Ivan hit the floor for him to realize Steinbeck *hadn't* joined Austen on the raft.

The man burst into the room. "Let's go."

Where? He didn't stop to ask as he followed Stein onto the sky lounge and down the stairs toward the bow deck.

"I hope you're not too attached to your boat." Stein paused in the dim lights of the deck.

"It's sort of named after my mother, so maybe a little."

"You'll have to upgrade." Steinbeck pointed toward the bow. "Let's get to those lithium batteries."

Declan nodded. "To be clear, once you start, you can't stop the chain reaction."

"I think that's the point." He motioned toward the front and Declan jumped onto the bow deck.

"Where's Sergei?" Declan asked as the door lifted.

"Time-out in the head," Steinbeck said. "But there are more roaming around the boat, so let's move it."

"Right." Declan took the stairs down to the locker, where they stored the fenders and the lithium batteries. Entered the code to unlock the garage.

"I can't believe you came back for me," Declan said to Steinbeck as the door opened.

"It took me a while to pick up what you were laying down," he said. "You were on the Cybernet op."

"You know about that?"

"It was talked about as a textbook operation that destroyed a Soviet complex that was aggregating our information, selling it to the world, and reverse engineering our technology. I especially remember how it ended."

"The lab was on a cargo ship docked in Vladivostok. Made a big boom."

"They thought you were one of them."

"That's what happens when you have a Russian mother and speak without an accent." Declan moved down into the storage bay, toward the batteries. "Apparently they haven't forgotten."

Steinbeck stayed in the bow. "So this whole operation? You're still running a Dark Horse op?"

Declan nodded.

"I should have figured that out when I saw my cousin Colt in Barcelona. He wasn't there to watch you. He was there to help you, wasn't he?"

Declan had unlocked the battery compartment, revealing the ship's lithium batteries—all twenty of them.

They would make a sizable boom too.

"I don't know who Colt is, but I did work with a clandestine government agency that helped me make contact with the Russian Bratva. I leased them the Mariposa land and watched them. As soon as I realized they'd gotten their first shipment of obsidite, I came up with the shell game."

"The three ships."

"We're down to one. They've been tracking the *Santa Maria* since we left Cuba."

"I should have trusted you," Steinbeck said.

"Give me your gun."

Steinbeck handed over the Beretta.

"I think your instincts are pretty good, Steinbeck. You suspected I was lying about something, and it wasn't really a lie, but I didn't want Austen to get involved. Maybe that was stupid, but I'm a little tired of living two lives." He gave him a solemn look. "I'm falling in love with your sister. I hope that's okay."

"I think I can live with that," Steinbeck said. "But first we need to find her. So let's get going."

Declan stepped back and shot.

The batteries sparked.

"Let's move." He turned and scrambled out to where Steinbeck stood by the anchor chain.

"Help me get this out." Stein had hold of a large bag.

Right. The secondary life raft. "How did you know this was here?"

"We did a couple of ops on boats like these back when we trained to repel pirates."

Declan grabbed the other side of the life-raft case, and then he and Steinbeck unzipped it, walked over to the bow, and dropped the case into the ocean. The water activated the raft, and it exploded out of the case, inflating. A four-man life raft, the boat wasn't big, and it was floating away in the night.

Shouts rang out behind them, and a bullet skimmed off the edge of the prow.

Smoke started to roll out of the garage.

"Go, go!" Steinbeck said even as Declan fired over his head.

"You go!" Declan kept firing.

Steinbeck took a step up to the bow and dove.

Declan tucked the gun into his belt, then followed.

The water shocked him, brisk on his body, and he surfaced as bullets pinged the water around him.

"Stein!"

No answer. He searched for the lifeboat in the darkness. It had floated away, but he spotted it some twenty feet into the swell.

He needed to catch it before the waves took it into the night. He swam hard for the raft, his hand catching the rope.

Behind him, the yacht caught fire. The flames burned across the bow toward the bridge. It lit up like a torch on the water.

Declan turned, searching again for Steinbeck.

Nothing but darkness, the waves cresting over him, burying any sight of Stein.

Then, just like that, the *Invictus* exploded as the flames hit the engine room. A billowing cloud of fire and black smoke churned into the night, reflecting upon the waves.

Declan treaded in the water, watching the *Invictus* burn, the decks, then the stern, and finally, the fire climbing to the pilot-house.

"Steinbeck!"

No answer in the orange glow of the sea.

No. No!

He nearly let go of the rope, the urge to swim back to search for Steinbeck rising through him. But if he lost the rope, well, he lost any hope of surviving.

Any hope of finding Austen.

Steinbeck, where are you?

He watched as the boat burned, a carcass of flame on the water, the pilothouse falling in on itself, cutting the vessel in half.

And nowhere in the flames did Steinbeck surface.

The *Invictus* finally sank, the flames quenched by the ocean, only debris remaining to flicker like stars on the water, until it, too, died.

He finally dragged himself into the lifeboat, lying on the bottom, his hands to his chest, breathing hard.

And then it was just Declan and his lifeboat and a sky full of stars floating over the great, hungry alone.

———•———————•———

"My God, my God, why have you forsaken me?"

Those words circled Austen's brain as she lay in the bottom of the lifeboat, the dawn cresting in through the nylon roof, heating her body. She'd survived, so far, a day, a whole night, and into the next day on the ocean. She was still alive.

At least, in body.

The raft came with a survival pack. A box of nutrition bars and pouches of water. She had enough rations for three weeks if she spaced out the nutrition bars and drank sparingly.

She'd also found the EPIRB and activated it, so hopefully anyone with an AIS-equipped vessel would see her. And maybe the EPIRB had transmitted her location to the COSPAS-SARSAT satellite.

Rescue might be on the way.

Now, to wait. And wait.

And pray.

And try to get the fire out of her head, her heart.

Her soul.

She'd spent most of the night singing hymns to herself—"Amazing Grace," "How Great Thou Art," "To God Be the Glory," and "Amazing Love."

She hummed that now. "Amazing love! How can it be that you, my God, should die for me?"

But her brain just kept moving back to the moment when she'd seen Declan's boat explode.

The sound had thundered across the water, her own screams echoing into the darkness as she realized that Steinbeck and Declan were somewhere caught in those flames. She'd watched the boat burn, watched the fire take down the navigation tower and the bridge, and finally, sink the vessel into the dark ocean.

No.

No.

She wept as the night crested overhead, and finally circled into herself and simply sang. Because she didn't know what else to do, and it felt like if she just kept singing, then it *couldn't* be true. None of it.

She wasn't lost at sea, again.

She hadn't just seen her brother perish.

She hadn't spoken those terrible words to Declan.

So she lay there on the bottom of the raft with her arms wrapped around herself, curled up as the waves tossed her hither and yon.

Mostly yon.

Somehow, she fell asleep. And Margo sat there beside her. In the raft. It didn't make sense, but there she was.

Funny enough, Austen asked her if she'd brought fresh shrimp.

"Of course I did, Tennie," Margo said, and because it was a dream, the container of peel-and-eat shrimp simply appeared. And then she wasn't in the life raft anymore but on the stern of her trawler, watching the sun sink across the water, seagulls crying from the golden sky, and Margo sitting on the back sofa, looking over a map of the Silver Shore.

No. Not a dream. A memory.

"Why is this statue so important to you?" Austen had asked. Margo had wanted to join the research team, but Austen had just gotten wind of a new dive outfit. One started by Hawkeye Marshall. Seemed like the right life. Diving every day, watching the sunset from the flybridge of her boat every evening. A simple life. Uncomplicated.

She liked uncomplicated. It meant easy choices, no regrets.

Margo had looked up at her. "It's not about the statue, Austen. It's about the hope that the statue has survived after all this time. It's about faith."

"But . . . you're not even Catholic."

Margo had taken a sip of the lemonade. "I don't have to be Catholic to appreciate the fact that Mary represents trust and hope and how God defeated evil and used a young girl who was obedient to do it. It is amazing to me that God can use anyone who simply *trusts* Him."

She'd folded the map. "In His sovereignty, God knew that she would say yes. In His sovereignty, He knew that He was sending her one of the most difficult jobs ever. To be Christ's mother, to watch Him die on the cross. To trust that He *really* was the Messiah as promised. God took the worst crime in history, the execution of Jesus, and turned it into the most important rescue. He took what the world meant for evil and turned it miraculous. And it all started with Mary saying yes. So yeah, I would love to pull her statue out of its watery grave. But not at the expense of dinner."

And then Margo had laughed, and Austen had too, as they reached for the shrimp.

But her words lingered, and maybe that's why Jesus's words on the cross hung in Austen's head as she woke to the sea churning and the light pouring into the life raft on her first morning in the vastness of the blue.

Her stomach churned, and she leaned over the edge and lost what little she'd eaten from the ration pack she'd found in the life-raft survival packet.

Outside the raft, the sea had awakened, turned confused, the sky dotted with intermittent clouds blocking the sun in one moment, letting it stream through in another. Wind caught her, and she shivered, still in her pajamas.

And because she had nothing else, she replayed her conversation with Declan as they'd walked along the cobblestones, her words pinging back to her. *"I didn't know that grief would feel so much like fear."* For some reason, she latched on to that now. Maybe because here, alone in the raft, with her knees drawn up to herself, she had nowhere else to run.

What had Declan said about looking at his troubles so he could figure out the problem?

And then her Hawaiian shark instructor was in her head. *"Stay still."*

But that was the problem, wasn't it? Staying still meant that she had to sit in her grief. Sit in her mistakes. Take a hard look at herself. And maybe come up with truth she didn't want to see. Like her own frailties. Her own weakness. Her own fear.

And at the end of it, she would always come down to the same reality.

She would never be enough to keep terrible things from happening. Tragedy and trauma and mistakes.

And of course, because she had nowhere to go, Margo's words stirred inside her, another memory, maybe from that day when she was looking at the map. But now the words seemed bright and vivid. *"The first thing the angel said to Mary was 'Do not be afraid.' It's the most common phrase in the Bible. God constantly commands us not to fear because He knows that we will constantly run from fear. In fact, most of the terrible things we do and the horrible choices we make are because of fear."*

And in her mind, she was holding on to the line and watching as Margo's hazel-blue eyes held hers, so much determination in them as she took the regulator out of her mouth. Then Margo had given her a thumbs-up. At the time, Austen had thought it was because she was about to ascend.

But what if it was actually a thumbs-up meaning No Fear?

Austen leaned her head down onto her knees. *"Be still."* The words rumbled through her, and she caught her breath.

"Be still, and know that I am God."

Right. Except it didn't seem like her own thought. It was deeper, like a hand had pressed on her chest and warmed it. And the words simply poured out of her, easy, whole. *True.* "Whom have I in heaven but you? You know when I sit down and when I rise up. The Lord is my strength and my shield. In him my heart trusts."

Yes. Trust the sovereign God. Who knows and ordains everything, from the past to the future. Who met her no matter what direction she ran in the past.

In fact, maybe finally, who got in her way to stop her.

So, no, she wasn't alone, was she?

She closed her eyes, sending herself back to the Cuban fishing boat, listening to her own words. *"I can guarantee you that God does rescue us. Not always in the way that we want, but definitely according to His great plan for us."*

Lord, I trust Your plan for me. Whatever it is. Future, and . . . past.

And weirdly, a breath, a freshness, the taste of hope broke from a terrible coil she hadn't realized was caught her chest. She breathed in the salty sea air.

"Be still . . . and know."

Yes.

Across the sea, a horn sounded.

She scrambled to the side and unzipped the door.

A boat. Not as large as Declan's yacht, but bright and white, coming right for her.

She waved, and again, the horn sounded. Then, from the back of the vessel, a skiff deployed and skimmed over the waves toward her.

The memory swept in of Declan standing at the bow, the wind blowing back his dark hair as he pulled her from the ocean.

Not this time.

No, this time it was a sailor in his early twenties.

He wore a white uniform and held a life preserver and reached out for her lifeboat as he pulled up alongside it. "Ma'am? Are you Austen Kingston?"

What? "Yes."

"Good thing your EPIRB is still working. Sorry it took so long for us to get to you."

She climbed over into the boat, and he snapped a vest onto her. They towed the life raft behind them. The boat sped toward the larger cutter, and now she read the words on its side.

A Royal Bahamas Defense Force boat.

"I don't understand. Who sent you?"

"We got an alert that said you were missing. Could be that your EPIRB activated and alerted our station. That's all I know." They pulled alongside the stern, and the back opened. They drove right up into the ramp area, and hands reached out to grab her.

And then she was aboard, a towel over her shoulders, someone handing her water.

"Are you okay, ma'am?" This from an officer who looked like a medic.

"Amazing love! How can it be that you, my God, should die for me?" Should rescue me?

He did. And He always would.

Time to stop running.

<hr />

Declan didn't know how long he'd lain in the bottom of the raft staring at the stars as they waned, the ocean casting him one way, then the next.

How was he supposed to tell Austen that he'd lost her brother?

He closed his eyes, the weight of it all clogging his chest, turning his body to rock.

Everything. *Everything* he'd done—and now Austen was out there in the darkness, and Steinbeck . . .

For a moment—no, *longer*—he wished Austen's words were true. *"I can guarantee you that God does rescue us. Not always in the way that we want, but definitely according to His great plan for us."*

Oh, Declan was tired of his own plans. He was suffocating, really, because the more he struggled to find the right way out, the tighter the noose entangled.

"Grace, son. And mercy. We don't realize it, but they surround us every day."

His mom, again.

She sneaked in, sat down beside him in the raft, her voice soft in his memory, praying over him like she had for so many years when she'd come home from a shift and checked on him, even into his teens.

"The Lord is my shepherd; I shall not want. He makes me lie down in green pastures. He leads me beside still waters. He restores my soul."

Declan put a hand to his chest, feeling his heart thump. His soul felt brittle, cracked and dry.

Of course, there was Austen again too, her words as they'd escaped the yacht: *"We set ourselves at odds with God all the time. Whenever we take control of our own lives and say, 'Thanks, but I'm in charge now.'"*

He nearly laughed with the horror of it all.

Oh, he was tired of being in charge. He opened his eyes, stared at the stars, the moon waxing bright against the black.

"Whom have I in heaven but you?" Again, Austen's voice, but . . . maybe . . .

God, I want to trust You.

But even as he thought it, his gut tightened.

No. No, he didn't want to trust. Because what if . . . what if God didn't show up? What if He didn't rescue? What if . . .

What if he was lost at sea with no hope of rescue? *"Like Paul being shipwrecked."*

He shook his head. Clearly God had a sense of humor.

"Sometimes God leads us into a place where we can't fix it so that He will. He lets us get in over our heads. 'Humble yourselves, therefore, under God's mighty hand. Cast all your anxiety on him because he cares for you.'"

Oh, Austen. Even in his memories, she was light and truth and hope.

Or maybe . . .

Maybe she simply *reflected* light and truth and hope. He sat up against the edge of the boat and scrubbed his hands down his face, looked again toward heaven.

Who else, really, did he have?

The wind caught his voice as he spoke. "God, I don't know. . . . I want to believe that You care. That You're not laughing at me right now. That I'm not . . ." He swallowed. "That I'm not lost from You."

"God opposes the proud but gives grace to the humble."

Right. He drew in a breath, the knots inside tightening. "Oh, Lord, please . . . please forgive me for my pride. Help me trust You."

He spoke the words aloud, but they echoed in his heart, right down to his parched soul.

"Even though I walk through the valley of the shadow of death, I will fear no evil, for you are with me."

"You. Are with me."

Even as he said it, his body reacted. His heart stopped thumping wildly, warmth settled through him. And he breathed. Full and deep and—

Untangled.

Oh. Oh.

"Surely goodness and mercy shall follow me all the days of my life." Amen.

Yes. Yes to it all.

Freedom from himself, from the need to control, to *fix*, everything. As if he could.

Yeah, what an idiot he'd been.

"Dec!"

He didn't believe it at first, the voice in the wind. Surely he'd dreamed it. Or hoped it. Still, he grabbed the flashlight stored in the small survival kit. Flicked it on over the water.

Nothing.

"Stone!"

He shot the light toward the voice.

There. A large orange fender floated in the water, and clinging to it—"Steinbeck!"

The man's face illuminated in the glow.

The life raft came with a flare gun and flare cartridges, an EPIRB (which he'd activated), and a couple of foldable paddles. Declan grabbed one and started to paddle to him, the flashlight in his mouth.

Steinbeck kicked toward him, finally grabbing the line that Declan threw to him.

He pulled himself to the flimsy ladder, clutched the edge of the raft, climbed up, and rolled onto the bottom.

He lay there, breathing hard, his hands on his chest. Only then did Declan see the wound in his arm.

"You get shot?"

Stein nodded. "Slowed me down a little. You're a hard man to keep up with." He looked over at him. "Good thing you left that fender garage open—it shot out all sorts of floating debris."

Huh.

"I am so tired of getting shot." Steinbeck pushed himself up, took a look at the jagged skin on his upper right arm. "Sorry about your yacht."

"Yeah, I'm not sure insurance is gonna cover the 'attacked by Russian pirates' claim," Declan said, but he smiled. *Seriously? Steinbeck, alive?*

Maybe God had heard him.

He chose to believe that. Even as the night faded to morning, the sunrise burning across the water.

Steinbeck had fallen asleep like the former SEAL he was—able to crash even in the midst of a tossing sea.

Maybe that was a twin thing too, because Steinbeck radiated the same hope Austen had, the kind that put Declan's soul at rest.

He slept for most of the day, and woke when Declan pulled out the sea rations. Food tablets the size of small bars of soap. He gave one of the wrapped squares to Steinbeck.

"Great. Steak and eggs for breakfast." But Stein opened the bar.

Declan found a pouch of drinking water and took a sip before handing it to Stein.

"There's enough for a week at sea, so if you need it—"

"I'm good," Steinbeck said after taking a sip. He passed the pouch back to him. "Seal it well."

He did and set it back in the accessories box. He also grabbed out a flare, just in case.

"I turned on the EPIRB last night, so . . ." He considered Steinbeck. "Why didn't you go with Austen?"

Steinbeck's mouth twitched. "Alosha."

Declan raised an eyebrow.

"You dropped that name to the guard on the boat. It triggered a memory."

He lifted a shoulder. "He's a little famous in FSB circles. Sergei finally figured out it was me."

"I'll bet. How long have you been working the Petrovs?"

"A few years. Back when the Russian Bratva tried to assassinate our president, I was approached by an old SEAL friend I knew from Afghanistan. He'd gone MIA last I'd heard, which made him a good fit for clandestine work. He was tasked by President White to start an off-books agency to keep an eye on the Petrov Bratva. They've been doing everything they can to drag us into another war."

Steinbeck nodded. "I caught wind of this from Phoenix. She said that the Bratva was working with the Russian government to make a supersoldier. And you were their key player."

"It looked that way, I know." Declan had finished his nutrition cube. It tasted a little like grass. "Because it had to. I had to get the Russians to trust me so we could unravel their blueprint."

"And the shell game you were playing with the boats?"

"I hoped they'd fall for it. Never did I intend for them to get the obsidite." He watched as the falling sun rippled over the water, turning it a deep blue with gold-tipped waves. "Now, hopefully, they won't."

Steinbeck went quiet. "But you lost your lead, and your cover."

"Probably. But . . ." He shook his head. "I'm ready to be done with all this. I hated lying to Austen. She deserved better."

Steinbeck made a noise of agreement. He'd finished his nutrition bar too. "Sun's going to get hot. You couldn't have purchased a tented life raft?"

"It came with the boat. Austen is on the bigger, tented raft. There were two others—one on the port side and the other on starboard. They were attached to the walls, so they probably went down with the ship."

Steinbeck looked away. "We hope."

Declan frowned. And then—"You think some of those Russians got off the yacht?"

"Could have. There was a lot of debris in the water."

"We need to find Austen before they do."

Steinbeck lifted an eyebrow. "Great idea. Which way should we paddle?"

"Funny. But help is on the way."

"How do you know?"

Maybe it sounded crazy to say "God put it in my heart." But the surety had landed inside him during the night, and with the cresting of the dawn, settled into his bones.

And also, "I made a call to my contact before you grabbed me at the hotel. I saw Captain Teresa at a restaurant and was already trying to figure out how to get the *Invictus* back. I figured that the US embassy could impound it and maybe I could pull a few strings to free her. Didn't see our siege on the radar, but I gave him my AIS signature to track."

"You're thinking that when the *Invictus* went down, it would have blipped off their radar."

"And they would have seen our EPIRB."

"That's my wild hope, but at this point . . ." He held out his hands. "We're at the mercy of the sea. And hope."

And he was back to *"His mercies are new every morning; great is your faithfulness."*

"I can live with that," Steinbeck said. He leaned his head back against the lime-green raft.

Hope. Yes. That's what had seeded in him.

Please, God, show up. For Austen. For me and Stein.

And Phoenix, because looking at Stein's drawn expression, maybe Declan was picking up his thoughts.

"How'd you meet her?" he asked.

Stein glanced over with a frown.

"I know you're thinking about Phoenix."

A muscle pulled in Stein's jaw. "She's probably fine. She's scrappy and smart and . . ." He sighed. "Truth is, she probably ditched us. Again."

"Why?"

"She's . . . Let's just say she has her own agenda. One that doesn't involve getting picked up by American officials. So my guess is that she took that off the table."

"Is she in trouble?"

"She *is* trouble." But Steinbeck's mouth hitched up one side when he said it.

Interesting.

"We met on a joint operation three years ago—both trying to rescue an asset who'd been kidnapped by . . . you guessed it, our friends the Russian Bratva. The Black Swans wanted him for their purposes . . . and we wanted him for ours." He shook his head. "We got tangled up together for a couple days sorting it all out. In the end, she won. Betrayed me and left me for dead after her team blew up a café trying to extract her."

"Left you for dead?"

He ran a hand across his mouth, sighed. "She called for help, but . . . I don't know. It's complicated."

"That's what bounced you out of the military."

"Medical separation, two bionic knees. I should have recognized her in Barcelona, but my brain just didn't click in fast enough. And then I caught her hunting your AI program in Mariposa, and . . . well, she's rather unforgettable. Even when she's disguised."

Declan grunted in agreement.

Steinbeck wore that distant look again, as if scrolling through memories. Finally, he sighed. "I should probably try to, though."

"Try to what?"

"Forget her." He met Declan's gaze. "Or maybe figure out why I can't."

Declan sensed there might be a third option, one that involved Steinbeck in something off-books and extracurricular. Yes, Stein definitely wore a "mission not over" expression.

Declan got it. *Please, God, let Austen's EPIRB be working.* So apparently, he was all over the humbly-asking-for-help thing. *"Whom have I in heaven but you?"*

The thought hung on to him as the sun settled into the sea, as the stars came out, glistened on the waves.

They drank more water. Shared another bar and huddled in the raft, trying not to freeze as the wind and night cast them into the waves.

He woke at the sound of a seagull calling into the dawn-lit morning. Declan sat up, watched it circle, then fly away.

They couldn't be that far from land.

Another seagull cried, and then he spotted a fin in the water.

"Is that a shark?" Steinbeck had woken too, and now sat up, watching it.

"I hope not."

The animal surfaced, sprayed water from its blowhole.

Dolphin. In fact, an entire pod of them, now circling the raft, blowing, diving again.

Steinbeck glanced at him, a half smile.

Declan handed him a protein bar and water. They ate in silence, watching the sun rise, and he didn't want to bring up her name.

Please, please let Austen be alive. Yes, it was a prayer.

He was trying to figure out if he should take off his shirt and drape it over his head to keep from getting burned when a horn sounded over the expanse of water.

Declan searched, a hand cupped over his eyes.

"There," Stein said, pointing. "A boat. Smaller than the Coast Guard, but there, on the horizon!"

Declan grabbed the flare gun, removed the barrel cap, loaded the flare, and shot it off.

It arched over the water, bright even in the rising daylight.

The boat responded with another long blast of its horn as it cut through the waves toward them, and it seemed he'd seen it before.

"It's Hawkeye!" said Stein, getting to his knees, waving.

How—

The boat slowed, edging closer, and Declan spotted a handful of men gathered in the bow, one he recognized. His contact, sandy-brown hair, with a cowboy aura about him. *Texas.* The man nodded at Declan, his expression tight.

So maybe something had happened to the *Santa Maria*. A stone formed in Declan's gut.

But first on his list was finding Austen.

"Seriously?" Steinbeck said as he grabbed the rope one of the men had thrown him. The man had dark hair and a strong build. "Colt? What are you doing here?"

"We're here for him," said Colt, the man next to Texas. "Heard he needed a lift. Didn't realize you'd be part of the package, cuz."

"That's your cousin?" Declan said to Steinbeck.

"Yeah, you met him in Barcelona."

"No, no, I didn't."

The raft bumped up against the boat, and Texas let down a ladder. Stein headed up first, glad-handed his cousin.

Then Declan climbed up.

Texas helped haul him aboard. "You okay?"

"Thanks," Declan said and shook his hand.

"Stein," Colt said, "this is Tate. He works with that group I mentioned."

Steinbeck extended his hand.

"Tate? That's your real name?" Declan said.

"I like Texas better," Tate said. "Easier to keep my worlds apart. Tate Marshall."

Declan got that. Except he was so very over his own double life as the Dark Horse. Alosha. He held out his hand to Colt. "Declan Stone."

"I know who you are," Colt said, giving him a nod. "Logan Thorne, my boss, can't stop telling us that you're his secret weapon."

Right. "No," Declan said. "Just trying to stay afloat."

"We got you now," Hawkeye said, coming out of the pilothouse. "Tate called Colt, and he called me. You guys hungry?"

"I ate a bar of soap a couple hours ago," said Steinbeck.

Hawkeye laughed. "Oh, you cracked into the sea rations. Yum."

"Any news on Austen?" Declan asked.

Hawkeye frowned. "What about Austen?"

"She's also lost at sea," Steinbeck said.

And the way he said it sort of punched Declan. *Lost. At sea. Alone.*

Because of him. *I'm sorry, Austen.*

Hawkeye's smile dimmed. He glanced at Declan, then back at Stein. "Then let's go find your sister."

And Declan shot another prayer toward heaven. Because apparently God was listening.

Please.

———————————•———————————

She'd been in her ratty pajamas for two long days by the time she was rescued by Alfonzo—*Fonzie*—Pinder, as he'd introduced himself on the Royal Bahamas Defense Force ship. The twenty-something sailor had seemed to make her his priority after they landed at the small defense post in Bimini, because he'd helped her make a call to Key West from the RBDF administrative office.

Hawkeye hadn't answered, so she'd called Mo. Thankfully the pilot had been between charter gigs and said yes, he'd fly over and rescue her.

And then maybe she'd never leave Key West again, *thank you*.

Except, she had nowhere to live, did she? So maybe it was back to Minnesota and ... that's when she shut down, sitting on a vinyl chair in the reception area, staring out into the blue ocean, the endless sky.

Fonzie found her, suggested food, and brought her next door to a tropical hole-in-the-wall café, and bought her bacon-flavored peas and rice and johnnycakes.

She'd never tasted anything so good as she sat in the air-conditioning overlooking the Resorts World Marina and the seaplane base.

Tall whitewashed ceilings, a couple palm fans circulating the air, and the smell of deep-fried conch fritters. And outside, at the long pier down the road, a Virgin cruise ship, with its big red stripe, had pulled up (the island wasn't so wide that she couldn't see the seventeen-story ship). Thousands of tourists streamed into the small town, shopping and maybe heading for Resorts World Bimini and its expansive golden-white-sand beach.

She watched jet skiers circle the turquoise waters, and a dive boat came into the dock and unloaded a crew.

She was back in fantasyland, a refugee standing on the outskirts, and it felt almost sacrilegious for the world to keep turning after ...

And she lost her appetite, unable to bear the gasp, the terrible swell of reality.

Finally she put her head in her arms, letting herself cry despite being nearly dry. How was she going to tell her parents that Steinbeck had died?

Died.

And Declan—

"Ma'am. Would you like to talk to one of our local clergy?"

Fonzie had come back, sat down on the opposite side of the yellow picnic table. He'd changed into a pair of shorts and a collared shirt and wore a baseball cap. It hadn't occurred to her until now that maybe he'd been out looking for her all night.

"I don't . . ." She wiped her face. "I'll be okay. What I'd really like is clothes."

He pointed at her, then snapped his fingers. "C'mon."

They hopped into a golf cart, and he motored her down the long main drag into Alice Town proper, past pink and turquoise and yellow homes, some on stilts, past rustic beaches, and boatyards with private marinas, a few food stands, and salt-licked office buildings and cafés, and bordering it all, the azure sea. And despite her ordeal at sea . . . the vastness of it still beckoned.

Run. The urge to just . . . ignore it all, put it behind her, not think about Stein or Declan, or even Phoenix, just . . . leave it all behind, swelled inside her.

Except. *"Be still."*

Fonzie finally turned into a neighborhood and pulled up to a church shaped like a pyramid in the middle of a cluster of small homes.

A wooden building with slanted walls and windows at the base. "This is a Catholic church?"

"Yes," he said. "They have a clothing shelf. I'll be back."

Oh. She got off and headed to the building while he drove away.

The door was open, and she walked inside. Light streamed from a tall triangular stained-glass window onto the gleaming wood sanctuary. At the side and front, small altars held Virgin Mary statuary, a crucifix at the head altar.

The place smelled of peace and quiet and sanctuary.

"May I help you?" said a nun. Her brown eyes, as warm as her smile, took one look at Austen and said, "Oh, I see. Let's get you some clothes."

And that's how Austen found herself at a rack, searching for the right attire.

And maybe the sun had gone to her head, turned her a little crazy, but she was actually considering the purple sundress with the puffy short sleeves and slit up the side.

"We get so many people discarding their clothing to make room for souvenirs," said the nun, who'd introduced herself as Sister Clare and opened the closet and allowed her to rifle through the offerings.

Probably not the purple sundress, but maybe too many choices. White linen pants, sandals, sleeveless shirts, sundresses, hats. Even bikini coverups.

She found a pair of flowered leggings that looked like something out of the seventies, and then, just because, a yellow crop top with puffy sleeves and a boat neck. She used the church bathroom to change, then donned a pair of worn white Converse tennis shoes. As she stared at herself in the mirror, she felt, well, nearly normal.

She dropped her pajamas in the trash. Not that she didn't love them, but she just . . .

well, Declan had purchased them for her. And Declan . . .

Was complicated. And kind. And sweet and . . . *Oh,* she should have trusted him.

Of course, his words tiptoed into her head. *"I am doing the right thing. But sometimes doing the right thing requires you to do some, well, some bad stuff to get it done."*

Wasn't that the definition of Stein, and his job as a soldier? And she didn't see him as evil. No, Stein was . . .

Had been . . . a good man.

She stood in front of the sink, stared at herself. Slightly sunburned, her hair a disaster, but her reflection surprised her.

She saw determination. Strength. Courage. And Declan's words strummed into her. *"You have this aura about you that doesn't seem to be shaken by the events around you."*

Maybe it had been an act before.

But not now.

Still was different from paralyzed, or frozen.

When she emerged from the bathroom, Sister Clare had disappeared. She looked around, wanting to thank her, and found the nun in a small chapel off the main sanctuary. She was lighting a candle in a stand before a statuette.

A black statuette of the Virgin Mary. About three feet tall, it wore a crown encrusted with pearls, and a red ruby necklace, its head bowed in prayer.

Austen gaped, staring at it.

Sister Clare turned. "You found clothing."

She'd found more than that. "Is this . . ." She stepped up to the statue. "Is this the Santa María de la Paz—the Black Madonna of Hispaniola?"

Sister Clare glanced back at the Madonna. "She is a replica of the sacred relic from Father Hagarty, a Benedictine monk who helped found this church. It was originally given to him by the Monastery of San Francisco, in Santo Domingo. Old, yes, but—" She sighed. "Not the original."

Austen stepped up to the statue. It didn't look worn by the sea, the marble polished and shiny. And light glinted off the red ruby inlaid in the necklace.

Sister Clare drew closer. "She is beautiful. And nearly as perfect as the original. So close, it's hard to tell the difference, isn't it?"

Austen nodded. Glanced at her.

Sister Clare smiled. "I'll leave you alone with her." She patted Austen's arm.

Austen stared at the statue. Glanced behind her. Then she scooted up to the platform and angled the statue up.

It was heavier than she expected, and suddenly she imagined the entire thing catapulting to the ground, cracking into a thousand terrible pieces.

She examined the base. No initials.

Well, it was worth a try.

Setting it right, she moved it to match the marks, her hand on the base. Her fingers rubbed against an etching in the footer of the granite, in the back.

She bent down, then picked up the candle. Her heart stopped.

D.P., clearly carved in the black granite, about as big as a widow's mite.

She heard footsteps and stood up, set the candle back, her heart thundering.

Fonzie appeared at the door. "Are you ready to go? I saw a float-plane come in over the island. I think your ride is here."

She looked at the Madonna, the flickering candle, the rise of flame and smoke to the ceiling. The smoke of the prayers of the saints.

"It is amazing to me that God can use anyone who simply trusts Him."

It's not in a watery grave after all, Margo. She looked heavenward, nodded. Then turned to Fonzie. "Yes. I'm ready."

Fonzie drove her back through town, past the palm trees brushing the blue afternoon sky.

She'd have to tell Mo.

Maybe.

Because the secret *had* been well-kept, hadn't it? Until now.

"Be still and know."

She closed her eyes, inhaling the salty breeze as they drew closer to port. She spotted the massive cruise ship at dock and a couple seaplanes in the harbor, one motoring up to the dock.

Fonzie passed under the entrance to the World Resorts area, then motored toward the sandy white kayak beach, past the central fountain roundabout, and finally stopped in the lot. An SUV and a couple sedans sat parked under the sun, alongside golf carts and scooters.

Fonzie pointed to the plane.

Yep, Mo's ten-passenger Cessna Caravan Amphibian with the navy blue belly was tied to the dock. And she spotted him standing on the deck, talking with a few men.

"Thanks, Fonzie."

"Ma'am. Stay safe."

He probably didn't mean for the words to bite.

"Stay safe."

She might never escape it, the terrible hole inside. But maybe you didn't escape the price of love.

Love. She stopped, letting an SUV pass as it pulled up to the curb in front of her.

Yes, maybe she loved Declan, or could have. Loved the man she knew he was despite the layers and the complications and the lies.

Loved who she'd become just knowing him.

She crossed onto the boardwalk, past the SUV, headed toward the dock, and lifted her hand. "Mo!"

He looked up at her from the far end of the dock and raised his hand too. "Tennie!"

And then the men standing with him turned.

Sunburned, their clothing soiled, and one of them wore a bandage on his arm, the sleeves of his shirt torn off. His blue eyes covered in a pair of wraparound shades.

But her gaze went to the man beside him. Dark hair, aviator sunglasses, wearing a white dress shirt, grimy and rumpled, a pair of shorts, and . . . flip-flops?

She stilled. Caught her breath. Then, "Declan!"

Just like that, he took off for her, running down the dock toward the lot.

Movement out of her peripheral vision. A woman with long dark hair moving straight at her.

She glanced over just in time to see Captain Teresa, holding a handgun. Apparently, the woman didn't have a problem shooting someone in broad daylight. Or double-crossing her boss.

Or betraying them to the Russian Mafia.

Who knew—maybe she *was* the Russian Mafia.

She lifted the gun and pointed it at Declan. Or maybe Steinbeck. Or even Mo—

And that was just *it*.

Because Declan just kept coming, and *no, nope, nyet,* she wasn't going to watch a man she was falling for—maybe wanted a future with—get murdered in front of her.

Austen launched herself at the woman.

Teresa turned and started to backhand her, but *sorry*—

Austen knew how to deal with sharks.

She deflected, slapping Teresa's arm away, then stepped up to her and—what was it Hunter had said? A shot in the nose?

Yeah. She slammed her fist into Teresa's face.

The explosion nearly crumpled her hand, but Teresa fell back, stumbling. Tripped. She fell with a smack onto the pavement, the gun jerking out of her hand.

Austen picked it up, breathing hard. "I know how to use this."

And that's when she spotted the Russian . . . Sergei?—appearing from behind the SUV.

"Stop!" She pointed the gun at him, then back at Teresa. Then back at Sergei, who just kept moving, so—

Her shot took out the back window of the SUV.

Sergei jerked, ducking, growled, and maybe would have launched himself at her—

But backup arrived in the form of Declan, who tackled the man.

She looked away from the fight, her gun on Teresa, whose nose had exploded, her face, chin, and chest covered in blood. She held her face, backing up.

"Stop!"

Austen looked up to see Fonzie running hard toward them.

One of the men with Mo had also run up, now stood over Teresa.

Then arms went around her, hands took hold of her wrists, and a body stepped up behind her, a low, perfect voice in her ear. "Good job, Wonder Woman."

She started to tremble, and he eased the gun out of her hand.

Steinbeck had taken over for Declan, put Sergei facedown in a submission hold, his other hand gripped on the back of the man's neck.

Fonzie ran up to Declan. "RBDF," he said. "Give me the gun."

Declan seemed to consider that, and for a second, she saw the former Marine in him, the man who'd been undercover, the man who'd been willing to die to protect her.

"He's a cop. Sort of," she said to Declan.

He let out a breath and handed Fonzie the gun.

"You okay, cuz?"

She looked at the man who'd walked up. Dark hair, he wore a black T-shirt over a pair of cargo shorts. Worry in his eyes. "Colt?"

A couple more men in white RBDF uniforms showed up, helped cuff Sergei, another man lifting Teresa off the ground and handing her into custody. The RBDF pulled her away for medical attention.

"Austen."

She turned, looked up, her heart thundering, still shaking. Declan's gray eyes searched hers, so much relief in them, it poured right into her, touched her bones.

Then she was in his arms, his embrace tight, his body steady, his heartbeat against her ear.

"I thought . . . I thought you were dead."

"Yeah. I get that," he said, and maybe he was trembling too, just a little. "When Mo said that you'd called—I lost it." He lifted his head. "I'm so sorry I left you out there, in the ocean. I thought— well, I guess I'm tired of thinking. I just . . ."

And then his eyes glazed and her heart simply exploded.

Forget it. Yes, she loved this man. This brave, complicated, generous, surprising man.

"Thank you for staying alive," he said, his hands cupping her face.

"Thank you for not dying."

He smiled then, blinked, and a tear fell down his dark whiskered cheek. "Anything for you, Austen. Anything."

And then he kissed her. His touch was soft and lingering, and he smelled of the sea, as if he might be a pirate who'd stolen her heart.

It belonged to him anyway.

So she wrapped her arms around his waist and stepped into the safety of Declan Stone and kissed him back.

"Seriously?" said a voice.

She broke away from Declan, met his eyes. "Can you not fire him?"

"I tried," Declan said. "Wouldn't take."

"You did *not* fire me," said Stein. "I quit."

Declan let her go. "Technically, you ghosted me. That's not quitting."

Steinbeck grinned.

She launched herself into her brother's arms, and he caught her up, pulled her into his embrace.

"Wow, you scared me, sis," he said, low and gruff into her ear.

"Ditto."

He put her down, held her arms, looked her over. "What are you wearing?"

"I like it," she said. "Peace, man." She held up two fingers. "Love, not war."

"I'm for that." Declan reached out and took her hand. "Mo, can you take us home?"

Mo had come up, now raised an eyebrow. "Um. Where's home?"

She sighed. Because, well . . . "Still no sign of the *Fancy Free*?"

Mo looked at her. "Oh, Hawkeye found her. She was spotted by a US Coast Guard cutter down by Jamaica, man."

"Can I suggest a trip to Miami?" Declan looked over at Colt. "I need to finish some business." Declan glanced at Austen. "And I think the lady needs to do some shopping."

"What?" But she grinned. "Only if you're buying." She slid her fingers through his, holding on as they walked out to Mo's plane.

"Do I get a say in what you choose?"

"Not even a little."

He nodded. "Thought so."

"Oh, Dec, you have no idea what you've gotten yourself into," Stein said, slapping him on the shoulder as he walked by.

Declan grinned, looked down at her. "Great. I love surprises."

She laughed. "Me too. But," she said as they waited to board the plane, "could we not get hijacked or bombed, shot at, or attacked by ground-to-air missiles on the way home?"

"Picky," Mo said as he undid the ropes from the cleats.

Declan helped her inside. Settled next to her on the leather seats. Wrapped her hand again in his.

Then Mo pushed them away from the dock, and they skittered along the water and into the pale blue sky.

And maybe, hopefully, on their way to happily ever after.

TWELVE

IT WAS A PERFECT DAY FOR A HAPPY ENDING.

Declan sat on a bench outside the Mariposa courthouse, sipping a cup of coffee, the palm trees rustling, the ocean combing the sandy shoreline, seasoning the air with brine.

He checked his watch. Should be soon now.

On Main Street, timber framing outlined the new bank, and new pavement already covered the street that had been swept away by the landslide. The sidewalk and beach were rebuilt too. And farther up in the community, new houses sat where the others had been torn from their foundations.

But best of all, he'd approved plans for the new trauma wing of Mariposa's small hospital.

A couple kids ran by, holding surfboards, their hair and bodies wet, leaving prints along the sidewalk.

"I brought you a johnnycake."

He looked up at the voice—Doyle Kingston. Tanned, wearing shorts, a collared T-shirt, and flip-flops. Doyle held out the pastry covered in powdered sugar, in a napkin. "Rosa says hello and to come by Hope House and get a real meal."

"Thanks." He took the treat. "How I miss Camille's French food. Apparently, she's done with yacht life."

Camille and the rest of the crew had gotten to safety in the Dominican Republic, thanks to Hunter. Declan had offered them a place to stay. Jermaine had taken a position as steward at the house, but Camille had returned to St. Kitts. Ivek got a job on another yacht, while Raphael had left them when they landed in the Dominican.

And somehow, Tyrone had *not* been shot after being thrown overboard. He'd found an abandoned dinghy and gotten to shore on his own.

Declan sent them all severance pay, although he doubted it would be enough to keep the nightmares away. He still woke with a start sometimes, Sergei growling in his head.

He hadn't seen the man—or Teresa—since the Bahamas Royal Defense had taken them away, although Steinbeck said they'd been handed over to American officials for questioning.

"Yeah, well, you don't have a yacht anymore, so I would guess that Camille would need to find a new job."

"Ouch," Declan said.

Doyle grinned. "Join the rest of us mere mortals." He glanced at the courthouse-slash-police-station-slash-judicial-center. A weathered two-story white building with a crow's nest, a bell tower, and the Mariposa flag fluttering in the breeze.

"It's taking a while," Declan said.

"Tia has to testify about Kemar's involvement with Sebold's gang, just to clear up any lingering ideas about him trying to escape consequences by being adopted and moving to the US."

"I thought the orphanage dropped all charges."

"We did. But Kemar was so against being adopted—that wasn't a secret. So we just need to make it clear that he's had a change of heart." Doyle bit into his johnnycake, took a sip of coffee. "Something about knowing you're wanted just . . . well, he's dropped the fake arrogance and is . . . confident, maybe. Or at peace. I don't know. But he's taking his soccer seriously. We're going to miss him at the upcoming inter-island game. You coming to it?"

"We'll see. You and Tia are doing a great job," Declan said.

Doyle nodded. He'd finished off his cake and now considered his coffee. "Heard from Austen?"

Austen.

Declan still wanted to laugh every time he thought of her seeing his house in Boca. *"It's always go big or go home with you, isn't it, Dec?"*

Mo had put them down at the Boca airfield, and while Tate and Colt had gone to Miami harbor to check on the *Santa Maria*, Declan had taken Austen and Steinbeck to his place on the waterway.

"It's hardly the biggest house on the block," he'd said as they drove into the circular cobblestone driveway to the white modern-style home. Two stories, four garages, the place looked out onto an infinity pool and sat on the inland waterway, where a small boat rested on a lift in the canal. White travertine flooring throughout the house's interior, with dark-brown trim, the place was clean and simple. "It only has five bedrooms."

"Oh, I don't know how you stand it," Austen had said as she'd gotten out of the car. The evening had already cast itself across the sky in lavenders and reds. Towering palms had flanked the front door, flowers bursting with color at the base.

"I bought it for the land. An acre in this area is unheard of," he said, feeling suddenly . . . Well, maybe he hadn't needed such a large place.

She'd turned to him then, the sunset lighting her hair on fire. "It's gorgeous, Dec." Then she'd touched his arm, slid her hand into his. Smiled, her green eyes catching the sheen of dusk.

Yes, yes, it was.

He'd ordered in that first night, then taken her shopping the next day, and had finally gotten the call from Texas, a.k.a., Tate Marshall.

The *Santa Maria* had arrived and been unloaded and the obsidite delivered to the processing center.

He'd been standing on his covered porch, Austen lying by the pool, Steinbeck brooding somewhere nearby, and . . .

"I need this to be over," he'd said quietly to Tate. "I need to have one life. No more secrets."

A silence at the other end. Then, "I get that, Declan. I really do. But some things are simply bigger than what we want."

Austen had looked up at Declan then and smiled, waved.

"I'm not lying to Austen anymore, about anything."

A beat.

"To be clear, I'm not negotiating. I'm telling."

"Right." A sigh. "Your country still needs you. We'll be in touch."

Declan had groaned and hung up. But he'd purposed to stop trying to control everything, hadn't he?

Now, as he sat in the Mariposa sun, he washed down the rest of the johnnycake with coffee and turned back to Doyle. "Austen's in Key West. I got her boat towed from Jamaica. It's still seaworthy, but it ran aground and needs some repairs. And it was looted before the authorities found it, so it's a little torn up. I tried to get her to stay in my suite at the Galleon Resort while she repairs it, but she's stubborn."

"You don't say."

He'd tried to talk her into letting him buy her a new boat, but, *"You can buy me a dress, but I have to draw the line somewhere."*

So he'd try to respect that.

But it had taken nearly everything out of him to leave her in Key West and return to Mariposa to oversee the dismantling of the Russian mining operation.

In the end, the crew had left, leaving a scar on the land, the Bratva players in the wind.

"And Steinbeck? I tried to call him."

Steinbeck. "He left with your cousin Colt, and I haven't heard from him." Although he'd offered Stein his job back, again.

Steinbeck had declined, and by the set of his mouth and the storm in his eyes, Declan had guessed it had something to do with Phoenix. And the photo that Texas had produced and shown them both in Miami.

Phoenix, taken into custody by the Cuban police. Except she'd vanished from lockup, so either she was in the wind—

Or—

That had to be what had Steinbeck in a knot.

He had probably gone digging for answers, despite his words about letting her go.

Yeah, right. Declan hadn't been able to get Austen out of his head either.

He missed her like a man missed the sun and the stars and, well, breathing.

"Steinbeck's always had his own mind," Doyle said. He glanced at Declan. "And he doesn't give up easily." He took a sip. "That stubborn-twin thing."

"It seems to be a family trait," Declan said.

Doyle grinned. And then the doors of the courthouse opened, and Jamal came running from the building, down the steps, and across the seashell-strewn path.

"Mr. D! I'm going to 'merica!"

Doyle had stood up, and Declan too, and couldn't help but smile at Jamal's toothless grin. Doyle threw his cup into a trash bin, then held open his arms to catch the boy.

As he hugged him, Declan spotted Tia, the codirector of Hope House, walking with Elise Jameson. Hunter came behind, his hand on Kemar's shoulder.

Kemar looked undone. Even from here, Declan could make out reddened eyes, tears on his cheeks.

Oh no . . .

Tia came up to Doyle and gave him a kiss, then crouched in front of Jamal and hugged him too. Elise stood behind Jamal, her hands on his shoulders as Declan walked up.

"Everything go okay?"

Elise wore tearstains also, and she nodded. Glanced at Kemar. "He had a hard time."

And again, the clench inside. "Did the judge dismiss the charges?" The poor kid had panicked and tried to run away with Jamal when he thought he'd be separated from his younger brother. Joined a gang and caused destruction at the orphanage.

But he'd also testified against Sebold in a closed statement and helped put the man behind bars, so . . .

"Yes," said Hunter, and he squeezed Kemar's shoulder. "Kemar has a clean slate."

Kemar wiped his eyes. Smiled, although it was shaky. "We're going to be adopted." He swallowed, then his eyes filled again and he smiled up at Hunter.

Oh. And now Declan's throat tightened a little.

Yes, this was what it felt like to be wanted.

"We're going to miss you," Declan said, and held out his hand to Kemar.

The boy shook it. "Thank you, Mr. Stone."

Declan tousled Jamal's hair. "You guys ready to go?"

"They're packed," said Tia. "Mo is on his way to pick them up, so we should head back to Hope House to say goodbye, huh?"

Declan turned to Hunter. "When are the proceedings in America?"

"Not for a few months. But it's just a formality," Hunter said.

"We're a family now." Elise pulled Jamal close. He put his arms around her waist, and she kissed the top of his curly-haired head.

"You coming with us to the Keys?" Hunter said as Kemar, Jamal, and Elise followed Doyle and Tia to the oversized golf cart.

Declan's mouth made a grim line, and he stuck his hands in his pockets. "There's still so much to do here, and—"

"And you don't have to be in charge of it all. Trust your people. Trust the Lord." Hunter put a hand on his shoulder. "Sure, you're needed here. But you get to live happily ever after too, Dec." He squeezed his shoulder, then walked over to the cart.

Declan watched them go, driving into the hills toward the orphanage overlooking the village.

The sound of machinery hummed down the street, along with the jangle of bicycles and *brr* of golf carts. The tangy smell of street food and the scent of the ocean hung in the air.

"*Grace, son. And mercy. We don't realize it, but they surround us every day.*"

Yes, they did. Time to start living like it.

———————•———————

Music spilled from the back of the small, almost rustic cottage, the sun dipping into the ocean behind it, the seashell path lit up with welcoming solar lights. Even from the driveway, the string lights lit up the backyard firepit area, and the scent of grilling burgers, brats, and shrimp seasoned the air.

Go. In.

Austen sat in her open Jeep, parked at the end of the drive, hands gripping the wheel.

Don't. Run.

"So. What's it going to be?"

She looked at Hawkeye in the passenger seat. Dark hair in tangles from today's wind, a tan, whiskers on his chin, he wore the required tie-dye shirt, one of Margo's originals. Austen had dug one out too—a crop shirt that tied in the front. She'd added a pair of green cargo pants that had survived the looting of the *Fancy Free*, and a coral necklace.

"You didn't have to come with me."

"And have Steinbeck hunt me down?" He held up a hand. "No, thanks. He's scary."

She laughed, then sighed. Closed her eyes.

"Sorry, sis. I want to stay, but I need to find her. I know, in my gut, she's in trouble."

What golden thread tied him to the woman who just couldn't stop betraying him, Austen didn't know, but she did know Steinbeck.

He simply couldn't leave threads untied.

Not unlike Declan, who'd headed back to Mariposa. And she didn't blame him, not really.

The fairy tale had to end sometime.

So yes, she'd returned to her life, and he'd been gracious enough to tow the *Fancy Free* back to her slip in the harbor. Poor girl had been stripped of her navigation equipment, her electronics, and even her watermaker before the authorities rescued her. At least she still had her engines.

Insurance would cover part of it. The rest—well, she'd fixed the *Fancy Free* before, she could do it again.

But it felt different without Margo to help.

"I can go in by myself," Hawkeye said softly. "You don't have to—"

"No. I do." She took a breath. "Let's go."

She climbed out of the doorless Jeep and grabbed the picture of her and Margo taken on the *Fancy* so many years ago, paintbrushes in hand. Wow, they'd been young. And naive. And full of hope.

Tucking the picture into her pocket, she followed Hawkeye across the white-shell drive and toward the back.

The waves lapped the boat ramp, and Mo's C-Dory listed against the long dock, quiet.

Sparks danced into the night as she came into the backyard. Bertie Higgins played from a speaker somewhere—"We had it all just like Bogie and Bacall . . . Here's lookin' at you, kid." And Mo stood at the grill, singing along, smoke lifting.

A fire blazed in a circle of stones, surrounded by Adirondack chairs and benches. Chip bags and a massive metal container of iced shrimp sat on a long wooden table, and a cooler held cans of soda and beer.

Austen raised a hand to Marci, who ran Hawkeye's dive shop, and her boyfriend, Jimmy Parrot, who was singing along, rather badly, with Bertie. Austen's dive buddy Ridley danced in the sand with a woman named Angel, who worked over at the Bahama Mama Hotel and had a little girl named Hannah.

Thomas, another diver, was there, standing with Gillian, a local artist who had shared space with Margo, at least those last six months. And of course Mo, and finally Parker, who docked his boat beside Austen's. He'd been sober for a few years and drank a Diet Coke.

Good for him.

He lifted the can to her, a smile on his face.

She nodded, and that's when Mo spotted her. He closed the lid on the grill and came over, holding out his arms.

"I knew you'd make it," he said as he hugged her, which she didn't deserve at all. He kissed her cheek, then held out his hand to Hawkeye. "So, you tie her up and throw her in the back of your truck?"

Hawkeye held up his hands. "This was all her."

Mo took her hand, considered her for a moment. "You got here just in time. The sun is nearly down." He looked out toward the dock, the darkening ocean. "It's a perfect night too. A calm sea, barely any waves." He pointed to a basket on the table. "The candles are over there."

"I'll meet you at the end of the dock."

He nodded, and she walked over to the table. The lanterns sat in the basket next to small wax candles.

She pulled one out and grabbed a candle, then headed out to the end of the dock, beyond the lights of the house.

The sun had just about settled into the sea, leaving a fiery blaze along the horizon, the last wink of day. A breeze carried the mystery of the night, twined her hair. She blew out a breath.

Footsteps, and she glanced back, saw others joining her, all holding lanterns. *Okay then.*

She unfolded her lantern and set it on the dock. Then she crouched and put the candle inside. Stood up holding the lantern.

Below the dock, Mo had waded out, standing waist-deep in the water.

The others joined Austen, and she realized they'd stopped the music. Good. She preferred the sway of the wind, the barest whisper of waves upon the shore.

Mo glanced up at her. "You ready?"

Her eyes burned, but she looked at him, then the others. "I'm sorry it took so long for me to . . . I just . . ."

"It's hard to say goodbye," Mo said.

She nodded. "It's more than that." She swallowed. "'Greater love has no one than this: to lay down one's life for one's friends.' Margo did that for me. And . . . she was okay with it. She knew where she was going and that this was not the end. Just . . . goodbye for now."

Mo nodded.

"I miss her," she said. "I miss her laughter, and her hope, and the way she believed that God was sovereign, no matter what."

Mo's eyes glistened.

Her throat thickened and she held out her hand. "I need a lighter."

Hawkeye handed her a torch.

She lifted the lantern down to Mo, who held it while she lit it. The square glowed, and Mo set it into the water.

"Goodbye for now," said Austen.

The lantern floated away, caught by the backwash of the current.

Hawkeye stepped up behind her, bent to hand his lantern to Mo, and lit his candle. Stood up and put his arm around Austen. "Goodbye for now."

She closed her eyes, her hands over her face.

Then she turned into Hawkeye and quietly sobbed.

An hour later, the lights still twinkled out at sea, just a bare glimmer. She'd peeled shrimp and sung "Summertime" with Kenny Chesney, roasted a marshmallow and laughed. And laughed.

And healed.

The fire started to die, and she got up. Walked over to Mo. "I'm going to take off. I need to get an early start on my boat." Then she took out the picture of herself and Margo. Pressed it into his hand. "I wanted you to have this."

He took the picture, ran his thumb over it. "Think anyone will ever find it?"

"The wreck?"

He looked up at her. "The statue of Santa María de la Paz."

Oh. "Maybe," she said, then touched his arm. "I think if God wants it to be found, He'll make that happen."

He nodded, then gave her a hug. "Thank you for coming, Austen."

She held on for a moment, then disentangled herself, took a last look at the fading lights, and headed to her Jeep.

Hawkeye jogged out to her. "You good?"

Sweet. She put her hand on his shoulder. "Yeah. I'm good."

Or mostly good. Because the truth was . . .

She missed Declan. And not because of his fancy lifestyle but *despite* it.

The man was good. And kind. And . . . maybe it was over—she hadn't heard from him since he'd returned to Mariposa two weeks ago—but maybe . . .

Maybe his life was too complicated to fit her in. Maybe she would just get in the way.

Aw, that wasn't fair. She could have gone with him—he'd invited her to Mariposa. But she had to face the rebuilding of her life sometime.

Still . . .

Margo, you would have liked him.

She got into her Jeep and headed back to town, over the bridge, past the naval base, and into the tight neighborhoods of Key West. Houses snugged together in shoebox yards with jutting palm trees and parrots calling, cats running across the narrow roads, and the historic ambiance of a town known for escape.

No wonder she'd landed here.

Music from the nightlife near Mallory Square lifted as she drove to the Galleon Marina. She made out the *Fancy Free* in the darkness, back at home in the slip, waiting for someone to love her again.

Austen parked, then headed out to the harbor, keyed in her code at the gate, and padded down to her dock.

The trawler's front light had been bashed on a rock, and the nav station on the flybridge looted, but her Magma grill and even her dive gear remained intact (it had been locked in the back benches, so that helped). The American flag hung in shreds from its mount on the stern, having been ripped as it wrapped around the pole. And the bimini she'd sewn flapped in the wind. Only the pole remained of her Starlink satellite system.

But the cabin navigation station remained intact, and her clothing in the forward berth had also survived.

Mostly, *Fancy* looked tired and ragged. But she'd made it home.

There was so much to be grateful for, despite the work of rebuilding.

Austen stepped into the stern. The door to the hatch remained closed, so she climbed up to the flybridge. Sat in the captain's seat. Put her feet on the console and leaned back, staring at the heavens.

"It is amazing to me that God can use anyone who simply trusts Him."

Yes, Lord. I trust you.

Footsteps below, on the bow, or maybe the stern deck. She sat up, her heart pounding.

She had no weapon, so she slipped off a flip-flop.

Got up and tiptoed to the ladder.

A man stood on her boat, in the darkness—

She held up her flip-flop. "Get off my boat!"

He held up his hands. Turned.

She threw the shoe at him. It bounced off his chest and he recoiled.

She reached for the other. "Get—"

"For the love, Austen—it's me!"

She stilled. And then her heart restarted and—

She moved.

Right down the ladder, launching herself into Declan's arms.

Because until this moment, she hadn't realized how much, how very, *very* much, she wanted this man. Him and his beautiful, complicated life.

He caught her, bracing himself as she wrapped her arms around his neck, her legs around his waist, holding on tight. "This is better than a flip-flop."

She leaned back, caught his face in her hands. He'd shaved, of course, but wore the slightest scruff, and she smiled down at him, the light from the moon in his beautiful eyes.

"You're back."

"I thought maybe you could use some help fixing up *Fancy*."

"I don't know. You might have to roll up your sleeves, get paint on yourself."

She lowered herself down, her arms around his neck.

"I love to paint."

"And then, you know, once the boat is fixed . . . who knows where we'll end up? Could be . . . we'll follow the current."

"Adrift. I'm in." He leaned close, the musk of him sweeping through her.

She lifted herself on her toes, lowered her voice, her lips close to his. "You do know that you're supposed to request permission to come aboard."

"Can I come aboard?" he whispered, his voice husky.

"This could get complicated."

"I love complicated," he said as his mouth skimmed her neck.

"As long as you don't get in the way. I have a big life, you know."

"I know," he said, leaning back. "But just so you know, I'm so going to get in your way."

"Finally." She lifted her mouth to his.

And then, as the night sky dropped starlight into the water, he kissed her. And very much got in her way.

Continue the adventure with the thrilling conculsion, Steinbeck!! A former soldier seeks redemption in a daring quest with a Black Swan.

There's Trouble in the North...

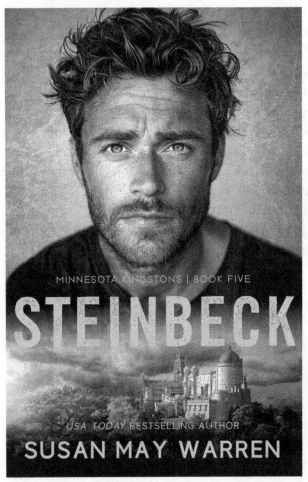

MINNESOTA KINGSTONS | BOOK FIVE

STEINBECK

USA TODAY BESTSELLING AUTHOR

SUSAN MAY WARREN

The greatest heist of all...

A thief behind bars, a soldier seeking redemption. Together, they embark on a daring quest to infiltrate a Russian stronghold, retrieve the plans, and dismantle the cyberman prototype. Failure is not an option. Don't miss the stunning conclusion of the Minnesota Kingston series by USA Today bestselling author Susan May Warren.

**The last person she can trust is the man she left for dead...
but he's the only one who knows she's alive, so...**

Emberly "Phoenix" Hart has spent years proving herself as one of
the Black Swans' most capable operatives. But when her mission
to secure a dangerous AI program leads to capture by the Russian
mob, she's forced to reach out to the only man who knows she's
alive...the man she betrayed.

Steinbeck Kingston left his SEAL career behind after a mission
gone wrong—a mission involving Phoenix. Now he's her only
hope of escape, but trusting her again could cost him everything,
including his reluctant heart.

As they race to prevent the Russians from weaponizing stolen AI
technology, Emberly and Steinbeck uncover a deadly betrayal that
threatens everything they hold dear. With the enemy closing in
and time running out, they must choose between protecting their
hearts and saving countless lives—including those of Steinbeck's
family.

When the traitor strikes at the heart of Steinbeck's home, can
Emberly finally trust in love enough to stop running? Or will her
instinct to survive alone cost her the only real family she's ever
known?

A pulse-pounding romantic suspense that delivers heart-stopping
action, soul-deep emotion, and a love worth fighting for.

This faith-filled contemporary romance features a protective
alpha hero, a fierce heroine learning to trust, found family, second
chances, and redemption wrapped in a high-stakes international
thriller that will keep you turning pages long into the night.

ONE

WHAT IF THIS WAS THE REST OF HIS LIFE?
Sweaty, covered in grime, reeking of frustration, rooting around the dungeon of his father's workshop, hunting for, well, in this case, a battery.

But Steinbeck might as well have been hunting for his future. For hope. For anything that could jostle loose a fragment of a lead as to where—

"You find it yet?"

His brother Jack stood in the open doorway, an outline against the bright light of the hot September day, the scant breeze off the lake not enough to stir the heat of the old shed. Humidity sheened Jack's skin, plastering to it the sawdust and woodchips that also littered Stein's slickened skin. The place smelled of its vintage, humble beginnings as a wooden garage built in the thirties.

Stein longed for the fresh, salty breezes of the ocean. "No. Are you sure Dad kept the extra battery in here?"

In here might have been a vague term given the mess of tools that scattered across the worn, chipped workbench, intermingling with old gum wrappers, rusty nails, oily bolts, crumpled sandpaper, and tangled wire.

"He said it's here."

Steinbeck shook his head pushing against the old drawer until it groaned against its runner, caught, and wedged sideways.

He gave it another shove, but it only jerked and stuck again, and he bit back a word as he lifted his hands in surrender.

"For the love. I don't know how he can find anything in this disaster." He pulled the drawer back out and reworked it in. Then opened the one below it. "This is like walking into a time warp. Grandpa's been gone for years and still—" He pulled out an aftermarket service manual of a 1973 Alfa Romeo Spider, the pages coffee stained and wrinkled, as if the old man had set one of his cracked *I Love Minnesota* mugs on it while studying the schematic of the dual side-draft carburetor that had endlessly plagued him. "It smells like stale coffee and old oil in here."

"And varnish and dirt. Grandpa must have spent thousands of hours in here.. Wow, I miss him." Jack came into the room, shirtless, wearing a pair of paint-stained khaki shorts and beat-up runners. "Forget the battery. We'll recharge the one we have."

"I wanted to get the table done today." Steinbeck closed the drawer and shoved past Jack into the sunlight and beyond, to the shade of the towering cottonwoods and birch that arched over the maintenance area of the King's Inn compound.

A twelve-foot table, handmade, stained white, awaiting a second layer of sanding, stood on the cracked cement driveway.

The story of Steinbeck's life—another unfinished project.

Finally a breeze, and he stopped, hands on his hips, staring out across the impossibly lush, meticulously kept back lawn—*good job, Jack*—to the deep indigo lake, where a handful of guests sat on the long dock or in lounge chairs on the sandy beach.

The perfect getaway. Or prison, depending on your view.

The wind skimmed over his body, the scent, just barely lifting from the lake, carrying with it not only the white pine but the aroma of his mother's fresh-baked bread in the kitchen of the nearby Victorian home-slash-Inn.

Steinbeck's stomach growled.

"You're a real peach today," Jack said, turning his ball cap around. Stein's brother needed a haircut and maybe a shave, but he'd been spending long hours at a nearby rented garage, working hard remodeling a city-bus-turned-mobile-home, so maybe he didn't care about his appearance. Stein could nearly smell the wanderlust emanating from his older brother.

"No word on your missing friend?" Jack asked.

Missing. Friend. Two words that didn't exactly describe Phoenix. First—not missing but *captured.* Imprisoned, and yes, missing because according to his contacts, no one had seen her since she landed in Cuban custody a month ago.

His gut tightened. She was valuable. And tough. And would hold out—

Nope. He blew out a breath. "She's not my *friend.* We worked together."

Jack had walked over to the table, started to wipe off the last layer of sawdust with a clean rag. "Yep."

"Really. We knew each other—well, in a different life."

"When you were active duty."

Steinbeck grabbed a thermos of water, took a drink. It went down cool in his throat, loosened the simmer in his chest. "Yeah. Met her on an op in Poland."

Jack stood up. "Wait—not the—"

"Yes. That one." Stein capped the bottle. "The one with the bomb and where I woke up in Germany, my knees blown out." Only when his body soaked in the sun, like now, could anyone see the straight-line scars down both knees.

"Was she there?" Jack had stood up, shaking out the rag. "At the bombing?"

"Yep." Stein ran his hand along the tabletop. It needed at least two more coats of stain, plus sanding, but his mother would have the outside table she'd hoped for when she plunked down the plans to her oldest sons last weekend.

Maybe he'd finish one project. And he was determined to finish it today, if he could just find that battery in all this mess.

Jack had retrieved his water, too. He had spent the last few years as a hero, searching for the lost, before returning home last winter. And now he was sticking around to take over maintenance duties at the Inn while their younger brother Doyle found a fresh wind down in the Caribbean, finally restarting his life.

Out of all of them, Doyle deserved a happy ending.

"So you ran into her again?" Jack said after taking a drink.

"Down in Mariposa when I was working for Declan, and then yeah, a month ago when I went to visit Austen." Not entirely true, but he *had* seen Austen. Well, more than seen her. He'd helped rescue her from Cuban pirates, and maybe gotten in over his head in said country, an escapade that had ended poorly.

And landed Phoenix in Cuban custody. It wasn't his fault, maybe, but . . . "Let's just say . . ."

"No man left behind." Jack met his gaze. "She means something to you."

"No. She's . . . Like you said, I don't leave people behind."

"Mmmhmm," Jack said.

"I just need to find her. Make sure she's safe. That's all."

"That's all." Jack smiled. "So, you're right. Not a friend." He took another drink.

Stein shook his head, but for a second he stood in the shadows of a Spanish-style hotel in Old Havana, Phoenix's voice soft. *"I think you should kiss me."*

No, *no* he should not—

"You okay, bro? You look like you just got body checked." Jack was staring at him.

Right. "Yeah. The fact is, I've run into a dead end. I can't find her. And I know...just know she's in trouble."

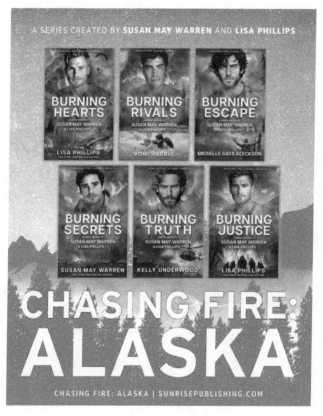

The skies over Alaska's vast wilderness are ablaze, not just with wildfire but with the flames of a dark and dangerous conspiracy. Join the Midnight Sun Fire Crew in another heart-pounding adventure as they find themselves fighting not only fires...but for their lives. Old romances reignite and new attractions simmer, threatening to complicate their mission further. Now, the team must navigate their tangled emotions and trust in each other's strengths as their fight for survival becomes a fight for justice in another epic, best-selling series created by Susan May Warren and Lisa Phillips.

Note to Reader

My heart is so full knowing you've experienced Declan and Austen's story! From shark-filled waters to midnight rescues, watching our brave diver and mysterious billionaire find love in the midst of danger has been such a joy to write.

We have one more thrilling book coming to wrap up this adventure-packed series! (Don't worry—I promise it'll be worth the wait!)

If you found yourself holding your breath through Declan and Austen's journey from distrust to devotion, would you consider sharing your thoughts in a review? Even a tiny note helps other readers discover their story (though maybe keep those sneaky Russian surprises our little secret!).

I'm blessed beyond measure by my amazing team. To my brilliant editor, Anne Horch—you always know exactly how to make these adventures sparkle and shine.

Special thanks to my incredible Rel Mollet—you're like a magical organizing fairy who keeps everything running smoothly. I honestly don't know what I'd do without your amazing attention to detail!

Huge hugs to my brainstorming angels, Rachel Hauck and Sarah Erredge, who always know how to help when my characters get themselves into impossible situations.

To my sweet husband, Andrew—thank you for being my go-to

expert on everything from scuba gear to spy craft. You make research fun and adventure even better!

Big love to Emilie Haney for creating such gorgeous, exciting covers, and to Tari Faris for making the insides just as beautiful.

Katie Donovan, you're a proofreading superhero, especially when deadlines are breathing down our necks!

To my dear readers—you make all of this possible. Thank you for bringing these adventures into your hearts and homes. I'd love to hear your thoughts at susan@susanmaywarren.com.

For all kinds of fun extras and sneak peeks, pop over to susanmaywarren.com or scan the QR code below.

Get ready—Steinbeck's story is next. Buckle up.

With joy and gratitude,

Susie May

P.S. Thank you for being the best readers in the world! ♥

More Books by Susan May Warren

Most recent to the beginning of the epic lineup, in reading order.

THE MINNESOTA KINGSTONS
Jack
Conrad
Doyle
Austen
Steinbeck

ALASKA AIR ONE RESCUE
One Last Shot
One Last Chance
One Last Promise
One Last Stand

THE MINNESOTA MARSHALLS
Fraser
Jonas
Ned
Iris
Creed

THE EPIC STORY OF RJ AND YORK
Out of the Night
I Will Find You
No Matter the Cost

SKY KING RANCH
Sunrise
Sunburst
Sundown

GLOBAL SEARCH AND RESCUE
The Way of the Brave
The Heart of a Hero
The Price of Valor

The Montana Marshalls
Knox
Tate
Ford
Wyatt
Ruby Jane

Montana Rescue
If Ever I Would Leave You (novella prequel)
Wild Montana Skies
Rescue Me
A Matter of Trust
Crossfire (novella)
Troubled Waters
Storm Front
Wait for Me

Montana Fire
Where There's Smoke (Summer of Fire)
Playing with Fire (Summer of Fire)
Burnin' For You (Summer of Fire)
Oh, The Weather Outside is Frightful (Christmas novella)
I'll be There (Montana Fire/Deep Haven crossover)
Light My Fire (Summer of the Burning Sky)
The Heat is On (Summer of the Burning Sky)
Some Like it Hot (Summer of the Burning Sky)
You Don't Have to Be a Star (Montana Fire spin-off)

The True Lies of Rembrandt Stone
Cast the First Stone
No Unturned Stone
Sticks and Stone
Set in Stone
Blood from a Stone
Heart of Stone

A complete list of Susan's novels can be found at
susanmaywarren.com/novels/bibliography/.

About the Author

Susan May Warren is the USA Today bestselling author of over 100 novels with nearly 2 million books sold, including the Global Search and Rescue and the Montana Rescue series. Winner of a RITA Award and multiple Christy and Carol Awards, as well as the HOLT Medallion and numerous Readers' Choice Awards, Susan makes her home in Minnesota.

Visit her at www.susanmaywarren.com

www.ingramcontent.com/pod-product-compliance
Lightning Source LLC
Chambersburg PA
CBHW022138090725
29394CB00007B/170